# THE MISADVENTURES
# OF MARGARET FINCH

CLAIRE McGLASSON

The Misadventures
of Margaret Finch

faber

First published in 2023
by Faber & Faber Ltd
Bloomsbury House
74–77 Great Russell Street
London WC1B 3DA

Typeset by Faber & Faber Ltd
Printed in the UK by CPI Group (UK) Ltd, Croydon, CR0 4YY

The right of Claire McGlasson to be identified as author of this work
has been asserted in accordance with Section 77 of the Copyright,
Designs and Patents Act 1988

*This is a work of fiction. All of the characters, organisations and
events portrayed in this novel are either products of the author's
imagination or are used fictitiously*

A CIP record for this book
is available from the British Library

ISBN 978–0–571–36372–8

2 4 6 8 10 9 7 5 3 1

For Dot and G.G.H. – Blackpool sweethearts

All perceiving is also thinking, all reasoning is also intuition, all observation is also invention.

— Rudolf Arnheim

# Prologue

He wears a solemn expression: lips parted, as if he intends to bestow some wisdom; his skin so pale where it meets the white crest of his hairline that you cannot see where it begins. Creases mark his suit, fabric pinched on the inside of his elbow, the flash catching the shine of his worn sleeve.

Behind him is a dark wall, papered with chains of vine; beside him, an aspidistra in a tall planter, its waxy leaves reflecting the momentary glare. But it is his collar that glows, like the moon, with borrowed light: a clerical collar which sits thick and starched around his throat.

He wears a solemn expression, and I wonder what thoughts are being shaped on his tongue. For he is looking not at the lens, but at a young woman, who sports the bobbed hairstyle of a starlet: jet black, cut into a blunt line to expose the curve of her neck. Strands fall across her cheek, curling forward into a sharp point just above her jawline. Are her lips parted in reply? Her eyes returning his gaze? It is impossible to see. She stands with her back to the camera, her head turned to his.

He wears a solemn expression. She is naked.

Some might swear it is meant to be, that everything preceding it was merely preparation for this time, this place, but Margaret Finch isn't the type to believe in foolish notions like fate. Still, no one could be more surprised than she to discover that, in both appearance and character, she is perfect for this mission. For the first time in her twenty-five years, being female is a benefit; being plain and wholly forgettable, an advantage. Following the rules comes naturally to her. There are those that she has been given: to watch but not participate, to listen but not engage. Then there are the strategies she has devised herself: a rummage in a modestly sized handbag can give her the appearance of being occupied for upwards of six minutes.

As a woman, she is not above suspicion, rather beneath it; as a woman she can go to places the male observers can't. Places like Blackpool's Open Air Baths. Specifically, the ladies' changing rooms. She suspects the stalls might have the effect of the confessional, that advice may be sought and secrets shared. But she has been put off the idea, for several days, by the thought of undressing or of seeing other people in a state of undress. Never having owned a bathing suit, she carries only the toolkit she was instructed to compile when she was recruited: a notebook and two sharpened pencils; a stopwatch; a packet of cigarettes and a lighter; five boiled sweets; and a hip flask filled with brandy. Offering a smoke / sweet / swig can be used to distract a subject if they should start to suspect they are under scrutiny.

She has only ever studied the lido from a distance, standing at a vantage point on the South Pier, which juts out alongside. The curved face of white stone always puts her in mind of the Coliseum. Today she steps inside, walking under one of the Renaissance arches leading to the centre, imagining that she will find herself in a combat ring, bracing herself for some distasteful spectacle. People crowd the edges of the pool, some watching from a viewing platform which runs the length of the roof, others trying to make themselves comfortable on the tiered seating which rises up to block the horizon of sea meeting sky. So many people. So much flesh on display. Young women stand in knitted bathing suits, adjusting necklines lowered by the weight of saturated wool. Young men wear only belted shorts, standing with their stomachs drawn tight. There are exposed chests, pale and hairy; legs arranged at lengthening angles; biceps tensed to maximum effect. She finds it all too much. Like meat set out in a butcher's window. The men and women give each other appraising looks. But all she sees is sinew and flesh. Spots of acne, yellowed toenails, skin blistered where it has burnt in the sun, dimples at the tops of thighs. To her the meat looks tainted. On the turn.

Reaching the changing room, she enters through the turnstile. She could hire a bathing suit from the kiosk, but since she has no intention of wearing one, decides to save herself threepence, and hire a towel for a penny instead. It will make her look as though she intends to swim and, if she carries it across her front, will be a good place to hide her notebook. Walking along the rows of changing stalls, she pushes the door of one that appears to be empty.

'Hang on!'

4

But it is too late: Margaret has already seen through the gap between the door and frame. The woman inside is bending over, pulling up her underwear.

'Sorry!' The cubicle door slams in her face. She moves on and, not wanting to risk making the same mistake again, waits until she sees an older woman emerge fully dressed. Congratulating herself for hiring a towel, Margaret hangs it over the top of the stall door to make it obvious it is occupied, and removes her shoes. There's a narrow bench, but she decides not to sit: the bottoms of her legs will be visible to anyone walking past and will look odd unless she gives the impression she is changing. Unpacking her bag, she tries to hear the woman on the other side of the partition, who seems to be talking to a friend further along.

'So quick,' one says in a lowered voice. 'Over just like that.'

'And did he . . . ?'

'I think so . . . There were . . . afterwards . . .'

'And did he say anything about . . . ?'

'No. Only that he hoped nature would take its course. And that it wouldn't be long before . . . well . . .'

The friend goes quiet for a moment then asks: 'Did he not try to . . .'

'No. Like I say, there was only that. *The act itself.* I wasn't sure whether I was supposed to . . . or . . .'

It is clear to Margaret that the two women think they are speaking in a code of modesty, but it requires very little intelligence to decipher it. Copying down their words, she writes *the act itself = intercourse* in the margin of her notebook. Her hunch that she would be able to collect shared confidences has proved correct, though she had not anticipated that they would

5

speak about such intimate matters. Is it because the screens are there to hide their blushes, or is it the removal of clothes that prompts a baring of the soul?

'It's all so confusing,' she hears the first woman whisper. 'I don't know what he wants. And it's not as if you can come right out and ask, is it?'

'Or come right out and tell him what *you* want!'

The woman shushes her friend with a laugh, and Margaret wonders what it is they would say if they could. She has overheard plenty of talk from her colleagues about working-class fantasies and patterns of desire. She was warned when she took the job that 'women like that' are much more inclined to speak in coarse terms about private matters. But she has not yet collected evidence about the specifics of what they *want*. As for herself, she has never thought about such things outside her professional role. To invent intimate scenarios would involve her own participation in the imaginary acts – something she has neither the capacity nor inclination to do.

Margaret transcribes every conversation, word for word, continuing to listen as another group of women arrives. Remembering they might see her legs beneath the partition, she takes off her stockings and undresses as far as her slip, grateful that she has chosen to wear a blue floral tea dress with a long line of fabric buttons to keep her occupied. When the neighbouring cubicles welcome new bathers, she makes a show of putting on the dress and stockings again. Her attempts to eavesdrop are thwarted several times by the loud protestations of children. One who (to her mind) seems disproportionately distressed that it is time to leave the swimming pool; two girls (presumably siblings) fighting about who gets to use a shared towel first; and a little boy who is begging his mother to buy him a sword (a word he pronounces with a heavy rather than silent 'w'). Margaret notes down every detail, next to the exact time, which runs as a ledger in a thin column on the left side of each page.

This cycle of observing, writing, partial dressing and undressing, continues for several hours. It reminds her of the night she took an inventory of men who fed pennies into the Mutoscope peep shows on the pier. They had put their eyes to the viewing window and turned a handle to see a stack of photographs flipping past. The machines had names like 'What the Butler Saw', but from what she had seen herself (her diligence required that she look for the sake of her report), the women undressed no further than she was doing now. In the one called 'Bedtime Beauties' three young ladies merely brushed their hair and arranged their nightclothes. Do men really find such mundane actions exciting? It all goes back to the moment Eve covered herself with a fig leaf, she supposes. It is the act of hiding parts of the body that makes them alluring because, considered on a purely aesthetic basis, they really have very little to recommend them. Elsewhere in the world, men and women expose every region of themselves. Private parts are considered public, imbued with no more significance than one's ears or elbows. Women can walk around bare-breasted and arouse no attention at all. But here in Blackpool men pay a fortune to see topless dancers on the stage.

These differences fascinate her: the unspoken codes that unify and define. Decipher those and you can identify transgression. In England, people rely on concepts of taste and propriety, ethics and morals, right and wrong. But there are too many variables in the formula: class, religion, education, gender. As concepts they are not consistent. If they were, she wouldn't be here right now, gathering data.

The curious thing is that some people seem to understand these unwritten rules instinctively. But from her own experience, Margaret knows it is all too easy to get it wrong: to cross a line, expose or shame yourself without realising. And by then it's too late.

Until she was eight, she thought people meant what they said, and said what they meant. But on the day she was introduced to Mother, she learnt that, very often, they say the opposite. Father had told her he had a surprise: he had found her a new mummy he was going to marry so they could all be a family and be happy again. That afternoon, a woman came for tea. She brought a cake and set it out on a stand on the table. It had cherries in it. 'I made it just for you,' she told Margaret. But when Father was out of the room, Margaret reached for another slice, and the woman looked angry. She ate it anyway, using her fingers to scoop up the last of the crumbs on her plate. And the woman said, 'Things are going to have to change around here.'

## 2

Four drinks in, Margaret acknowledges that she may be a little tipsy. It's a hazard of her profession, a necessity when her work takes her into public houses. She can't nurse the same half-pint of stout for hours; she might draw attention to herself. It is always wise to order two drinks as soon as she gets to the bar. Brandies. That way she looks as though she is expecting a friend or sweetheart to join her at any moment. Though in reality she has neither.

A quick glance at her watch tells her it is 9.33 p.m., almost closing time. She has been sitting here since seven, having emerged from the outdoor baths to find the promenade significantly quieter than when she left it. At that hour, families have returned to their boarding houses for an evening meal. Margaret has noted that the locals describe this as their 'tea', and takes care to use the same term in her reports, for the sake of accuracy. Perhaps it is the fact that she has failed to eat anything herself that accounts for her light-headedness now. She should have stopped to get some refreshment, but her attention was caught by two men as they crossed the tramlines to the other side of the street. One was wearing an overcoat, much too big for him and much too warm for the season. She could tell by the worn fabric that he was a man of low pay. A mill worker, a side-piecer perhaps. There was something about the way he moved that struck her as odd: the inside pockets of his overcoat looked full, the hems uneven as though weighed down by whatever was inside them. The fabric did not sway with each step he took, rather his body seemed to move inside it. Margaret followed, dashing to catch up.

'Just a lickle favour,' she heard him say to the other man (who was much more suitably dressed), his accent confirming her assumption that he was from Bolton (the way he said 'little' as if the word contained no Ts at all). It is Bolton's turn after all. Every worktown in the north-west stakes claim to its own Wakes Week: when the mill machines fall silent for repairs, and the workers make their annual pilgrimage to the seaside. When it comes to the names of these towns, she has noticed that a disproportionate number start with either a 'B' (Bacup, Barnoldswick, Blackburn, Burnley and Bury) or an 'R' (Radcliffe, Ramsbottom, Rochdale and Royton): tongue-twisters of cobbled streets and grime-stained bricks. For seven days a year, each is rendered a ghost town – roads emptied, shops closed, church bells silenced – until its sons and daughters return home with sunburnt skin and empty pockets.

'Strictly between us, mind,' Overcoat Man said, patting his nose with his forefinger before parting company with his companion, and stepping into a pub.

*The Mermaid Public House. Man enters at 7.06pm. Mid-40s, average build, sandy brown hair, modestly dressed in over-sized coat which he does not remove despite the warm atmosphere. Orders one pint of ale. Drinks (7 mins) and orders another. Woman arrives 7.25pm. Approximately 20 years old and moderately overweight. Honey-coloured shoulder-length hair (pinned back in rolls from her face), red short-sleeved sweater and pencil skirt (ill-fitting) with make-up applied thickly enough to be obvious (from distance of approximately 12 feet). Sits at empty table nearest the bar and suggests that Overcoat Man might like to buy her a port and lemon. He refuses and turns his back on her. Woman stands and joins table of four young men, one of which goes to the bar for a round of four pints and one port and lemon (for the lady). Woman touches her hair frequently (13 times within five minutes). 7.56pm, she leaves with one of the young men. Exit met with laughter and jeering from the remaining three.*

Margaret records her observations with the detachment of an ornithologist. You cannot walk up and ask a wagtail or a linnet how it attracts a mate or guards its territory, you stay distant and watch them, and she finds the technique works just as well when it comes to human behaviour. She is careful to keep her notepad hidden in her lap beneath the table, jotting times and prompts in her own form of shorthand, which she has developed since she was recruited five weeks ago. Listening patiently through hour after hour of complaints about the poor performance of football teams, the unreasonable expectations of wives and the cost of living these days, she dutifully copies down every detail.

There is a white-haired man sitting alone at a table in the far corner. He is reading a newspaper but keeps looking in her direction. Margaret is slow to turn away and he catches her eye. 'Can I get you another?' he says, nodding towards her glass.

'No thank you,' she tries to keep her voice steady. 'I'll wait until my gentleman friend gets here. He won't be long. But terribly kind of you.' Too well-spoken. Margaret is usually careful not to give herself away, but sometimes when she gets flustered, she forgets to tone down the accent her stepmother was so desperate for her to perfect. In the days when she still visited her grandparents, she would stand in the parlour and recite the poetry she had learnt in elocution classes, basking in the look of pride and wonder that her speech would prompt. But by the time she returned home for dinner, her words had become lazy and they let her down, which let Mother down, and 'reflected badly on her father who already had more to prove than most, what with the state the war had left him in'. The wrong vowel sound. A tut. A head shake. 'After all the sacrifices I've made . . .'

But now here she is in Blackpool, having to round off the sharp edges of her consonants, having to unlearn all the lessons of her childhood. It's an irony that isn't lost on her.

The man returns to his newspaper, a satisfied smile crossing his face (perhaps he has solved a crossword clue). Margaret does not catch him looking up again, but his attention has shaken her. She feels exposed; worries that other people in the pub may be watching her, that she may have given herself away, missed something obvious, broken some sort of code. She fights the impulse to stand and walk out. Reminds herself that she is here to work. She lifts her glass and tilts it, pretending to study the brandy inside.

By now, Overcoat Man is a quarter of the way through his sixth pint and she has noted that he seems to be well-known to both the landlord and the majority of customers (unlikely to be on holiday then, probably a local). He nods at every man who walks into the lounge. Twelve have responded with a shake of their head, seven by nodding or tipping their cap. Margaret has observed that, at intervals, every one of those seven has left the pub, followed shortly after by Overcoat Man, who resumes his post at the bar between two and eight minutes later. It is difficult to time him precisely without a stopwatch, but she doesn't want to take hers from her bag. She has witnessed enough to convince her of two hypotheses: that a) the nods signify some code of communication and that b) they relate to surreptitious meetings, which probably involve illicit or illegal activity. She forgot to note down a description of the most recent man, and now she's having trouble remembering what he looked like, distracted by the turn the conversation has taken at the bar.

'They're getting uppity,' the landlord says. 'Nothing more. They need reminding who lost the last time.'

'That's the problem, right there. You can't keep people down forever. It's that as'll make them fight back. They've learnt their lesson.' Overcoat Man puts his pint down so forcefully that ale spills out of the top.

Alert, Margaret tunes out every other sound in the room. Some people are said to have a photographic memory but, since she took this job, she has discovered her talent is aural. She can remember conversations, hold them in her mind in their entirety, until such time as it is safe to write them verbatim in her notepad.

'Don't be soft, lad. He'll be playing up again soon as we let him.'

'Force him into a corner and he will!'

Margaret knows to whom and what they are referring and she feels a flash of anger. They talk as if the threat is no more serious than a playground spat. As if it won't happen, could never happen again. As if men like them won't be dragged into it, shot at, blown to pieces. As if they won't return changed. Just like her father was. If they return at all.

Exchanges about Hitler's intentions and what should be done about them often begin just like this. But they frequently escalate into fist-fights depending on the amount of alcohol consumed. While the rest of the country looks to Europe for signs of war, she watches the brawls playing out here in England. She sees the copies of *The Blackshirt* left on bar stools, and the salesmen selling subscriptions to the Left Book Club. The government's busy tying itself in knots about which poses the greatest threat – Germany or Russia – while all along the argument is being settled here, in the pubs and working men's clubs. Pride and honour, belligerence and belief. For Margaret it always comes down to statistics, probability, percentages. Three quarters of the population are working class, and since they were given the vote, they run things now. That's why it is vital that she carries out this mission. To understand them.

'If it happens, I'll be fighting for the *right* side.' Overcoat Man finishes the last of his pint and nods at a young man who is leaving the pub. 'Our lot could learn a lot from him, if they stopped to listen. He makes a lot of sense.'

# 3

A thought comes to Margaret so suddenly that she feels it as a physical sensation, a moment of clarity that makes her senses sharpen. That's what Overcoat Man is up to. The British Union of Fascists have headquarters here in Blackpool. Perhaps he's one of them. He has disappeared outside again and she needs to follow. She stuffs her notepad into her handbag, and in her haste, drops her pencil, but she mustn't draw attention to herself by bending to retrieve it. Instead, she finishes the last measure of brandy in her glass, taking pains to look unhurried as she stands, slips on her jacket and walks outside. Her legs feel shaky after sitting in the same seat for so long, and she stumbles on the step down to the pavement.

Overcoat Man is not here. She left too long an interval before following him, but he can't have gone far. There's a narrow cut-through that runs beside the pub, but it is too dark to make anything out. Giving her eyes a moment to adjust, she starts to walk, meeting the junction of an alleyway that runs behind a row of terraced houses, the glow from their upstairs windows too weak to cast much light into the shadows. With her arms held out wide she can't touch both walls at once, but with each step she pushes a hand against one, then the other, to keep herself upright.

Hushed voices. Two men. She edges forward and sees an open gate leading to one of the backyards. Another step and they might have seen her. Hiding herself closer to the wall, she stands perfectly still to listen.

'It doesn't work like that.'

'You can trust me. I'm good for it.'

If only she could see them, she'd have a much clearer idea of what they are up to. Are they passing on information? Making plans for a meeting or some sort of rally? There's another sound. She holds her breath. Footsteps. They seem to be coming from some distance. She turns back, but there is no one there. It's as if her mind is lagging behind her senses, as though she has to will the cogs of her brain to turn. Unsure now whether to move or stay. The voices from the backyard are suddenly louder.

'Rule's the same for everyone—'

'But—'

'I'm the one taking all the risk. Forget it.'

She is slow to register the moment of silence. By the time the gate hinge squeaks, it is too late. Overcoat Man is walking at such a pace that he crashes into her.

'What the—?'

'I'm sorry.' Margaret steps away, her back hitting the wall.

'What's your game?'

The younger man is beside him now. 'Who's this?'

Margaret tries to get past them but they are blocking her way. 'I was just . . . If you'd excuse me, I need to . . .' But her words have no effect on them; they continue to talk as if they haven't heard her.

'A snitch?' the younger man asks the other. 'Think they'd use a woman?'

'Wouldn't put anything past 'em these days.'

Margaret speaks up again. 'I'm not . . .'

'Just as well, because I'm not going to let them put me away again.' Overcoat Man pats the other man on the back. 'We were just having a little chat about boxing. He is very keen on sports aren't you, lad? And why shouldn't two friends have a little wager on it? Between the two of us. Just a bit of fun.'

'Bet she likes a bit of fun herself,' the younger man says, grinning to reveal a missing tooth. He steps forward and takes a strand of her hair between his fingers. 'She doesn't look the type. But they're the ones as can surprise you.'

She can smell the ale on him. She knows she should fight but her body is rigid. She closes her eyes tight and wills her arms to hit out and her feet to run. But nothing happens. She can feel his breath now, on her cheek, and his hand reaching around her waist. Can hear both of them laughing. And then, a third voice, much more well-spoken. She opens her eyes and sees something moving behind the two men. 'There you are, dear girl! I've been looking for you everywhere!' She can't see who is speaking, but she can't be imagining it because the hand is gone from her waist. The men have swung round to face the stranger. Undeterred, the voice speaks again. 'Ah good evening, gentlemen. Thank you for looking after her. So kind. I hate to think what might happen to a young lady out on her own at this hour.'

'Look, we're not wanting any trouble,' says Overcoat Man, his tone suddenly conciliatory. 'We were just having a private conversation and—'

'Dear fellow, fear not. I have no interest in your affairs. No harm in a man having a wager or two to make the sport a little more exciting eh? But I really must get my niece home.' Niece? A hand reaches out to her through the gap between the two men, a gold signet ring on its little finger. She grasps it. 'Come along, dear girl. Come along with Uncle.'

She no longer has to will her feet to walk, she simply surrenders to the pull on her arm and follows its lead, moving
forward without looking back. She dares not risk letting go of
his hand. 'You're all right now. Don't worry, I'm here,' he says.
'Just keep going.' And that is what she does, not slowing even
to glance at him, in case her body stalls again. Even without
looking she can sense he is no threat. He has the voice of a man
but the figure beside her is as small and slight as a boy. Taller
than her, granted, but he can't be more than five foot three
under the top hat he is wearing. His presence stirs a memory in
her, of walking beside her grandfather: a small, wiry man who,
even in old age, had the energy of a child. Constantly on the
move, constantly talking. His body insufficient to contain all the
thoughts and ideas he had.

When they reach the main street, he drops her hand and
turns to her, lifting his hat and placing it on his chest, as if to
subdue his own heartbeat beneath. And she recognises him.
'You're the gentleman who . . .' The gentleman who offered to
buy her a drink in the pub. The one with the crossword. 'Thank
you for . . . back there . . . I . . .'

'Catch your breath,' he says. 'We're safe now.'

'What if they follow—'

'They would have been here by now.' He looks around and
nods towards a low wall outside the pub. 'Why don't you sit for
a moment?'

'I'm fine. All just a misunderstanding. I was about to explain
to those men . . . that I . . .'

'Not men you can reason with, I'm afraid. What if they had
turned nasty?'

She fears they had already turned nasty, but she dare not consider what might have happened had he not intervened. 'But why did you . . . ?'

'It's what I do,' he says, bowing theatrically. She is not sure if he is poking fun at himself or at her, only that she does not understand the joke. 'If I can ever be of help to someone then . . . well . . .' He sighs. 'I don't always stop to consider the consequences. But then you already know that . . .' Does she? 'I thought they were going to give me a good beating for my trouble, but we got away with it this time, eh? I think it was the element of surprise. And this . . .' he replaces his hat and taps the brim of it, '. . . makes me look far taller, and far more important than I really am!' Smiling widely, he shows no desire to hide a set of overcrowded teeth, which jostle for space either side of a large gap in the middle.

'Are you quite sure you are all right?'

'Yes. Thank you. I can't tell you how grateful I am . . . that you stepped in.'

He seems to stand up a little taller. 'Thank goodness I was able to.'

'But how did you know I . . . ?'

'I followed you out of the pub to return this,' he says, taking a pencil from his top pocket and handing it to her. 'You dropped it.' He lowers his voice and leans closer. 'And if I am to be completely honest, I wanted to talk to you about what you were up to . . . all those notes you were taking. I could see what it was all about.'

'Oh!'

'Yes, yes. Quite obvious really. Though I'm surprised our paths crossed so soon. I only arrived in Blackpool yesterday. No one knows I'm here yet.'

The relief she feels at being rescued turns to confusion. Does this stranger know her? Is he part of the same mission? Perhaps it is Tom Harrisson, the man who is in charge of the whole operation. She has heard his name mentioned frequently, but has never met him.

'I understand.' He taps his nose conspiratorially. 'You're not the first.'

'I'm not?'

'No, no. When you've lived a life like mine you tend to attract . . . well, you know . . .'

She doesn't.

He grins again. 'Good. I think we understand each other very well! So, the only question is when I am going to take you out to discuss what we are going to do about it.'

Do about what? She is trying not to stare at those teeth, looking down instead at the street light reflected in the shine of his shoes. He really can't stand still, rocking very slightly from the balls of his feet to his toes and back again, just like her grandfather used to do.

'Yes. My treat of course. Tea on Friday afternoon.' He stands back and considers her, then extends a hand. It hovers there for a few seconds before she realises she is expected to lift her own to meet it. But instead of a handshake, he clasps her fingers between his two palms. He squeezes her hand with a gentle pulse, or perhaps it is the beat of her own heart, skin burning where it is being touched, as if every pore is gasping for air. She is desperate to pull free from his grasp but that would be rude, after what he just did to save her.

'Marvellous!' he says, unaware of her discomfort. 'I am glad we've met! The Metropole, let's say three p.m. I'll get a longer break on Friday afternoon before the onslaught of the new arrivals on Saturday.' He winks as he lets go of her hand, touches the corner of his hat and strides away, calling back over his shoulder. 'Until then, Miss . . .'

'Finch,' she says.

But he has already disappeared into a side street.

# 4

The curtains are so thin you could spit peas through them. The thought comes to her now as she covers her head with a pillow. She remembers overhearing the phrase from a housewife at the market. Margaret had written up her observations afterwards: how the woman had appraised the quality of a tablecloth between her middle finger and thumb, unfolded a layer of cotton and held it up to the light. 'Proper pousey,' she'd concluded, shaking her head. But she bought it anyway, though not before she had bartered on price. Margaret collects these colloquialisms like pressed flowers. For as long as she can remember, she's had a sense of the power of these words: dangerous enough to be banned in her own home. As a child, she whispered them under her breath, naming objects around her in a forbidden tongue: perfume instead of scent, sweet instead of pudding. Imagining, in her childish mind, that each item had another, secret life.

She marvels at how differently Blackpool's holidaymakers see the world, and how different their world is from her own. Though in her lodgings she gets a taste of it: observers are required to live among the study group to get as close as possible to the true experience. It has taken her a while to acclimatise, the change so sudden that she suffered with headaches in her first days; muscles tensed, breaths shallow, as though she had been plunged into cold water.

She was in her final year studying Mathematics at Newnham

College in Cambridge when she saw the job advertisement in the *New Statesman*. The salary was minimal but living expenses were covered, which meant she would not have to return home to her parents in Northampton. There had been no opportunities to stay on at Cambridge; she had proved she had a natural aptitude and an unusually high intellect, but there was, of course, the handicap of being female. Nor could she meet the expectations of her parents, having no inclination towards romance, matrimony or procreation. The girls she had been at school with had already 'settled', a term which she pictures literally, imagining them as particles of sediment piling up, one generation on top of another.

Margaret wants a life of purpose. She wants to solve problems, find solutions. It's not that she is arrogant, just realistic: a talented mathematician for whom marriage offers very little opportunity to use her skills (beyond household budgeting). She would undoubtedly be hopeless at holding dinner parties to further her husband's career. Research might aid her in choosing the right clothes, or menu; she could perfect the skill of flower arranging to make a fashionable centrepiece for the table; but when it came to making suitable conversation with the other wives, she would be found lacking. No, it would not be fair to inflict herself on a husband.

Mother, however, resolutely miscalculates her suitability for marriage, and assumes that she will move back and take an administrative position at the bank where Father works, until she finds a match. She has told Margaret, with some pride, that she has recently taken it upon herself to make enquiries about the marital status of her friends' sons (taking care not to mention 'Cambridge' or 'Mathematics', lest it put them off).

Blackpool is a necessary compromise to Margaret's escape, but she has discovered that it suits her better than she could have imagined. If only she can prove herself, there is a real possibility she might be asked to stay on after the summer season is finished, or be invited to take up another post elsewhere. Who knows where the opportunities might lead – to which organisations or government departments? And if she can only stay away long enough to become an irredeemable spinster, even Mother will have to admit defeat.

The secretive nature of her role provides the perfect screen behind which to hide. She can say, with all honesty, that she is not in a position to discuss the important work she is doing. And Blackpool is too far away for her parents to make an impromptu visit. Not that her father is capable of acting impulsively. Not any more.

Mother would be horrified to know that the curtains hang limply at her window, that the brass bedstead is tarnished, the mattress sagging. Some of the other researchers have been blighted with an infestation of bed bugs. The spots on their arms add an air of authenticity when they try to infiltrate a group of sunbathers on the beach but, having seen how persistently they scratch, Margaret has become fastidious about prevention: she regularly strips off the mattress and applies Keating's insect powder to the crevices between the slats. Last night she woke convinced that she could feel the crawl of something on her skin and jumped out of bed to check every inch of the sheets. After that, she could manage only a fitful rest, turning over the events of the evening, trying to make sense of what had happened. But every time she was on the verge of an answer, sleep would interrupt her logic and lead her on a winding path.

Thank goodness for the stranger who stepped in. What was his name? She is unsure whether she failed to ask or has forgotten the answer. At the time, her pride did not allow her to imagine the full implications of what might have happened if he had not been there, but in her sleep the memories return: the smell of ale, fingers clutching at her waist. She wakes again and finds red marks on her skin where she has been scratching.

Usually, Margaret applies the principles of mathematics to everyday life. Like every other woman, she makes thousands of these assessments every day: the result of a particular meal on her figure, the probability that the group of men on the street corner might jeer or attack. The difference is that Margaret knows she is doing it, understands the mechanics of the process, draws comfort from the reliability of the numbers. But last night she ignored the risks and put herself in danger. She got carried away and did not stop to make the calculation. Had she done so, she concludes, it would have been obvious that she was at a significant disadvantage. The combined physical strength of the two men, coupled with her suspicions about their moral weakness, should have been enough to make her think twice about following them outside. And the environmental conditions, a dark passageway with limited options of escape, should have made her abandon the plan altogether. Margaret is disappointed, not in them, but in herself.

The man who came to her rescue had followed her out of the pub, he told her so; she remembers that much. The pencil he returned is lying on her bedside cabinet. She tries to retrieve the rest of their conversation from her mind, but it is incomplete, and makes no more sense now than it did at the time. He said he knew what she was up to, which surely means he is part of the organisation. Perhaps he was carrying out his own observation of her and, if so, she can only conclude that she has disappointed him too. But he seemed keen to take her for lunch at the Metropole, excited to discuss something with her. That much she can remember. And she is duty-bound to go and find out.

She steps out of bed and onto the rag rug, which is all that decorates the worn floorboards. She needs to use the loo (not the lavatory, as Mother would have it) but until she is properly dressed, she does not want to risk seeing the other boarders. They often leave their doors open and call between rooms, rushing to share clothing or gossip.

Margaret keeps her own door closed to ensure she is never included in these conversations. It is partly for this reason that she washes with cold water every morning, filling a jug before bed and carrying it to her room. With only one indoor toilet and one bathroom serving the entire property, there is competition for a slot. The girls congregate on the landing while they wait their turn, the last in the queue rewarded by a sink that's snarled with hairs of varying shades.

'What I wouldn't give to stay in bed today,' she hears a voice say. 'Cramps are terrible this month. I went proper faint yesterday. I was glad to have a quiet minute in the stockroom, but his nibs caught me leaning again the shelves and told me to look smart. They have no idea, do they?'

'They wouldn't care if they did.'

'One of these days, I'm going to tell him where to stick his job.'

'Make sure I'm there to see it!'

It is much more efficient and private for Margaret to wash

in her own bedroom, a task she never lingers on. She keeps a heavy dressing gown around her, opening it just enough to reach in and wipe a flannel under her arms and between her legs. The act of dressing is similarly hurried. She is never quite able to shake the impression that she is being watched as she slips on another tea dress (identical to the one she wore yesterday in all but print). When she first arrived, she noted this particular style was considered fashionable among young women on their holidays and bought three in different colours to make sure she would blend in. Gloves are not necessary here and her hat is a plain one: navy straw with a white trim.

Shutting her bedroom door behind her, she makes her way down the stairs as quietly as possible, hoping to evade the notice of her landlady. Maude Crankshaw takes a keen interest in the comings and goings of her guests and is perpetually primed to catch them in an act of rule-breaking. A stout woman with strong arms, she wears an apron that creates the effect of one large breast across her front. She is always ruddy-cheeked. And always sweating.

Margaret is relieved to have the chance to tip out the dirty water from her jug in the drain outside before Maude appears in the back doorway. 'You're up bright and early. In late again last night. Were you out with a young man?'

'No, Mrs Crankshaw. Just enjoying the evening air.'

Maude wears a momentary look of disappointment but refuses to be diverted from her course. 'Well think on – if you do find yourself *enjoying the evening air* with a sweetheart, don't you let him take you under the pier.'

Grown so accustomed to deciphering eavesdropped conversations, Margaret wonders for a moment if this is a euphemism for something unspeakable. 'Take me how?' she asks, immediately regretting that she might learn the answer.

'Under the pier, where the sweethearts go . . . or the sand dunes at Lytham. That's another spot. I'll take that.' Maude grabs the jug, changing the subject before Margaret can enquire how she came to be so well-informed about such things. 'An egg is it this morning?'

'Actually, I'm not that hun—'

'Sit down,' she says, directing her into the front room where a small square table is set out for breakfast. 'Chucky egg'll do you good.' Maude steers her to one of four seats around a small square table, and leaves the room. The wireless is on low in the corner. The announcer is reading a headline, but Margaret can hardly make it out. Something about gas masks. She stands, intending to walk across and turn the dial, but Maude returns almost immediately with a small speckled egg rattling in the top of a two-legged egg cup, designed to resemble Humpty Dumpty. Margaret sits again before she is told to.

'There you go, love.'

'Thank you. Would you mind turning up the news a moment?'

Maude does as requested.

'. . . *roll-out to the general population will begin next*—'

'All right for you?' Maude says, returning to stand over Margaret.

'Thank you, yes. I was hoping to . . .'

'. . . *Check for local instructions about where and when you will be issued with*—'

'You don't mind it cold.' Maude says it as a statement rather than a question.

'Cold?'

'Your egg.'

'I just want to listen to . . .' But it's too late. The announcer has moved on. Sometimes Margaret feels like standing in the street and screaming at people to pay attention. She is not sure whether they just can't see the truth, or they do not want to. But she is not the type to scream. Instead, she lifts a teaspoon and calmly shatters the top of the shell. Inside she finds a white that's greyish and a yolk that has the consistency of a rubber ball. She wonders how long it was boiling for. 'Lovely, thank you.' But Maude does not take this as a cue to leave, and continues to stand over her with a look of maternal enjoyment, rubbing her hands on the front of her apron. Margaret has no choice but to add a liberal sprinkling of salt to every spoonful, well aware that she is playing directly into her landlady's hands. At the end of each week, she is handed a bill of 'extras' including the use of the cruet, and any bottles of fizzy drinks she may be tempted to take from the display set out along the top of the piano. On her first night here, she accepted an offer to try the dandelion and burdock only to discover, six days later, that an additional penny had been added to her rent.

'I'd better be off then,' Margaret says, pushing her chair out from under the table.

'Always working aren't you, love? All times of day and night. What is it you do again?'

Always the same question, which Margaret always answers with the same vague reply. 'Secretarial work.'

Maude thinks this to be a rather posh occupation and, not wanting to betray her ignorance about exactly what it entails, never presses for more detail. Instead, she finishes their conversation as she does every morning: with a wink. 'Well, I hope you're doing your *secretarial* for some bachelors.' As far as Margaret can tell, Maude does not have a husband of her own to speak of. Perhaps Mr Crankshaw has left this earthly life, or left his wife for worldly temptations. Perhaps there never was a Mr Crankshaw in the first place.

# 5

Margaret does not want to linger in the passageway that leads from the back door to the street, but she has to step carefully to protect her dress from the damp brickwork. It is so narrow that the sun never ventures below the rooftops. Water has dripped from loose guttering and bruised the red bricks. Seagulls have left their mark too: grey and white streaks like old scars on raw skin. She turns right onto Cocker Street, directly into the sharp wind that cuts channels between the houses. It rushes past, taking her breath with it. The sea breeze is a fickle thing, never seeming to blow in the same direction. On one road it can be strong enough to knock you off your feet, but turn a corner and the air falls still again. She could walk through the town, past the railway station and the Winter Gardens, but she chooses a route along the seafront instead.

There seem to be as many animals as people: horses tethered to carriages, dogs tethered to owners by a lead or length of string. There's a man smoking on a bench with a monkey on his shoulder. Margaret has watched his act before. He stands and plays the accordion while the animal rocks backwards and forwards in a kind of dance. Every few songs he stops and passes a hat around and, if those listening are slow to show their appreciation, he sends the monkey out into the crowd. The little beast is adept at parting people from the spare change in their pockets. Jumping from shoulder to shoulder, climbing up trouser legs, it proudly holds up every shilling stolen, baring its teeth in an expression which onlookers mistake for a smile. 'What a cheeky little beggar,' they laugh. No one argues when the monkey returns to the front with its little hands full and drops their money into the hat.

She draws level with the North Pier and the start of the Golden Mile, a nickname she has learnt is not entirely accurate. It runs, in fact, more than a mile and a half along the front, to the town's South Pier. But every house along it is, undoubtedly, a gold mine: front gardens, ground floors and basements rented out to sideshow acts and refreshment sellers. Come lunchtime the air will be filled with the smell of black peas and vinegar bubbling in copper vats. Margaret watches as men with rolled sleeves lift boxes onto trestle tables and unfold large umbrellas to protect their merchandise from the rain that is forecast to arrive by the afternoon.

On the beach, attendants are putting out the deckchairs, arranging them in battalions, each frame placed an equal distance from the next; the lined canvas pointing towards the sea. Margaret enjoys the sight of them at this time of day, before holidaymakers disturb the uniformity and drag them into smaller huddles or turn them to face the sun. The rock seller is setting out his stall. He's another she has written about in her reports. A fortnight ago she stood on this spot for two hours, noting down exactly what his customers bought and in what quantities; whether they took off the wrapping and started to enjoy their treats straight away or saved them for later. Her findings were, initially, curious. She thought that she had identified a pattern. Every person who approached the stall was greeted in the same way, 'Ah tha wants some toffees!' leading her to wonder what it was that made the working classes favour that style of confectionery. But after a few minutes she realised toffees was a generic term denoting sweets of all kinds. And once again she felt as though she had learnt a secret.

Leaving the prom, she turns into Lytham Road, which dog-legs from the seafront, carrying buses into the parts of town that most holidaymakers never see. Glad of the shop awnings that shelter her from the breeze, she carries on until the three- and four-storey hotels give way to more modest houses. Left into Bloomfield Road and past the football ground which, though she has never attended a game herself, provides a good source of material for surveillance on match days. Then into Shetland Road, where semi-detached Victorian villas are arranged in pairs like shoes or gloves, each couple married by a porch that runs across the front, and divided from its neighbours by a low red brick wall topped with curved tiles. As the street stretches further on, the gaps between buildings become fewer, and the rows of terraces longer.

It is in one of the three-bedroomed houses that headquarters has been established: the offices where reports are written and records kept. She lifts the latch on the wrought-iron gate and walks up the path to the front door, ringing the bell beside it. Just as she expects, she has to ring a second time and then a third to summon her supervisor, James Timoney, to answer it.

'Ah! Come in,' he says, as though surprised to see her. He shouldn't be: she comes almost every day. And he is usually here to let her in. In fact, she cannot fathom how or when he carries out his own observations, because she rarely sees him venture outside. She guesses he is in his early thirties; an unusually thin man, his slight frame is accentuated by a close-fitting knitted waistcoat which causes his shirt sleeves to billow about his arms. His wide-legged trousers swing around his ankles like flags on poles, his dark hair swept to the side by a generous dose of oil which has left a smear on his wire-framed glasses.

'How are you, Margaret?' His familiarity never fails to make her uncomfortable. She had been the one to suggest politely, in the first week of her posting, that he call her by her first name. But she wasn't expecting him to actually do it. The other observers all insist on calling her 'Miss Finch', lingering over her name with mock reverence to emphasise the fact she is a woman. To them, the 'Miss' denotes the fact that she fails to hit the mark. But James Timoney never seems to notice her sex at all, apparently unaware that in their team of six, she is the only female. To him, she is solely a researcher.

He ushers her into the front room, the room that in neighbouring houses is set out as a parlour with armchairs and a sideboard. But here the walls are lined with glass cases, charts and diagrams. 'Anything for me?' He walks to a shelf near the window and studies a glass bowl, half-filled with water, in which a goldfish is swimming in circles. As far as she knows, one of the other observers won it at the fair, and brought it back to HQ intending to flush it down the loo. Yet here it is. James Timoney has given it a home, and a name: George Formby, after the film star who plays the ukulele and sings songs about voyeurism. She suspects it has fin rot.

'Not today, I'm afraid,' she says, refusing to call him James but reluctant to address him as Mr Timoney for fear of seeming old-fashioned. He is hoping for another treasure to add to his collection. The shelves of every case are crammed with novelties: a china ornament of Blackpool tower among sweets in gaudy wrappers, trick novelties and picture postcards. There's a toy dog hanging from the mantlepiece by a length of elastic, a bottle of Bass with a stick of pink rock sitting atop it. Taking a seat at his desk, James brings a jeweller's loupe to his eye and, squinting to hold it in place, begins inspecting the sails of a toy boat. Does he know about the white-haired man from last night? She wonders if there's a way of introducing him into conversation without giving herself away. 'I've been working on a report about public houses. Some illegal gambling.'

'Very good,' he says. But he does not seem particularly interested. 'Mention it to Reardon, he's following up a lead on that.'

'Right.'

Reardon is one of the others on the team. There are four of them who meet in the room next to this office after hours, and she has noticed James never chooses to join them. He is their supervisor, so perhaps that's the reason. There is an unspoken understanding that Margaret would not be welcome: they would feel they have to watch their manners in her company. But she has no inclination to sit and talk with her colleagues anyway. She is happy to work alone. And James seems satisfied with her progress so far. Though it is Tom Harrisson who will decide whether she stays on after the summer season. James speaks of him with great reverence; from what she can gather, they studied at the same college, though at different times. Harrisson is an anthropologist, who studied exotic peoples of the world and decided to turn his attention to Britain.

Margaret had arrived in Blackpool for an interview, knowing only that researchers were required and, greeted by the chaos of James's office, she had wondered whether the project was a serious undertaking at all. James had told her that she would be working for a social research project called Mass Observation, which had been 'established to record every aspect of life among the lower orders: from talking to sleeping, fighting to drinking, dreams to hysteria'. She could tell it was a speech he had rehearsed beforehand. There were already teams of researchers in London. Harrisson himself had worked undercover in a mill in Bolton but he wanted to see how workers behaved on holiday, to understand how they spent their money and their leisure time. He was convinced that they would be caught doing things they would never dream of doing at home.

'Not all of it is suitable work for a woman,' James had told her, 'but you can play your part. Do things that are difficult for the chaps to do. Family activities.' She had feared that he would ask her about her own family. Under the scrutiny of a man with his observational skills, perhaps she would give away a clue – a word or a pronunciation – that she was not who she seemed. That she had never really belonged at university with the other girls. But he made no mention of her life before Cambridge, too busy reminiscing about his own days studying: The Eagle public house, the meadows at Grantchester, the buns at Fitzbillies. She greeted each memory with what she hoped resembled a smile of recognition. She knew of all those places of course, had heard the others making arrangements to meet there, but had never been invited herself.

'So,' James had said, looking down at his notes, 'Miss Finch. Are you going to join us?' In that moment she decided she would. She nodded as he told her it was vital to understand the psyche of working men and women in order to know how to help them. She agreed when he explained how real change could be brought to lives of hardship and despair. Though she has still not got to the bottom of exactly when and how all the information will be used, or to what practical purpose the knowledge will be applied.

She looks at him now, so engrossed in the study of his toy boat that he seems to have forgotten she is standing there. 'I've made some observations in the lido too.'

'Oh?' James looks up at her; the jerk of his head is so sudden that the loupe is dislodged. He catches it as it falls. 'Was that Irish fellow outside? Selling yo-yos?'

'I'm not sure,' she says. 'I didn't see—'

'Yo-yos. You know, little discs of wood. With string wrapped around them.' He lays the boat on the desk, flicking his arm up and down in demonstration, and she glimpses the child he once was. '*Yo-yos*; you bounce them.'

She does know. She knows exactly what he is describing but he is so earnest in his excitement that she doesn't have the heart to stop him. She imagines his mind is much like this room: a miscellany of oddities and memories. Poorly organised.

'Come in all different colours . . .' he says. 'He was selling them last Thursday. Or was it Wednesday? But no one's seen him since.'

'I'll look out for him.' She takes off her jacket and goes to hang it on the stand in the corner, which is being gradually taken over by James's collection of flat caps.

'Put that back on,' he says, standing suddenly. His tone is abrupt. Perhaps he does know what happened last night. 'We're going straight out again.'

'We are?'

'There's something I need to do. Can't put it off any longer.'

She can see his discomfort. Disciplining a member of his team will not come easily to a man like James. The white-haired man reported back. And now she is going to lose this job. Is going to have to return home. To Mother.

Is it too late to make her case? Explain? 'Can I just—?'

'No time.' He picks up a black box and hangs it on a strap around his neck. 'Come along.'

# 6

James strides past her into the hallway with the obvious expectation that she should follow. Easier to just hand in her resignation, spare them both the embarrassment, get it over with here and now. But 'Time to go!' he says. And she knows that there is little point in registering any objection. He won't listen. It is not that he is stubborn or arrogant like other men she knows, it is that he is all too often in a world of his own. And today he is even more distracted. Anxious to get to wherever they are going.

'I need a decoy,' he says, ushering her out of the front door and leaving the key beneath a garden gnome on the front step.

A decoy. Such an unexpected word. Margaret's shame is usurped by curiosity.

'I've been working on it for several weeks,' he says, his knuckles white as he grips the box around his neck. 'I think it's pretty much there. That's why I need your help.'

So, he doesn't plan to send her home? The relief she feels is instant, her body stalling as she takes a breath. 'What is?' she says, struggling to keep up. 'Would you mind if we . . . Could you slow down a bit?'

'Yes, sorry, you're right. We should walk together. Makes us look more convincing.'

She isn't sure what they are supposed to be convincing people of. He hasn't answered her question. There only ever seems to be room for one subject at a time in James's brain. As

soon as a new thought comes to him, the one before is eject-
ed. She can tell he has already forgotten her request to slow
down, his pace now akin to a gallop, and she briefly considers
asking him where they are going but, already out of breath, she
can't afford to expel energy on needless words. The pavements
become busier as they draw close to the seafront and James
seems to grow smaller; he walks through the crowds with his
head down, his elbows tucked into his body, saying not another
word until they reach the Golden Mile.

She has never seen so many people. There must be thousands,
swarming and clamouring. Since she walked the prom, not an
hour before, they have multiplied. The sea beside looks cowed
by so much humanity; gentle waves beating an apologetic retreat. They step between parked cars, which sound their horns.
Not parked at all, but stuck in a queue. Carts, buses and trams,
brought to a standstill by the people who have spilled out into
the road. Every window is filled with figures, the roof of every
stall supporting several bodies. One man has even climbed up a
flagpole to get a better view of the scene.

'Dear God,' says James, drawing closer to her. 'Let's cut back
and go through the backstreets. Too many people, it's—'

'What's going on?' There's something about the mood of the
crowd, a sharp edge, which makes her stomach contract; fear
or excitement, she can't be sure.

'Margaret . . .' James tugs on her sleeve and she turns to him.
He's pale. 'We need to get on. Somewhere much quieter.'

She is torn by a desire to find out what's happening and a
reluctance to disobey her supervisor. 'But I've never seen anything like it,' she says. 'It must be a rally or march or something.
Don't you think? Perhaps we should—'

'We need to concentrate on why we're here. Come on.'

Before she has a chance to make argue further, he turns and takes a route away from the seafront. She follows after, walking quickly to catch up with him, and calls out to a passer-by who is rushing to join the crush. 'What's going on? Why is every-one—'

'Harold Davidson,' the man shouts over his shoulder, with-out slowing his pace. It's a name she recognises but can't place, and she feels foolish for her ignorance. She makes a point of reading up on all the various union and party leaders.

'Did that man say Davidson?' James says, as she draws level with him.

'Yes.'

'Well I never . . . The man himself!'

She is too proud to admit that she has no clue who the man himself might be. 'What do you suppose has brought him to Blackpool?' she says, calculating that the question will not be-tray her.

'Money I should think. He must be trying to raise funds for his case.'

'His case, yes.'

'There was definitely more to that trial than met the eye. Things that were hushed up for . . . well, obvious reasons. Seemed to go on for months. One of the chaps I was at school with is a newspaperman. I might see what he can tell me on the QT.'

'Good idea.'

'And if he really is here in our patch, Margaret, it's definitely worth looking into what the people make of him.'

'Definitely.' The things people say in private are much more revealing than what they say in opinion polls. More honest. More authentic. It's what this project is all about.

'We need to get into the thick of it,' he says. 'Do they believe him? If there's one thing the working man can be relied on to do, it is to follow his heart where these matters are concerned. His view of the world is not diluted by intellectualism. He is content to feel the truth rather than to know it. It's something the rest of us could learn from.'

'It is,' says Margaret. Though in truth she could not agree less. She has come to Blackpool to learn *about* the working classes not to learn *from* them. She spent much of her childhood unlearning their habits.

'Might shed some light on their view of authority. Religion too, of course.'

'Of course.' Religion. She's got it! Harold Davidson. *Him.* 'The Prostitutes' Padre!' she says.

'Yes, I rather suspect he came up with that name for himself. Seems to revel in the attention.'

A vicar – no, rector – from somewhere in East Anglia. Norfolk. Defrocked by the Church of England for something improper. It was a sordid business which had irritated Margaret at the time. All depressingly predictable as far as she could tell. She is not condoning such behaviour but it hardly warrants the kind of attention it generated in the press. News, by its very definition, is that which is new, or at least surprising, and the weakness of men – even the clergy – could be considered neither. She could not fathom why the country had paid so much attention to the salacious details. There were several days that Davidson's trial kept even Hitler off the front page and so, on principle, Margaret had refused to read about it.

They turn back onto the promenade. 'Here we are then,' James says, finally slowing his pace, as they reach the domed roofs of the North Pier. It is noticeably quieter at this end of the seafront. He looks around, his fingers tapping a march onto the case round his neck. 'Almost torn in half last year you know,' he nods towards the pier. She does know. Repeating stories he has already told her is another of his eccentricities. 'A paddle steamer. On the way back from Llandudno.'

She should let him continue. Men, like parents, must always be made to feel they are right, otherwise they find a way to exert their authority. But she finds the task of making other people feel comfortable exhausting. She decided long ago that biting her tongue was the best stratagem, but it has never come naturally, and occasionally her thoughts become words before she can stop them. 'You have mentioned it.'

'Oh, have I?'

'The *Queen of the Bay*? The name of the steamer, I mean.' It is irrefutable proof. Realising he must indeed have told her the details on an earlier occasion, she expects to see disappointment on his face but he looks confused, then impressed. She goes on. 'Ripped a hole ten—'

'—feet wide!' he smiles. A tight smile, at odds with his other features. But it seems to soften. 'That's right! No one—'

'—was hurt but several people were marooned at the far end.' She realises, quite unexpectedly, that she is smiling too.

He makes a noise under his breath as he tilts his head, almost imperceptibly, to the side. She finds the gesture difficult to decipher but concludes it is amusement. Or confusion. Or both. Either way, he seems to have relaxed a little. *She* seems to have made him relax. Though she didn't mean to and she is not sure exactly how she achieved it. The drumming on the case has stopped.

'Champion!' he says, with a little too much enthusiasm. 'That's what the locals say, isn't it?' It is. One of the colloquialisms she has collected in her observations.

'Grand!' That's another common one. In Blackpool no one says 'capital' or 'splendid' like they do in Cambridge.

He takes a deep breath. 'Here we are then.' He has already said that but it would do no good to point it out. 'Busy . . .' he adds, looking over his shoulder.

'Always,' she says. 'That's Blackpool.'

'Yes,' he says, 'that's Blackpool.' A pause. 'Shall we get down to it?'

'I'm sorry?' she says.

But he is distracted. Opening the clasps at the back of the case around his neck he releases a concertina of black ridges.

'A camera!' she says. 'That's why you want me to . . . I thought for a moment it might be a . . .'

'What?'

'There was talk of gas masks on the wireless this morning.'

'Margaret, you are a one! No, it's definitely a camera.' He grins widely, but his lips are shut tight, as though trying to stop a secret from spilling out. 'Ready?'

She nods, unsure what she is agreeing to.

'Over there then. Pose for me.'

## 7

'Pose?'

'Yes. In front of the railing.'

Everything is moving too fast. Not a moment before, they were sharing a smile and now he is asking her to stand and arrange herself for him. She is horrified at the thought that he might be sweet on her. He has not shown any interest in that regard before. But, though it has never happened to her personally, she knows the signs to look out for. Wanting her to pose for him surely qualifies. She has been overfamiliar, must have inadvertently said something she shouldn't have; something that made him think she was interested in romantic interaction.

'I'm not sure it's . . .'

'Hmm?' He is busy adjusting the dials on his camera.

'Appropriate. Professional. For me. To pose. For you.'

He looks up and his eyes widen momentarily. 'Oh . . . I see. I'm sorry. Yes . . .' He drops his voice to a whisper. 'It's not what it looks like.'

Margaret has eavesdropped enough conversations to know that when someone uses that phrase, it almost certainly *is* what it looks like. And she can feel him drawing closer to her now. They are standing side by side.

'I've made some . . . adjustments.' He brings the viewfinder to his eye and falls silent while he focuses on the sea. Then in a low voice says: 'Don't look now but there's a woman to your left.' Taking her time, as though scanning the crowd for something or someone, Margaret moves her head first to the right, then to the left, confirming that he is correct. 'See her?' he asks, giving the lens a quick wipe on his shirt before raising it again. 'Her ice cream is melting quicker than she can eat it. It's dripping down the front of her dress.'

A trick camera. James must have modified it so that he can stand and watch a person, while appearing to be looking elsewhere. He wasn't planning to take a photograph of her at all. She is here to serve exactly the purpose he has said: a decoy. Nothing more. A momentary sense of relief is swept away by a wave of mortification. She has just used the word 'appropriate'. She implied that he had dishonourable intentions. Out loud. But he has no such thoughts about her. Of course he doesn't. He wouldn't. Should she apologise? No, she won't do that. She feels like turning and running away but that would only draw more attention to her mistake. So instead, she forces herself to speak. All she can do now is pretend the misunderstanding didn't happen.

'It's ingenious,' she whispers, feigning an interest in the dials and buttons. 'Do you just use it to look, or does it take pictures?'

'Oh yes, it still takes pictures. I think it is going to come in very useful. Best to go out in pairs though. Don't want to get so caught up with what I am looking at that I end up inadvertently pointing it at some chap's wife!'

Yes, she supposes that would be a very bad idea. She has seen how territorial men can be, especially when they are inebriated.

'Stand just there,' James instructs her. 'That's it.'

She does as she is told, reminding herself that he cannot see her. She tries to remember the times she has observed other young ladies arrange themselves for photographs, considers lifting one arm above her head (like the girls in bathing suits she has seen on postcards), or standing with her hands on her hips (a common trick used to emphasise a female's child-bearing credentials).

'Left a bit,' he shouts across to her, fiddling with the focus ring. 'A bit more.' Then in a voice designed for passers-by to hear: 'Beautiful, darling! That's one for the album.' He is going too far now. There is no need to play the role with such commitment. But she is impressed that he has done his research. The North Pier is the posh end: sweethearts are careful to address each other as 'darling' to set themselves apart from the 'luvs' further down the promenade. Though it is unlikely anyone would give Margaret and James a second look here anyway. Too busy worrying about keeping up their own appearances: wives straightening their husbands' lapels, mothers pulling up their sons' socks. Everything has to look just right. But Margaret feels all wrong. Still unsure how to arrange her limbs, whether to show her teeth or smile with closed lips, she settles on standing with her hands clasped together and reminds herself that people aren't staring at her, it only feels like it.

There are no signs of embarrassment or offence in James's manner; no awkwardness or resentment. Perhaps he was so excited by the thought of using his camera that he didn't realise she was suggesting – well, she mustn't think about her foolishness now. She must be grateful she got away with it. She won't make the same mistake again.

For several hours they continue their double-act, working

out a series of code words in whispered exchanges: 'say cheese' means stay still while he composes the covert photograph, 'give me a smile' means she should stall for time by smoothing her dress or fixing her hair. He suggests she use a compact to pretend she is checking her reflection, but she doesn't carry one. The only mirror she owns is wrapped in a handkerchief in the back of her dressing-table drawer in Northampton. Her parents presented her with a small box on her thirteenth birthday, but she has rarely thought about it until now.

As soon as she held it, she was convinced. A box that shape and size. It had to be jewellery. A necklace. The pendant from the wedding photograph that used to stand on the mantlepiece at her grandparents' house. She had spent hours studying exactly what the woman in it was wearing. Elizabeth. Lizzie. Her mother. Her real mother. Who died when she was three. The pendant just a delicate smudge on the photograph. Was it a leaf or feather? Now she would find out. Would see it. Hold it. Wear it.

'Go on then!' Her father is smiling at her. She eases off the lid. Slowly. Carefully. But before she can remove it, Mother is speaking. There's warning in her words. 'It wasn't cheap, Margaret. The man in the shop said it's inlaid with mother-of-pearl.'

The man in the shop. Suddenly the box feels heavy in her hand. Too heavy for a necklace. The lid comes off and she sees a flash of emerald green, criss-crossed with a grid of white lines. She can feel tears rising, but she mustn't let them reach her eyes.

'I told you she was too young to appreciate it, William,' Mother says, folding her arms.

'She's just a bit overcome, aren't you, Margaret?'

'Yes, Father. I just . . . I wasn't expecting . . .'

'I'm glad you like it. But your mother's right – we're trusting you to keep it safe. We wanted you to have something special.' It is too much. Too precious. She doesn't deserve it. She feels as though, through carelessness, she has already lost or broken their gift. 'Try the clasp,' he says and she does as he instructs. 'You're a young lady now.'

She brings the mirror up to her face, finding her reflection; sees the woman in the photograph looking back. Father used to say she was 'the spit of her' until Mother pointed out that the phrase sounded common. But her grandparents never shied away from marvelling at how much she looked like 'Our Elizabeth'. Grandma would raise her eyes to the ceiling as she spoke, leaving Margaret to infer that her mother's soul was somehow hovering above them. 'A real credit to you, this one, Lizzie,' she'd say. And Margaret would take the reward she was offered for her resemblance: a bowl of 'winkers' (tinned clementines so tart that they made her eyelids twitch). She had lived with them for three years until Father returned home from fighting in France. She wishes now that she had taken her time and savoured every segment, enjoyed the sharp stab of flavour on her tongue.

She packs the compact back into its box, and her father speaks so softly she can barely hear him. 'More like her every day,' he says. 'It's the eyes.'

'Precisely,' says Mother. 'Margaret, I'll show you how to make them look less . . . well . . . a little powder can work wonders.'

The afternoon is spent taking lessons on the correct application of make-up in which she learns there is a fine line between looking polished and looking cheap. 'When you are a naturally plain girl, you need to work a little harder at it than everybody else.' Mother's excitement turns to exasperation as Margaret fails to master the techniques to 'add shape to her thin lips' and draw attention away from her 'unfortunate jawline'. She should be trying hard to make the best of herself. Mother talks as if there is another version waiting to emerge, like a butterfly from a chrysalis. But painting her face only emphasises Margaret's shortcomings; proves that she has tried, and failed, to make herself more desirable. She is more of a moth than a butterfly.

She still has no use for a mirror. But James is right: it would serve a practical purpose here. 'I'll bring it next time,' she tells him. She will have to buy one if he wants this to be a regular partnership. And to her surprise she finds she is not averse to the idea. He is delighted with his new contraption, taking photographs of young boys fishing from the end of the pier and young women adjusting their dresses to expose their legs to the sun: collecting people much like he collects his souvenirs. While he changes his umpteenth roll of film, she takes the opportunity to sit down on a bench and look out to sea. The water is calm today, sunlight catching on rivulets that trail like ribbons behind the disappearing tide. It feels good to look but not observe; to watch a child build a sandcastle without timing how long it takes before they knock it down; to hear snatches of conversation and not commit them to paper. It's as if she has been given permission to tune out for a couple of hours, to turn down the noise.

She is grateful that James is too busy for conversation. The skill of making small talk, which seems to come so easily to everyone else, has always been something of a mystery to her. The constant fear of saying the wrong thing always leaves her depleted. But today she is required to do nothing more than stand and pretend. And pretending is a skill she has honed over her lifetime. Her role demands no more exertion than forcing a smile. And there are moments when even that seems to be occurring naturally.

Another click. She looks back over her shoulder just as he lowers his camera; sees him tilt his head again and stare at her intensely. His expression is strange. He looks as if he has just remembered she is there. Just noticed her for the first time. Typical James.

'I almost feel like I'm on holiday myself today. Takes me back. Where did you go when you were a child, Margaret?'

She feels her cheeks flush, and turns back to look out towards the beach. What can she tell him? That her family didn't believe in holidays? That Mother made sure that every penny was spent on creating the right impression, living in the right area, wearing the right clothes? Trips were made with purpose rather than leisure in mind. Train tickets to London were an investment because it meant they could go to the dress agencies: shadowy places hidden behind unmarked doorways and up flights of stairs. To get the quality Mother insisted on, they had to buy second-hand, travelling to an address across the city to collect previously worn garments she'd seen advertised in *The Lady*, occasionally making short detours past St Paul's Cathedral or Buckingham Palace so that she could gather just enough detail to convince the neighbours that they had spent the day sight-seeing. 'Oh, all over the place,' Margaret says.

'I have fond memories of being by the sea. Not like this. Wild places. Quiet coves. No one else around. I used to wish I could live there all year.' He pauses, starting to put the camera back into its case. 'Did you grow up near the coast?'

'No, Northampton.'

'You don't get much more landlocked than that!'

He looks up at her but she darts her own eyes away to watch his fingers trying to coax the camera's concertina closed. 'Do you think you've got the hang of it?' she says.

'Hope so. I'll find out when I develop the photographs. Beautiful day for it anyway.'

'Yes.'

He pauses. 'It's not nearly as bad as I thought it would be.'

'We were lucky with the weather.'

'We were. And I was so busy with this,' he nods at the camera, 'that I quite forgot about . . .' She wants to prompt him. Not finishing his sentences is another of his habits. But he is distracted again, turning to look over his shoulder. 'So many people. We should . . .' His words falter. She has studied enough conversations to know that she is expected to step in and say something. But she is not quick enough and silence takes hold – the easy atmosphere between them shifting quite suddenly. And she is at a loss to explain why. She wants to leave now, be somewhere else. Be by herself. She feels this awkwardness as a physical sensation: a prickling fear that makes her skin itch and her stomach burn. A drink will calm her nerves, slow her thoughts. A drink to take the edge off.

'I couldn't have done it without you,' he says, stepping forward to stand beside her again, so close that his shoulder briefly brushes hers. She resists the urge to tell him this is a ridiculous assertion. Of course he could. He is the one with the camera.

She didn't do anything. Not really.

'Well, I'd better get on,' she says.

'Of course. Sideshows again?'

'Not sure I'll get anywhere near them today. But I've been thinking about Davidson,' she says. 'I'll go back tomorrow once it's calmed down. See what I can pick up from the crowd.'

# 8

At school, Margaret was taught that there were seven wonders of the world, but when she arrived in Blackpool she found one on every corner: 'The Missing Link from Borneo' and 'The Glamour Twins: Identical In All Ways!' Every building along the Golden Mile is emblazoned with giant billboards that advertise the acts within; hoardings jut out to corral punters inside. 'You won't trust your own eyes' they promise, or 'you've never seen the like'. It upsets her to see families handing over money they can't afford to spend; confuses her to think that they are taken in by this sham or that; angers her to think that these tricksters make their living by cheating others of money they have worked so hard to earn. She tries to understand why people crave the outlandish and the grotesque, why they gasp in collective amazement and recoil in collective disgust. James says it's a hunger for the exotic. They travel no further than 40 miles to Blackpool for their annual holidays, but they want to deceive themselves that they have seen something of the world. They want to return home with a story to tell in the pub.

She has seen the new batches arrive into Blackpool's Central Station, spilling from the carriages even before the trains have reached a standstill. They swarm the platforms and the streets outside, moving as though in thrall. Oblivious to the cars that are trying to navigate the roads around the station precincts, they crane their necks upwards instead, thirsting for a glimpse of the Tower that stretches up to greet them. The moment they satisfy themselves with a sighting is the very moment their holiday begins in earnest. They slow their pace and fan out in different directions. Some carry their luggage straight to their boarding houses, others waste no time in rolling up their trouser legs and going for a paddle in the sea.

James told her when she arrived in Blackpool that, until recently, it had been the busiest railway station in the world. She couldn't fathom it until she went up the Tower herself and, from the viewing platform 380 feet above the ground, watched the queuing trains pull into its fourteen platforms.

So far, she has spent a fortnight taking a full inventory of the attractions on the Golden Mile. At first, she struggled to fight her way through the hordes but, after two exhausting and unproductive days, she had a breakthrough: succumbing to the flow of people like a boat being carried in a current. Now she travels south along the full length of the promenade before finding a bench or low wall to sit and make her notes. Then she crosses and is swept northwards on the other side of the street.

It's not yet 7 a.m. but there's already a crowd gathering for Davidson halfway down, beneath a board so big that it covers both the ground- and first-floor windows.

*STRANGE! BUT TRUE! THE RECTOR OF STIFFKEY!*

On the street is a low platform: a stage built of rough wood that runs right across the front of the building. Those turned away yesterday are already staking their claim to a place in the queue, determined not to be disappointed a second time. They huddle together for warmth, silently urging others to join the ranks and prove that they were right to get here early. At this hour the sun has not yet taken the sting out of the wind. Women shiver in their holiday dresses; children whine about the wait, fathers forced to subdue them with the threat of a slap (it will be a good hour before Pablo's ice creams offer the option to silence them with sugar). Standing at just five foot two, Margaret can see only the backs of heads, tanned necks, the stripe of braces and the clasps of handbags held tight. At times like these, like so many others, her size is a blessing. Small and slight, she is able to pass unnoticed.

'Can you see?' shouts a woman just in front.

'Not from here,' comes an answer from a few rows ahead of her.

'We'll be lucky if we get sight of him.'

There are two older men beside Margaret, taking great delight in discussing the merits of Davidson's trial. 'It's a rum thing in't it? How the mighty have fallen.'

'If you ask me he should've worn his trousers back to front the way he wears his collar. Would've saved himself a lot of trouble!'

Margaret finds it distasteful that they have come in their droves to see the rector, to revel in the lurid details of the charges made against him. But she can recognise that he's the perfect draw. Vulgarity, the researchers have been told, is an idiosyncrasy of the working man who wields it as both weapon and shield. And never more so than here in Blackpool, where even the most innocent of comments or innocuous of items can be twisted into a bawdy joke. The Tower, standing erect on the seafront, the biggest punchline of all.

'Watch it!' A thick-necked man beside her turns and pushes back against the row behind. The atmosphere is becoming fraught. She can feel the crush of the crowd. It carries her forward, her body moving but her feet slower to catch up. If she wasn't packed so tightly between other people she would fall. She is trapped, stifled by the odour of so many bodies sickly with perfume and pipe smoke. But the men beside her are showing no signs of flagging.

'Well I never believed it of him. Those two women—'

'One. The other didn't give evidence in the end.'

'One then. And she was no better than she should be. Bet she led him on.'

'He were already making a nuisance of himself in the tearooms. Chasing the nippies.'

'Good luck to him if he could catch 'em!'

The crowd starts to stir and she looks up to the raised platform to see two men emerging from behind a hoarding. They are carrying a barrel, the kind you might expect to see on the deck of a galleon, with a small metal pipe jutting out from the top, their task made more difficult by their marked difference in height. One of the two is shaped like a barrel himself, the other as lean as a strip of bacon. Margaret watches them heave it onto the platform then rock it onto its rim, spinning it slowly towards a curved wooden support that has been fashioned to hold it in place. They shake the barrel to check it is wedged firmly, before the stouter man steps back and rubs his hands together in confirmation of a job well done. Communicating silently with a nod, they both climb down from the platform and push their way into the crowd. Margaret will include this detail in her report. They are 'gees': plants paid to blend in with the paying public. There may be a dozen or so in total. Some at the front to lead the way to the ticket booth, some at the back to encourage wavering families to join the queue and part with a shilling each.

She can feel the crush of bodies building behind her, a thickening of the air as the numbers grow. Like the splitting of cells, the crowd seems to double in size with every passing minute. She can understand why they've built the stage outdoors; the logistics of getting so many people in through the front door would be difficult and possibly dangerous. Blackpool has never seen the like, has never seen so many people mustering for a sideshow act. All for a glimpse of a man in a clerical collar, which they could get for free in church on any Sunday.

Someone steps onto the platform now. A spieler: the most important component of any sideshow. Because, Margaret has observed, it is never about the act itself, not really. They come for the story. Anticipation is always the most satisfying part of the experience. Good spielers can make a customer believe that what they are about to see might be the strangest and most remarkable sight of their life. The very best can make them leave convinced it really has been. Margaret supposes this one would be considered handsome for his age: dark hair, greased back, and a dash of grey at his temples. He wears a grey three-piece suit, and lifts a watch from his pocket which he swings on its chain. 'It is time, ladies and gentlemen.'

There's a cheer from the crowd and a lone voice shouts: '*About* bloody time!'

'An innocent man, much maligned by the newspapers. An innocent man thrown to the lions by his own church. An innocent man whose only crime was to help those in need, to extend the hand of Christian kindness to girls with nowhere else to turn.'

'It was where he was putting his hand of Christian kindness!'
someone jeers. The spieler raises an eyebrow (whether in censure or encouragement, Margaret is not sure) but hastily drops
it back to the required expression of solemnity.

'The Rector of Stiffkey is the most famous man in England.
More talked about, surely, than the new king. More talked about
than the old king, his brother! He has been defrocked . . .' he
pauses for the inevitable wolf-whistle from the crowd, '. . . he
has been defamed. He has been derided. What next? Why, you
might ask, has Mr Harold Davidson come to Blackpool?' He
pauses again and chatter breaks out in the crowd. He does not
raise a hand to hush it. He stands instead with a feigned look of
disinterest. Experience has taught him that this will make them
more eager to come to him. Only when there is absolute silence
does he go on. 'Why has he come to Blackpool? A very good
question. One I have asked him myself. And if you will permit
me, I will share with you his answer.' There's a thud behind the
hoarding at the back of the stage, but he does not miss a beat.
'Mr Davidson has come to demonstrate his innocence. To seek
from you – the good, the fair, the just – the judgement he has
been denied. To seek from you, the righteous and the pious—'
howls of derision from the crowd now, '—understanding of his
plight and help for his predicament.'

'Where is he then?' shouts a man on the front row. 'And
what's the barrel for?'

'Another excellent question, sir! The barrel is a contraption
built to the exact specifications of Mr Davidson himself . . .' He
pauses for dramatic effect, knowing this is the point he could
lose them. 'A design inspired by the Greek philosopher Diogenes.'

('Dioge-whats?')

'A humble man who lived in a barrel to demonstrate the virtues of poverty.'

('There's no virtue in being skint!')

'Diogenes lived in a barrel in the middle of a marketplace to make his point. Ladies and gentlemen, the Rector of Stiffkey has a lesson of his own. He will imprison himself every day until the Church considers his appeal.'

('What – you mean he's—')

('Look at that!')

A single line of smoke coils up from the pipe on the top of the barrel.

('He's inside the bloody thing!')

Word is passed from the front of the crowd to the back, carried on the drift of cigar smoke which rises from the makeshift chimney. If Davidson really is inside, Margaret deduces that there must be some sort of hatch or doorway in the hoarding behind it. Either that or he has crawled through a cavity underneath the stage.

'Ladies and gentlemen. The most famous man in England has put himself on display. You've seen him on the front page of every newspaper in the land. Now you can see him for yourself.' The spieler strides across the platform and gives a small knock on the front of the barrel. 'Mr Davidson,' he says, bringing his mouth close to the chimney but projecting his words out into the crowd. 'Are you ready to meet your public?'

Perhaps she imagines it but Margaret thinks she hears a muffled knock from inside.

'Very well,' says the spieler, returning his watch to its pocket. 'I am proud to present Harold Davidson, the Rector of Stiffkey!'

With that he opens a hatch on the front of the barrel, revealing a small window covered in wire mesh, the kind you'd find on the side of a rabbit's hutch. The rows of people behind her surge forward to try and get a glimpse, but invisible forces (which Margaret suspects may be the gees) begin to organise them into a queue. They line up in front of the ticket booth: another opening which has appeared in the hoarding.

'He's a brave 'un to do it,' says a man to another. 'Wouldn't get me all shut in like that.'

'That's not bravery. It's good sense. In a barrel no one can see 'im. Not unless they pay up.'

'True! And he's a wet bugger from what they say. Ran out during a sermon once because he saw a church mouse. Terrified of animals.'

'He'd have been better doing that when he saw those girls. I'd sooner trust a wild bull than a female – more predictable!'

Margaret is jostled to the front where she finds a surly woman taking coins without greeting or acknowledgement. Ordinarily it is the pretty girls who are given this job, but this woman is middle-aged, her face crumpled into an expression of disdain and disappointment that the locals would liken to 'a bulldog chewing a wasp'.

When Margaret's turn comes, she climbs onto a single step below the barrel and looks inside, her eyes struggling to focus. It is like a scene inside a doll's house. A toy man sitting, head down, in his study. He looks perfectly relaxed, perfectly oblivious to the absurdity of his situation. He scribbles a line or two onto the notepad on his knee then pauses, staring thoughtfully at the cigar in his other hand and taking a puff before resuming his writing. A single lightbulb above his head illuminates the inside of the barrel, making his white hair glow. He looks up. She sees the gap between his two front teeth and steps back.

It is him. The man from the pub. The man who saved her.

## 9

Even as she makes her way to their appointment, Margaret has not decided whether to go through with it. Her initial calculation had been simple: she must keep her word and meet the white-haired man who rescued her. But her discovery that he is Harold Davidson has thrown her certainty off-balance. No matter how she tries, she can't seem to find a resolution. This is a man found guilty of making a nuisance of himself with young girls, yet he was a perfect gentleman who had come to her aid. He said he knew what she was up to, yet she can't fathom how he could have prior knowledge of her work. He is one of the most famous (or infamous) men in England, yet is desperate enough to display himself inside a barrel. If she did give herself away in the pub, if he somehow guessed what she was doing, he could blow the cover off the whole project. And it would be her fault.

The weather is cooler today. A breeze that feels as if it belongs to autumn. She turns onto the prom, and can see the Metropole, the only hotel on the beach side of the road: a red-bricked island topped with white cupolas. But she paces up and down the street for several more minutes, wanting to arrive precisely on time. A doorman, wearing a navy uniform, opens the double doors and ushers her through. Passing the reception desk, she navigates a path through staff who make no effort to avoid her as they carry suitcases and hat-boxes, and finds her way across plush carpets to the atrium restaurant. It is domed with glass, the walls Wedgwood blue, every surface and pillar covered in gold plasterwork; mahogany chairs and white-clothed tables arranged at precise intervals.

'Can I help you, miss?' A young man is standing behind a lectern in the doorway.

'I'm meeting someone.'

'Are you?' As he says it, he looks down the length of her body and back up again. 'Another lady?'

'A gentleman.'

'And has the gentleman made a reservation?'

'I'm not sure.'

'The gentleman's name, then?'

'Davidson. Mr Davidson.'

He checks his list, using his finger to scan the column of names written on it. 'No Mr Davidson here. We've got a Donaldson.'

'That's not him.'

'Are you sure he was expecting to meet you *here*? There are dozens of establishments further down the promenade.' She knows what he is getting at. She's beginning to wonder herself. She remembers mention of the Metropole but perhaps she has got the day, or time, wrong.

He goes on: 'Is it possible he may have used a different name? Occasionally our patrons like to keep their appointments . . . anonymous. Oh, excuse me.' He looks past Margaret as a young lady steps in behind her. 'Ah, Miss Angus, welcome. Let me see you to your table.' She watches the woman follow him to a spot near the centre of the restaurant. She can't help narrating the scene in her head, as if she is taking notes for a report: Female, early twenties, mink-coloured day dress, gabardine, with a brown velvet collar and cuffs, tan heels and matching handbag.

Margaret looks down at her own pea-green tea dress, the shade garish against the red of the carpet. She should have bought something more suitable to wear. The maître d' seems in no rush to leave the woman's side, pulling out a chair for her to sit on, unfolding her napkin and placing it across her lap, before engaging in a short exchange which Margaret cannot hope to hear across the chatter of the restaurant.

'Still no sign of your gentleman?' he asks, finally returning to his post behind the lectern after pausing to make enquiries with several other guests on his walk back. He gives her an exaggerated smile and for a moment Margaret considers turning round and leaving. This was a bad idea. Her physical safety may be guaranteed in such a public place, but what about her reputation? Does she really want to associate herself with a disgraced man like Davidson?

'Would you like to wait for him to arrive? Perhaps you could . . .' The maître d' gestures for her to step to one side.

'I . . . I'm not sure. I . . .'

'Very well.' He sighs. 'Follow me.'

She does as he instructs, walking behind him, feeling the other diners watching as she passes. The volume seems to drop, chatter falling quiet, teacups held suspended midway between saucer and lips. But she must be imagining it. Margaret prides herself on being the person who goes unnoticed. That's why she's so good at her job.

She pulls out her own chair, unfolds her own napkin and busies herself by studying the gold-trimmed card on a holder in the centre of the table, which offers only one option (tea with a selection of sandwiches, scones and cakes). It leaves her wishing there was a more comprehensive, leather-bound, à la carte menu to keep her occupied while she waits. It is seven minutes before a waitress, dressed in black skirt and white blouse, arrives to enquire whether she'd like to order.

'I'm meeting someone,' Margaret says, despising the apologetic tone she hears in her voice. 'He must be running a little late.'

'Perhaps some tea while you wait?'

'Please.'

'Earl Grey?'

At the mention of it, Margaret is laid bare. She is ten years old again. Sitting opposite Mother in one of the big hotels in Piccadilly, a treat during one of their annual pilgrimages to London. She is trying to concentrate on every muscle in her body all at once. But the effort of keeping her back straight, stopping her hands from fidgeting in her lap, resisting the urge to uncross her ankles, is too much. She can feel a tightening in her limbs, a prickle of heat rising up the backs of her legs and into her spine. Her body is going to betray her. It always does. She is trying to remember the list of rules that Mother drilled into her during the train journey from Northampton. *Remember, Margaret, we do not stir our tea in a circular motion; it is not proper. Do not slice into a scone, but tear it instead.*

Mother is already drawing too much attention to herself, clicking her fingers to get the attention of a passing waiter. 'Yes, good afternoon. Tea for my daughter and myself please,' she says loudly, then, turning to a woman on a neighbouring table, 'Shopping does make one thirsty, don't you find?' The woman smiles politely and looks away. And in that moment, Margaret knows. She knows that Mother doesn't belong here. With every attempt to speak like them, sit like them, be like them, she is showing herself up. The more she tries to fit in, the more she singles herself out. She is nothing more than a mimic. A bad one. And Margaret despises her for it. For putting her through it. This is supposed to be a treat. Mother told her so. She is supposed to be enjoying it.

'Tea for two.' The waiter places a silver teapot and milk jug onto the table. Margaret lifts her teaspoon from her saucer but her shaking fingers make the metal clatter against the china. She is sure everyone in the restaurant has heard her mistake; a look tells her Mother certainly has. 'Remember, Margaret,' she whispers, in a tone disguised as kindly, 'remember your manners.' Margaret watches with some satisfaction as Mother tries to grasp the handle of the teapot, surprised by the heat of the metal.

'A good conductor,' she says, without thinking.

'I beg your pardon?'

'Of thermal energy.'

'Margaret, what have I told you about showing off.' With some irritation, Mother opens the lid of the teapot and stabs a teaspoon inside to mash the leaves. 'It's not befitting of a young lady.'

This time she lifts the pot and pours two cups. All Margaret has to do is stay quiet, pick up the milk jug, tip it just a little, let the very smallest drop dilute the rich brown of her tea. But when she reaches for it, she knocks the jug over, sending the contents spilling across the table. And Mother's incensed whisper grows to a volume that neighbouring diners can hear: 'I've spent months putting my housekeeping money away and you had to spoil it!'

*

'Earl Grey?' The Metropole waitress repeats the question slowly, as though Margaret is incapable of understanding English.

'No. I'll have a sherry instead. Thank you.' As soon as she has ordered it, Margaret feels a sense of being rescued. The right drink at the right time can be all it takes. A moment of punctuation. Like a mathematical symbol in an equation, it makes sense of everything that comes before and after. The first time her Cambridge professor handed round glasses of sherry at the end of a seminar, she felt she had passed some kind of test. It became a Friday afternoon ritual. A moment of belonging.

The drink arrives in an ornate tapered glass, cut crystal, a single cat's tongue biscuit on the saucer beside it. She leans back in her chair and takes the first sip, savouring the warmth of familiarity, the certainty that she has made the right choice. She is grateful to have something to keep her hands busy, tilting the liquid in the glass (the pale liquid of a dry sherry, not the dark amber of the sweet stuff Mother keeps in the decanter at home). She tries to pace herself but the drink is gone quicker than she means it to be and she orders another, handing the empty glass to the waitress to be sure she takes it away, fidgety in the short interval before a full one arrives to replace it.

She hears Davidson before she sees him. His appearance is causing something of a commotion in the dining room, but he seems oblivious. She looks up to see him pointing at her, his top hat beneath his other arm, his clerical collar clearly visible against the black of his shirt. And she prepares to greet him with some pleasantries. A comment on the weather perhaps. 'Good aftern—'

'Goodness! I'm a terror for timekeeping!' he says, snatching out the chair across the table and appearing to fall into it.

'Yes . . .' The moment for 'Good afternoon' has passed. But she is at a loss for what to say.

'Always in trouble with my congregation for being late!'

'Is that where you've . . . ? Why you're late, I mean. You've been in church?' She realises this is a ridiculous question in the circumstances.

'I am no longer permitted to preach. And I have no desire to listen to others in the pulpit, Miss . . . I'm afraid you'll have to remind me.'

'Finch.'

'Like the bird, very good. And you know who *I* am of course.' He winks and takes a large cigar from his top pocket, which he lights, closing his eyes as he takes his first mouthful of smoke. 'What was I saying? The pulpit, yes. I would find it too painful. Phariseeism and superficiality is, unfortunately, characteristic of England's religious respectability. For all its talk of charity and love for one's fellow man, I have seen the Church for what it truly is: ineffectual when it comes to striking at public vices, vindictive towards those who take on the challenges it is too timid to face itself, not to mention how sly the—' He interrupts his train of thought to hail a passing waitress. 'Excuse me, I'm famished. Could we get the ball rolling? Quick as you like.' He grins.

'Of course, sir. Earl Grey?'

'You're very kind.'

Margaret does not mention that the ball could have been rolling twenty-five minutes earlier, when he was supposed to be here. The waitress nods. 'Very good, sir, and for the lady?'

'A sherry please.'

Davidson turns to watch as the waitress walks towards the

double doors into what Margaret presumes must be the kitchen. 'Pleasant girl,' he says, absentmindedly. 'Now, back to business. I'm very glad we met so fortuitously the other night.'

'Yes, I wanted to thank you again. I'm afraid I was rather foolish to get myself in that situation.'

'Don't mention it! I can imagine it gets rather perilous sometimes. When you're on the trail, so to speak.' On the trail? 'But you know what curiosity did to the cat.'

Margaret wants him to slow down. He is talking in riddles.

'You're like me, Miss Finch; you find yourself drawn towards drama.'

'I'm not sure I—'

'But we both have a dedication to the truth. As soon as we became acquainted, your kind manner convinced me that you would give me a fair hearing – something I have been cruelly denied by the Church—' This thought is interrupted by another. 'Oh, do take out your notepad if you'd like to. No need to be shy. We both know why we're here.'

She doesn't want to admit that she still has no clue exactly what he expects of her. 'It's all right, I'll just . . .'

'Whatever you prefer.'

The waitress returns with a teapot, a sherry and a three-tiered stand of food. Davidson does not hesitate in digging into the cakes before the sandwiches. 'I was tricked into coming to Blackpool – well perhaps not tricked exactly – but it was not until my arrival that I discovered I would be put on display in such a manner. But what choice did I have?'

'I . . .' Margaret begins to speak but realises it was a rhetorical question. She busies herself with selecting a sandwich from the stand instead. He does not pause to hear her respond. He does not pause to chew his food. He does not appear to pause to take a breath. She had been worried he would be the sort of man who would look at her intently, and had prepared for their meeting by planning ways she might employ herself to avoid returning his gaze. She has observed that avoiding eye contact usually means people's attention passes over you, so she often busies herself with checking her pockets for lost keys, counting loose change in her palm or fussing with a stray thread on the hem of her coat (which she leaves dangling there deliberately for just such occasions). But Davidson, eating a finger of sponge with an intensity of purpose she has rarely seen, hardly looks at her at all.

'I have, I'm afraid, run up significant debts in an attempt to clear myself of the charges made against me,' he continues. 'I need to raise sufficient funds for my appeal. Long before the unpleasantness in court, I was spending more money than I could afford, trying to help those unfortunate girls in London. Think of me, if you will, as Robin Hood taking from the rich to give to the poor. Then understand that the theft was from my own modest coffers!' Every part of him seems to move as he speaks: the cigar, still lit in his hand, jerking to reinforce each point; his gaze constantly darting around to the other tables in the dining room. He is nimble, spritely, full of the energy she'd expect of a man half his age. His eyes shine, the lines around them crumpling as he smiles. She remembers the skin on the back of her grandfather's hand, so loose upon his bones, which fascinated her as a child. She used to pinch it gently into a ridge then count the seconds it would take to flatten. Davidson's hands are speckled with the same spots: the marks of age that Margaret thinks of like the rings of a tree, denoting years passed or disappointments overcome.

'You see – and I'm keen for you to understand this – God brought me to my true calling.' Davidson reaches for a napkin and wipes his mouth. Before she can avoid them, his eyes have met hers. Her first impulse is to look away, to lift a sandwich or take a sip of tea. But she doesn't. And she is surprised to find welcome in his gaze, solace even. Not a feeling of being looked *at* but looked *to*. As if he is, very gently, asking that she simply listen. 'I was walking across London Bridge when I came upon a woman – no more than a girl – who was intending to end her life. Can you imagine how wretched one would have to feel to contemplate such a thing?'

'I can't,' Margaret says.

'I don't know how long I stood and talked to her. It was cold, that much I remember. But not as cold as that grey water beneath us. I stayed until I was reassured that she had changed her mind. But I returned home that night disturbed. The thought haunted me – what if I had not been there? What if I had not seen her?' His voice catches and she fears he is going to cry. Right there in the restaurant. 'And that's why I vowed to . . . We all deserve to be noticed, don't we?'

With that, Margaret looks away. He is being noticed right now, making a spectacle of himself, blowing his nose on his napkin. The couple on the next table are probably staring at them. The waitress too. But Mr Davidson seems unaware, or uninterested, his voice increasing in both emotion and volume. 'I dedicated myself to looking at the sights from which others turn away.' She looks to him again. Compelled, fascinated, because she thinks she finds sincerity in his eyes. In fact, she is almost sure of it. A look that greets her without expectation or judgement. So much of her life spent trying to read the thoughts and moods of other people, but this stranger communicates something so clearly, so directly, that she has no need to analyse or decipher. 'Do you see?' he says.

'I think so.' He rescued Margaret, after all. And now here she is, sitting across from the most famous man in England. What would Mother think of that? She'd be appalled. Margaret stifles a smile.

'My motives have been so cruelly misunderstood,' he says, his eyes leaving her to find another treat from the cake stand again, and settling on a scone. Something has shifted; a moment passed. A feeling of what? Connection she might call it, which only took shape once it was broken. The change is so sudden that she feels disorientated. He slides something across the table to her. It is a postcard with hand-drawn headlines.

*STRANGE! BUT TRUE!*
*(in other words) the whole case against*
THE RECTOR OF STIFFKEY!
*was conducted in the strangest manner it is possible to conceive of*
*& it is quite*
*TRUE*
*when we say that everyone is puzzled by the very strange*
*happenings!!*

'Designed it myself,' he says, noticing a spilt dollop of jam on the tablecloth, wiping it up with his finger and licking it off. 'I had copies printed. There are questions to be asked and the answers will be very illuminating.' She studies a cartoon strip drawn rather crudely on the bottom. 'My accuser – my *sole*

73

accuser, Barbara Harris – being paid £1 7s 6d a week pocket money whilst the case was in progress,' he says, tapping his teaspoon on the sketch of a stick man and stick woman shaking hands.

'You think they bribed her?'

'They backed her into a corner. If she refused to testify, she risked losing the help she was being given. In court they cast me as a predator when, in fact, my only role was protector. The young ladies I helped were in dire need of moral guidance. They did not have the strength of character to look after themselves. I ask you, did Our Lord Himself not extend the hand of kindness to Mary Magdalene? Did I not have a duty to follow His example?'

He continues in this way, answering questions which she has not posed. Margaret stares right at him, willing him to look up again. But he doesn't. Instead he talks and eats and gestures around the room. She should be trying to memorise every detail but she can't keep up with the sense of it. All she can think is that a guilty man would not go to so much trouble, or put himself through so much humiliation. Surely he would have gone quietly. As she understands it, he was given every opportunity but refused to step down.

'My fellow clergymen proclaim to follow Christ's example but when it comes to going into battle on His behalf they choose to stay in the safe havens of their parishes,' he says, the words tumbling out between mouthfuls of cucumber sandwich. 'The Church cast me out and we will make sure the world hears of it. And it will hear of the hidden and shameful lives that those young girls are forced to endure. A class of persons, numbering thousands, compelled to exist under degrading conditions, haunting the streets like painted vampires.' He looks at her finally, to make this point, but it is no more than a glance this time. 'Those are the very words I spoke in my first sermon after I was accused. I arrived to my parish to find the church packed to the rafters. They were standing six-deep at the back. Motorcoaches had brought parties from Wells. A contingent of the British Legion had marched from Blakeney. A newspaper man counted fifty cars parked near the church. I stood before them and posed a question that day: were they, I asked, taking their part in raising those whom life had dragged down?'

'It must be a great source of regret that—'

'Miss Finch, I cannot regret the circumstances in which I find myself. I can only rejoice that my suffering is bringing the plight of the forgotten and the neglected to the fore. I trust in God that the truth will out.'

With that he checks his watch, takes out his wallet and removes two ten-bob notes. 'My treat,' he says. 'I have a tendency to ramble on but I hope you can extract something from it. Get a sense of the story.'

He winks at the waitress and makes a show of sliding the banknotes under his side plate, before getting to his feet.

'One thing I wanted to ask you—'

'Next time. Must dash. I do hope you will look in on me in the barrel sometime soon, Miss Finch. You can always wait for me backstage. Just ask for Uncle Harold. Oh, and you can keep the postcard. A gift from me.'

## 10

Smoke is rising from the chimney on the top of the barrel. Margaret has come to regard it as a signal to her alone. A message from Davidson, that he is still staging his protest, still resolute in proving his innocence. Logically, she knows he has no idea that she is there. But she feels a kind of responsibility to watch over him and, besides, she does not sleep well, dreaming as she does of crawling insects and disembodied feet. Venturing out to observe Davidson's arrival most mornings gives her a reason to leave her boarding house before the others wake. Though, in reality, she needn't hurry: she often finds herself waiting for ten, fifteen, even thirty minutes before she sees him dashing along the pavement, a hand planted on his top hat to stop it flying off his head.

In many ways, his confinement makes him the perfect subject. She can watch without having to hide. From that simple smoke signal she can decipher the exact time he steps into the barrel, the precise moment he leaves. As far as she can tell, there is barely a moment that he is not smoking a cigar. The only cessation is when he is forced to discard an old one and light a new.

It is two weeks since he arrived in town and the crowds are only just starting to thin. Margaret has not been formally assigned to write a report on his show, but James did suggest – no, insist – when Davidson first arrived that she should find out what the working classes made of such a man. So, she has made a point to come back every day since. And though she would not admit it (even if she had someone to admit it to), she would come anyway. She is determined to unravel the truth of his purported guilt. She is determined to solve him.

She suspects his popularity is the simplest trick of all, a sleight of hand. It is not really the Rector of Stiffkey that the crowds queue to see, it is his scandal. Not the man himself, but an idea invented by the newspapers. They don't get to listen to the real Davidson, the one Margaret met, because they don't want the truth. They want a spectacle. But she is different, he said so himself at the Metropole. He sensed that she would give him a fair hearing.

She makes a record of what other people think. There are the usual responses: spectators leave struck by the cramped conditions he sits in, or disappointed that he did not look up at them. The vast majority seem to buy one of his postcards, which they will send to 'Auntie May' or 'Joan and Ronnie'. She knows he takes food in there because she heard a spectator wondering 'what kind of butty he were eating' but she has decided not to give too much thought to the arrangements for toileting (noting only that, at intervals, a shutter is pulled across the wire mesh at the front of the window). He is exhibited from 8 a.m. until 9 p.m., six days a week, and Margaret makes an effort to vary the times she comes. Sometimes at night, when the last in the queue are sent away disappointed, she has seen Davidson emerge from a side door of the building and go to various public houses. She has followed him, three times, as far as Bonny Street, a passageway barely noticeable from the main road, where the tiny houses are crammed so tightly that they appear to be holding each other up. On the first occasion she waited ten minutes to be sure Davidson had gone inside, then she turned down the narrow passageway herself. There she found the cobbles strewn with chip papers and smashed bottles; a series of mismatched windows lit by gas lamps, glass cracked, panes partly covered by grey net curtains. Behind them, rooms that made Maude's boarding house look salubrious by comparison. And as she stood there, she pitied Davidson. In the past he had lived in a rural vicarage with a drawing room, a garden, a servant perhaps. And a wife and children. He definitely had those. Where are they now? she wonders. Presumably respectability is still important to them, even if it has ceased to have meaning to him.

He has no idea she has been following him, she has made sure of that. Only once did she fear he had spotted her, when he turned unexpectedly and looked in her direction. But she saw no flicker of recognition on his face. And was surprised to find that, once the initial wave of relief had retreated, it exposed something beneath. Something stranded, like flotsam. Something like disappointment.

She does not record these sightings of Davidson in her notebook, waiting instead until she gets back to her room, and writing them in her diary. Dates and times. Descriptions of people he speaks to and places he goes. He has found himself in court again since arriving in Blackpool. Margaret joined the crowd outside. Several hundred began to gather nearly two hours before the hearing, standing with little shelter from the heavy rain. When the doors opened, she watched them rushing pell mell up the stairs, and saw several slip and hurt themselves. Only the first few got a seat inside; the rest had to make do with a glimpse of Davidson as he arrived, greeting him with a cheer when he finally made an appearance (fifteen minutes late). The evening paper reported that he had been fined £1 16s for setting up a temporary structure without permission. And on the following morning, she discovered that his barrel had been moved inside a shopfront, where he could operate within the perimeters of the law. If anything, his appearance in court had caused the crowds to swell again. She has seen them turn nasty only once: a few agitators threatening to turn the barrel into the sea with Davidson inside; a woman shouting at people not to hand over their money to a man who has exploited vulnerable girls. Otherwise, the spectators are always excited to get a glimpse. What they wouldn't give to meet him properly, as she has done. No doubt they'd think her mad not to have paid him a visit backstage, but the longer she waits, the more uncertain she is that he meant the invitation. That he wasn't simply being polite. And she still cannot decipher what it is he expects from her. Perhaps she should call on him. Perhaps when her Golden Mile report is finished.

She has been methodical in her study of the gawdy catchpenny stalls, the street sellers and the fairground games. And towards the end of every day, when her weary feet begin to complain more insistently, and she longs to leave the eddying crowd, she chooses one of the other sideshow acts to visit. This afternoon she joins the queue to see 'The Headless Girl'. She has observed that those who advertise themselves as 'unsuitable for children or ladies of a nervous disposition' seem to draw the biggest numbers of both. Noting that she has waited for twenty-three minutes, and been warned no fewer than seventeen times that what she is about to see is not for the faint-hearted, she pays her shilling. Then, following the instruction to brace herself to witness 'the harrowing and the grotesque' (unsure whether the description is intended as a warning or a promise), she steps through the front door of what would once have been a house.

Discordant music plays from an unknown source, the parlour knocked through to the dining room to create one long gallery. Red curtains cover one wall, a thin man in a dinner suit using a cane to hold back the crowd as it pushes forward. 'We keep these drawn to give you one last chance to change your mind,' he says. 'Many have thought themselves strong enough to stomach the sight and have never recovered.'

At this the crowd laughs a little too loudly. Friends draw closer to each other; a child buries her head in her mother's skirt. The music stops and there is a moment's pause before someone replaces the needle on a hidden gramophone. 'Very well, if you are sure . . . I present to you a medical impossibility. A girl whom science says cannot exist. And yet she lives! Ladies and gentlemen, The Headless Girl!'

On his cue, the curtains are pulled back. On a dimly lit stage, raised a foot off the ground, Margaret sees it, and for a moment she forgets why she is here, her eyes no longer primed to study the reaction of the crowd. She cannot look away from the thing arranged on a chair. A collection of body parts that makes no sense. Two long legs, one crossed over the other, the seams on their stockings running like stitches down their length, disappearing into black patent heels at one end and a dark red pencil skirt the other. Sitting above them is a body encased in a flesh-coloured blouse that clings to every contour, large breasts shaped by the architecture of a brassiere. Arms are arranged neatly either side, elbows tucked in, one hand lying on the lap of the skirt, the other holding a lit cigarette. But there is no mouth to smoke it. Nothing where the head should be. No neck, no jaw, no hair or face; the void is marked by a metal scaffold that juts out from the neck and supports rubber pipes that spout towards the shoulders. It looks like a cage, without a bird inside. And then the body moves, the legs uncrossing then crossing again, and there is something obscene about the sight of it.

Margaret can picture exactly what sort of head the woman would have; knows her lipstick would be pillarbox red, her hair bleached and arranged into blonde curls. The image makes her think of Davidson. The girls. The accusations. She imagines this is how they looked. Girls like that always do. The men in the room know it too. She turns to see the knowing smiles they pass between them, the shared fantasy that their own wives would have the body of this girl. A body without a head to think or a mouth to scold them. But why is Margaret imagining what she *would* look like? It is simply an illusion. She just needs to work it out. Most of the sideshow 'magic' is so obvious that she can see through it in an instant. But occasionally it takes patience and determination to unlock the secret. And she prides herself on never failing. While others are content to stand and marvel at the spectacle, she works out how the artifice is achieved: the decoys and distractions, the stacked odds, the sleight of hand. While others are blinded to the mechanics of the deception, she alone can see the strings being pulled. She is not suggestible. Not like the rest of them.

'The remarkable thing is that this girl is normal in *every* other respect,' the spieler says. 'She has been examined by eminent doctors who have confirmed that every other function is in perfect working order.' The Headless Girl's hand twitches and flicks the ash from the end of the cigarette. Margaret observes the spectators from the corner of the room. She notes the questions that they ask, the vast majority concerning the practicalities of surviving: the mechanics of eating and breathing. But when she returns to type up her findings later, Margaret will note that there was much whispered innuendo about other functions of the mouth. The experience leaves her feeling that a joke has been told, but she cannot quite understand the punchline.

She considers the scene from various angles. Tilts her head, stands on tiptoes. It is nothing more than smoke and mirrors. Her best guess is that the woman's head is hidden in some sort of mirrored box, built to reflect the onlookers' fears and fantasies back at them. And suddenly she does not want to linger. Cannot bear to look.

As she makes her way towards Shetland Road, Margaret's stomach reminds her that she has missed both lunch and dinner, her hunger prompting an uncharacteristic urge to step into a fish and chip shop. She finds herself waiting behind an elderly man who speaks so loudly that she can only assume he is deaf. She'd be surprised if any sound could penetrate the rampant growth of hairs that cover the route to his eardrums, and has to repress an urge to tell him to trim them.

By the time they reach the front of the queue she is convinced that the condition has affected the clarity of his speech as well as its volume. 'Babbys' yead,' he says, taking a small leather purse from his pocket and pushing the coins around with a poke of his forefinger.

The man taking the order confers with the man wrapping the food, who in turn confers with the man frying it. But all three are at a loss to understand what it is he wishes to eat.

'Babbys' yead.' The old man gestures, pretending to cradle a baby with one hand and tapping himself on the head with the other. 'Babby's '*ead*!' It's a shame, thinks Margaret; old age has obviously addled him.

'How about a nice steak and kidney pudding instead?' says the man who is serving.

'Tha's what I said!' The old man counts out the correct change on the countertop, turning to Margaret and rolling his eyes. Then making no attempt to lower his voice: 'These jokers have obviously never been as far as Wigan!' He shakes his head with a look of wonderment. 'It's another world in Blackpool!'

It is, thinks Margaret, then she realises she has forgotten to look up at the board and decide what to order herself. 'A portion of chips please.' She is still so distracted by the question of why anyone would want to eat something that resembled a baby's head that when the server asks if she would like pea-wet with her order, she nods.

It is only as she starts to walk to HQ that it becomes apparent that the hot bundle she has been handed is starting to leak. Green liquid is soaking through the newspaper wrapping and onto the front of her dress. Pea-wet, she realises, must be the discharge that comes off the marrowfat peas that are boiled until they become mushy. It certainly smells like it.

By the time she gets to the front door, strips of sodden newspaper are sticking to her hands. There is a light on in James's office but, even when she rings the bell for the sixth time, he does not come to let her in, so she bends down and lifts the gnome that stands sentry on the spare key. Though she would never come here after hours herself, she has suspicions that some of the male researchers use the empty building to further their study of the sexual morality of working-class women. Crossing the threshold, she rushes down the hallway with the chips held at arm's length, keen to get them to the safety of the kitchen dustbin as soon as possible. What a mess! Gravy she can just about understand, and the peas themselves have nutritional value at least, but the water they've been boiling in?

She grabs a handful of cloths from underneath the sink and sets to work retracing her steps, cleaning up the trail of green liquid. Though it is not part of her job description, it has fallen to her to keep headquarters clean. It would not occur to any of the men to wash their own teacup or sweep up the sand that they walk in on their shoes. Yes, she hates herself, hates that it merely confirms their view of her, but she isn't doing it for them, she is doing it for herself. She cannot not bear the chaos to reign and the dirt to fester. Would not be able to concentrate on her report knowing there were puddles of pea-wet on the hallway tiles. And so, on her hands and knees, she does what she always does: she restores order. She crawls across the black-and-white chequerboard, pausing when she reaches James's office to stand up and turn off the light he has left on. In the dark, the souvenirs in the glass cabinets really do look like artefacts, light from the bulb in the hallway settling on the edges of ornaments and toys. She knows she shouldn't, but she steps in. There are pieces of paper on every surface, open books lying spine-up on the floor. How can James work in such an environment? It makes her agitated just to look at it. She can't resist replacing the top on his fountain pen to stop the ink from drying out but, the very moment her hand touches it, she hears a bang. A pulse of air in her ears. A breeze must have slammed the front door shut. She mustn't have closed it properly when she dashed in.

'Hello?' She can hear a man's voice but can't work out where it is coming from. It's as if the sound is coming from the floor beneath her feet. 'Hello? Is someone up there?'

She has the sensation of being watched, is suddenly aware of where she is standing and how it would look to anyone who found her. 'Yes! I'm . . .'

Footsteps on the stairs. She has to leave the room. Shouldn't be in here alone. But she can't bring herself to put the fountain pen down until she has screwed the top on it. '. . . coming!'

Stepping out into the hallway, she is just in time to see the doorway under the stairs open, and James emerge.

'Ah, Margaret, it's you,' he says, relief in his voice. 'I thought I was going to have to fight off a burglar!' He raises his fists and spars with the air, nervous energy running through him. He really had expected to find an intruder. She thinks him rather brave for coming to find out. 'Gracious, it's bright!' he says, lifting a hand to shield his face. 'It's pitch black down there.' He nods to the doorway behind him, still protecting his eyes with something like a salute. 'Rather frightened myself when I heard someone walking around up here. Silly really.'

She doesn't think it was silly at all, but she can't understand why he was lurking in the cellar in the first place.

He turns and heads back through the doorway. She hears him walk down two steps and pause on the third. 'Are you coming, Margaret?'

She is not sure she should be following a man into the dark. Even James. She hesitates and peers around the doorway. The hallway light touches the first half a dozen steps or so but below that she can see nothing.

'Shut the door behind you,' he says. She does as he asks, then turns back to find a head in the darkness. A head detached from its body: James illuminating his face with a torch. He directs the light onto her feet, then down onto the tread below them, to guide her. She follows its path, stepping after it. James walks backwards into the darkness, but as soon as she has safely reached the bottom he turns from her, snatching the light away. She fights an impulse to rush after it, forces herself to quieten her breathing, puts out her hand to find the wall, the bricks slick with damp. There's a smell that catches in the back of her throat. A medical smell. A chemical smell. She edges her foot back and wedges her heel against the first step, in case she needs to find her way out.

The torchlight jerks around the room as James walks across it, flashing into cobwebbed corners. Margaret hears the bang of something metallic, and there is darkness. Sudden. Complete. At the same moment, James cries out. She has an instinct to run but she is not sure whether towards him or away.

'Are you all right?'

'Yes. Dropped it on my foot. Where's the blasted light?'

She hears a click, then an amber glow spills from a lamp on a table set out in the centre of the room.

'Sorry about that,' James says. 'So – what do you think?'

It takes her a moment to understand what she is looking at. A washing line pegged out beneath the low ceiling. A table covered in bottles and trays, tools and papers.

'A darkroom?'

'Yes. All fairly crude I'm afraid. I'm a beginner. But this is perfect timing. I had just got everything set out and was about to start.' She recognises the spy camera he used a couple of weeks ago, as he lifts it from the table. 'Are you quite all right, Margaret? You look . . .'

'I'm . . . just surprised.'

'We gave each other a fright I should think!' He picks up something that looks like an empty cotton reel and puts it in his shirt pocket. 'You remember the photographs we took?'

'Of course.'

'Time to see if that cloak-and-dagger routine paid off.' He checks the temperature of the liquid then reaches across her. 'Shall we?'

She says nothing but he seems to take her silence as assent. Another click and the amber light disappears back into the lamp. There is nothing but darkness. No chinks of light, no shadows. She can see nothing. Nothing at all.

'A fiddly old business in the dark,' James says, his voice suddenly a whisper. 'The key is to have everything to hand and know exactly where to find it. Any light at all could damage the film.'

She waits for her eyes to adjust but there is no change; it remains as dark as if she were wearing a blindfold. She feels as though her body is swaying, set adrift. She wants to reach out and hold onto the edge of the table. But she dares not move in case she breaks something. In case she accidentally touches James.

'Are you all right there, old girl?'

'Yes.' Old girl? No one has ever called her that before.

'I'm opening the film cassette now. I just need to cut off the end and . . . hold on . . . not quite . . . that's it . . . now I can roll it.'

There's a rhythmic crackle as the film is wound. It is a trick of her brain. She knows it is. But she imagines she can see what he is doing, can see the look of concentration on his face. And she can hear every breath he takes.

'Thanks again for helping. At the pier.' His movements stop and she can sense he has turned his head to look at her. 'It's important we keep Harrisson happy.' She smiles in reply then realises that, of course, he cannot see it. 'He wants results,' he says.

'Yes.'

'He hopes to prove certain . . . hypotheses. I'm concerned that I'm not quite giving him enough . . . how can I put this? I'm under some pressure to provide . . . colour.'

'My report about the Golden Mile isn't far off now.' As she says the words, she is surprised to find they sound defensive. 'I went to see The Headless Girl today.'

'Ah – did you? What did you make of her?'

'The crowd certainly found her convincing.'

'And what about you?'

'I could see how the illusion was achieved. A mirrored box and—'

'But did you not find it unnerving?'

What does her reaction have to do with anything? It is not significant. She was there to study how other people behave, not to be entertained by the spectacle. 'I suppose. When they first pulled the curtain back. Have you seen her?'

'I . . . no. I've got a postcard from the show somewhere. All the tubes coming out of her neck and . . .' She hears a soft gulp as he swallows. 'I'd like to see her for myself . . . of course . . . but you see, I'm so busy here.'

A feeling comes to her now, a feeling that has been creeping up on her this past fortnight. Of thrill and unease. She should have finished her report by now. Should have typed up much more of it. She'll put in more hours. It won't take her long to catch up. She won't let James down. 'I've got a postcard you might like – for your collection.'

'Oh?'

'Harold Davidson, setting out his case.'

'That will make a great addition. Did you go back to see his act?'

'Yes.' It is not a lie. But she doesn't mention that Davidson gave the postcard to her personally.

'So what do the people make of him?'

'Very mixed in their opinions.'

'That's disappointing. I thought there might be a clear view.'

'I'm sure there's more I can gather.'

'Leave it, if it's not yielding anything obvious.'

'Like you said – it could tell us a lot about people's opinion on authority, religion. I think the crowds see something in his story.'

'A diversion from the mess the world is getting into!'

'Perhaps, but I think it is more than that.'

'How so?'

'He's been treated pretty badly by the Church, by all accounts.'

He laughs. 'By *his* account.'

Margaret can see he has a point. 'But if he really has been made a scapegoat, then shouldn't we—'

'It's not our place. The mission is to understand working-class views, not influence them. And Harrisson is looking for something quite specific – people away from home, in the holiday spirit . . . but there have been very few recorded sightings of . . . misbehaviour. Fights and . . . well . . .'

She knows what he is getting at. She wants to tell him that he needn't be shy with her; she has heard a lot worse in the conversations she has eavesdropped on in pubs across the town. But she appreciates his attempt to protect her modesty. 'I'll be sure to keep an eye out.'

'No, Margaret, I wasn't suggesting that *you* . . . It's just on my mind, that's all. Oh, I shouldn't be burdening you with my thoughts.'

How strange that he should think them a burden. This is her

job after all. 'I want to help. If I can,' she says.

'If your report is nearly ready, I'll tell Harrisson to expect it. That would be help enough. Thank you.'

He returns to his task, talking her through every stage of the process and every tool at his disposal. She joins him in counting down the precise number of minutes that the film is processed in the chemical baths, and hears the liquid lapping against the sides of the tank as he agitates it (five seconds of gentle turning for every thirty seconds of development). He describes each stage of this conjuring act with a rigour that pleases her: the developer washes away the silver compounds of the unexposed areas, while the fixer freezes the rest so they are no longer light-sensitive. Every so often he asks if she is all right, but never if she is keeping up, never if she understands. And by the time he tells her that the steps are nearly complete, she realises that she has come to enjoy the lack of any light. While she has been busy learning the science of photographic development, the blanket of darkness that felt as if it might smother her has become a comfort. In the dark she does not shy away from asking questions about the composition of the fixing agent, or the effect of dust on the grain of the image. For those few minutes, the voice inside her head is silenced. In the dark she doesn't have to observe other people; in the dark she doesn't have to watch herself.

The moment James switches on the lamp again, she feels that she has been woken too soon, too violently. Her eyes hurt and she hopes that the sudden rush of light will blind him a little longer so that he doesn't look at her before she has had a chance to compose herself. It's a term that has always made sense to Margaret: as though she is a melody she can write and perfect. As soon as she came to see every interaction as a musical performance – laughter like the trill of a piccolo, condolences delivered with the solemnity of bow on cello – she started to see the patterns, to understand when a conversation suddenly dipped into a minor key or soared into a major.

'Looks like they've turned out well,' says James, inspecting the photographs hanging on the strings above their heads. 'Good definition. Good contrast. It only takes one chink of light to get in and everything starts to blur.'

At night, the Golden Mile shines as brightly as its name: lurid yellow flaring so brazenly that the moon appears to blanch in shame. Businesses compete to over-stimulate the senses and stun passers-by into stepping inside. Everything is over-sized and dazzling. The biggest, the best, the brightest. Children (staying up far too late, in Margaret's opinion) drawn by the promise of a treat or prize; parents turning to find their sons and daughters have disappeared into a shop or arcade. Organ music plays from an open window, a cluster of men sing in a doorway, stallholders overcome the weariness of the day to shout above the constant chatter. At this time of the evening, the briny air feels stagnant, lost beneath the smell of beer and tobacco.

It has been a long day and Margaret wants to escape. It is all too much. She could never hope to capture it all, and disappointment has been taking hold. A feeling that she can only liken to indigestion. A physical sensation of burning in her chest, a growing unease planted when she found a memo pinned up on the noticeboard at HQ. 'More evidence on promiscuity,' it said. And though the request was directed at the entire team of researchers, she read it as a criticism of her alone. Harrisson's theory, that people lose their inhibitions on holiday, is certainly sound, but she has done little to help James prove it. So far, her reports have contained nothing more than sightings of kissing couples. She is not significantly knowledgeable about the subject to judge whether they are French kisses, or those denoted by another nationality. So, she has devised her own scale of measurement: where the two participants do not part for air for a period exceeding eight seconds she lists it as 'passionate kissing' (she recorded no fewer than eighteen examples on a single night after a dance at the Winter Gardens). It is common for her observations to be peppered with 'sexual touching: uninvited/ unwelcome'. Men grab at women's body parts with no more ceremony than one might scratch an itch. She wonders whether they even realise they are doing it. Margaret has, on occasions, felt a hand on her breast or a sharp pinch on her bottom. She cannot fathom why such an act would give a man pleasure and why it has to be done with such force. Perhaps it is nothing more than an involuntary compulsion, an occurrence so common that she need not make note of it at all. She has failed to confirm sightings of any touching beneath clothing, or removal of garments, but Maude's implication, a few weeks ago, that couples go under the pier for consensual sexual interaction, has set her thinking. She wants to record a sighting of illicit commune, veering between fascination and fear at the thought of witnessing the act.

Margaret walks into the nearest pub to find a corner to sit and think, and orders what her father would refer to as a 'stiffener'. She begins by making a note of the competing risks and benefits of venturing under the pier, careful to consider what could have happened had she not been rescued from those men in the alleyway. But the objections grow quieter with every whisky, their edges blurring. Any voice of consternation now almost inaudible. She can do this. Wants to. For her career. For James.

Male researchers are encouraged to participate in this kind of research directly: to fraternise with young female holiday-makers and report back on how far they manage to take their courtship. Sexual intercourse is often performed standing up, against the outside wall of a dancehall or public house; it is referred to in reports as 'a knee-trembler'. But relieved that, as a woman, there is no expectation for her to deploy such sordid tactics, Margaret resolves to gather evidence from a distance.

Heading back to the pavement of the Golden Mile she takes the steps down to the covered pathway that runs behind the beach. Benches are positioned at intervals, looking out to sea between stone arches. Courting couples sit holding hands, one pair sharing the same ice cream, another the same coat that covers their laps. She supposes they might consider the view romantic. The light spilling from the prom snags the crests of waves, which soothe the night with an insistent whisper.

The tide has gone out, pulling back the curtain on the South Pier's illusion: exposing the metal struts that make it appear to hover just above the surface of the sea. Margaret steps onto the sand and walks towards the pillars, the pale moon lighting her way through strands of seaweed discarded by the waves. In the daytime, she has watched groups of children on the pier, seen them lying on their fronts and putting their eyes to the gaps between the wooden slats with delighted terror. Now, she is the one looking up through the cracks, glimpsing stars floating on a midnight sky. She feels that the world has been turned upon its head and that she could fall right through them. The pillars are scarred with the shells of living creatures, hanging on until the sea returns again. There's a smell of sulphur, of stagnant water. An empty bottle lies unbroken at her feet. In a few hours, she thinks, it will be dashed against the metal posts, shattered into a hundred pieces and swallowed by the waves.

She should perhaps have brought a torch, but that would make her presence too obvious. Fearing that even the moon might give her away, Margaret walks in line with the posts, and peers around them before continuing. Silhouetted beside a pillar further ahead, she can see something moving against the metal, flapping back and forth like a flag. She would have said it was a figure, but the proportions are all wrong: height stunted, legs misshapen, head missing. Its movement is becoming more rapid, more insistent. Noises carry across the still air. Ragged breaths like the rhythmic panting of the sea. The damp sand muffles her footsteps and she is able to make her way closer. And what she sees suddenly makes sense. Two figures. One pressed flat against the metal of the post, the other pushing against it. The head is not missing but bent over the shoulder of the other person. The legs are not misshapen, but half covered with trousers which have been unbuttoned and left to drop to the floor. And all she can think is that they have fallen into the seawater that pools around the man's feet. That when he pulls them back up he'll have wet trousers.

This is what she came here to see. She should be delighted. But she is surprised to find that she is not. She has a feeling of having failed somehow. She had wondered whether actually seeing the act being committed might excite her in some way, that it might ignite a sensation that she had long feared she would never feel. But it hasn't. Just the opposite, in fact.

She can hear the rolling sea, taste the salt on her lips, but she can no longer see it. The moon has hidden its face altogether, cringing behind a single strip of cloud, and Margaret turns away, heading back towards the walkway. Since moving to Blackpool, she has taken very little notice of the landscape. But at night the distractions are packed away, and what's revealed is wild and untameable. She has come here to observe people when they aren't pretending. To see what they do when they think no one is watching. To hear whispers in the dark. And now all she can hear are her own.

She is exhausted but she knows, if she goes back to her lodgings now, that she will not find sleep there. She needs to find purpose and her first thought is Davidson. She is not far from his sideshow and she has observed that he usually waits until the crowd has dispersed before he leaves – would no doubt be mobbed if he didn't. Perhaps he is still there. She could just see where he goes then call it a night. Make sure he is all right. Perhaps she might even speak to him this time. Has he been wondering why she hasn't taken him up on his invitation to pay him a visit? Has he given it a second thought?

Following the path back towards the stairs that lead back up to street level, she avoids the pools of light thrown by the streetlamps, as though stepping directly through them will make her a target, but for whom or what she does not know. It's not far to walk but it is slow going. There are still plenty of people out enjoying the warm evening, couples dancing the foxtrot and a group of women trying to do a fling. A young man falls and his friend picks him up and puts him over his shoulder. Margaret reaches Davidson's show, now closed for the night. Taking a seat on an empty bench on the opposite side of the road, she places her handbag on her knee, pretending to search for something inside it, while glancing up to look for any signs of Davidson. One last look across the road and she can make out a top hat, sees him turning onto the seafront and walking north. She stands and follows, crossing the road so she can walk behind him. Rushing to get closer, then holding back as he slows to speak to two young women. One of them takes something from her pocket and hands it to him. There's the spark of a flame, the smell of cigar smoke reaching Margaret seconds later.

She looks down, watches the shoes of the women as they step towards her, laughing. 'He'll hear you!' one chides the other as they pass.

'Don't care if he does. What's he going to do? There's nothing of him – couldn't knock the skin off a rice pudding!'

Margaret looks up to see Davidson striding away. No top hat now, but white hair, weaving between the small groups gathered along the pavement. He is heading for something, walking at quite a pace, as if he has a purpose and a destination in mind. He takes only the most cursory of glances left and right before crossing a junction then taking the next side road inland. It is much quieter here. If he turns, he'll see her. She pulls her hat down lower and raises the collar of her jacket. The street is deserted apart from a man walking towards them with a black dog on a lead. Davidson stops suddenly, glances back towards her then steps left, ducking out of sight. From this angle she cannot see where he has gone. A doorway or passageway perhaps. Nodding politely at the dog-walker, she stays motionless for a moment, considering what her next step should be. Then, deciding she has come this far and may as well see which building Davidson has gone into, she walks very slowly to the spot she last saw him, and edges up to the entrance to a narrow passageway at the side of a terraced house. She decides to risk a look.

'Has it gone?' Davidson's face is so close it is almost touching hers.

'Dear God!'

'The dog . . .' There is no chance he hasn't seen her this time. 'Has it gone?'

She looks back down the street and finds it empty. 'Yes.' She should walk away herself. If she goes now – if she doesn't turn back . . . Perhaps he didn't get a good enough look at her.

'You're sure?' he says again, and she can feel him peeking past her to see for himself. 'In that case, let's go . . .' He is right behind her now. 'We can't keep meeting like this. Hanging around in dark alleyways. What will people think?' She can hear a smile. 'And there is obviously more you wish to discuss. Otherwise you wouldn't have been following me.'

'Following—?'

'Did you think I hadn't noticed?' That's exactly what she had thought. What she had been sure of. 'Not to worry,' he says, stepping past her into the street, 'practice makes perfect! But, there's really no need. I'm only too happy to give you all the information you require. When's your deadline?'

'Deadline? I . . . it's late . . . I—'

'A drink,' he says as he strides up the street. 'I insist.' And she is already following him again. This time at his request.

# 13

They do not stop at the first pub they pass, the second, third, or even the fourth. Davidson leads her several more streets inland. Margaret has started shaking, and tells herself it is the adrenalin of being discovered. But there's embarrassment too. That she has made a fool of herself, and that he spotted her failings so easily.

'Go on then,' he says. 'You must have a list of questions.'

'I . . .'

'Ask me anything you like. Anything at all.'

She chases her thoughts but cannot grasp a single one of them. Did he do the things he was accused of? Is he the kind of man they say he is? Has he known all this time she has been keeping an eye on him? He could not have known. He was inside the barrel for most of it. She could ask him if he knows about Mass Observation, but if he doesn't, she will have given herself away. She needs to say something neutral.

'That dog . . .'

'Horrible things.'

'They were right about you being frightened.'

'Who?'

'I heard some people talking in the queue for your act. One of them said you had run at the sight of a mouse.'

There's a look on his face, something like pride. 'You really have done your research! Yes, unlike much of what's been said about me, that story *is* true. I was right in the middle of my sermon when I saw it. And I screamed. Top of my lungs. They must have thought I'd seen the Devil himself!' He chuckles but his eyes remain wide. 'Running right along the top of the pew. Fast as lightning. And I . . .' his shoulders shake in an impression of a shiver. 'I climbed up into the pulpit until one of the congregation scooped the monster up in his hands – his bare hands! Can you imagine? – and took it outside to set it free.'

Most likely took it outside and killed it, Margaret thinks. Probably knocked it over the head. No use letting it go; they always find their way in again.

'After you,' he says, as they reach the door of the Red Lion. Margaret hasn't been here before. It is busy, but he cuts a path through to the bar, Margaret following in his wake. There he greets the landlord, a man whose burst capillaries suggest he drinks almost as much alcohol as he serves. In another town, it would not be considered respectable for her to stand here. But there are (she counts them) five females of varying ages already at the bar. In Blackpool the rules are relaxed, even the rules about what a woman may or may not do.

'A ginger ale for me please.' Davidson turns to Margaret. 'And for you?'

'I'll have the same,' she says.

'Very good.'

'With a whisky. A double.' Her voice is louder than she intends it to be. Davidson looks down, disappointed in her perhaps. Interesting – she didn't have him down as a teetotaller. Not necessarily a beer man either, but she had pictured him as the type to sip a good port.

'Let's take that spot that's coming free,' he says, nodding towards a table at the end of the bar. 'You sit and I'll go and get our drinks.' He takes off his jacket and folds it carefully, as if it is made of the finest cashmere rather than creased wool. It is only now that she notices he is not wearing his clerical collar, just a slightly crumpled white shirt with the top button open. 'I'm off duty tonight,' he says, bringing a hand to his throat. 'Wearing the full get-up rather draws attention to who I am.'

'Yes,' she says. 'I suppose it would.' He wasn't wearing it on the first night they met, but she remembers seeing it in the Metropole, and she wonders whether he should be wearing it at all – even for his act – since he has been defrocked by the Church. Surely there are laws about such things.

He returns to retrieve their drinks and she watches him chat easily with two old men. 'What do you reckon, sir?' the first says to him. Margaret can see from his uniform that he is a postman. 'This one,' he goes on, pointing at his companion, 'says he's an 'ero. He'd have you believe he won the Boer War single-handed.'

'Bloody right I am. I've got medals. More bloody bars on 'em than a stepladder,' says the man in question. Margaret suspects the only bar he has any familiarity with is the type he is sitting at.

'You both look like brave fellows to me,' says Davidson. 'Men like you are the backbone of this country. How about I stand you both a drink?'

'Ah, that would be very good of you. Very good.'

The two men salute as Davidson pays and walks back to Margaret. His generous gesture distracts them only momentarily before they find another cause for argument.

'Do you miss them?' Margaret asks him as he places the drinks down on the ring-stained table.

'Who?'

'Your parishioners.'

'I miss feeling that I am doing good. Isn't that the purpose we all crave?' She supposes it is. Or at least it should be. 'It was God's will,' he says. 'It was in my blood. My father and his father before him. Inevitable that I would one day have a flock of my own to tend to.'

She nods but says nothing. She has learnt that people share more that way. Give them silence and they fill it, offering up the odd-shaped pieces of themselves to fit into the awkward corners.

'But it wasn't always my calling. It may surprise you to know that I had another life before the Church.'

'Really?' She resists the urge to get her notepad out.

He laughs. 'Really. In my younger days I was an actor. Rather a good one – so I'm led to believe. Left school and joined a touring theatre company. Played the title role in *Charley's Aunt*. Do you know it?' She nods. But she doesn't. 'Trod the boards in the West End too. At the Steinway Hall. I like to think it was a good foundation, that I brought some of that performance to my Sunday sermons. Light and shade. Comedy. Tragedy.'

'I can imagine.' She can't. 'But your family were . . .'

'Not exactly what my father had been hoping for, put it that way. He indulged me for a short while. I got a few paying jobs to see me through my studies at Oxford. I met my wife, Molly, during that time. She was an actress. Such a beauty . . .'

'What does she make of your—'

'I was a chaplain to the Actors' Church Union for a while. Ministering to spiritual needs in Music Hall.'

She tries to draw him back to the subject of his wife. 'Does Mrs Davidson still perform?'

The expression on his face suggests amusement, as though she has told a joke, but he straightens his face and says, very solemnly: 'No. It has been some time since my wife has *performed*. For me at least.' Margaret decides that he is being unnecessarily cryptic. And when he gives her another smile, she does not return it. 'Forgive me. To answer your question, no, she has not graced a stage since we were married.' Margaret considers the irony that his wife's circumstances have since become just as dramatic as any play she might have acted in. 'She settled down to church life much more easily than I did. I'm afraid I missed the excitement of showbusiness. For a while God gave me a way to return to that world and do his work. Good days. Thrilling times. The magic of it! I'd very often stand and watch the shows from the wings; the atmosphere back there . . . But it wasn't to last.'

'Why not?'

He shifts in his seat. 'The accusations. All unfounded! Close-minded people who didn't understand the freedom of theatre. There was nothing inappropriate about me being back-stage. Yes, the girls are required to do quick changes but I am a professional. I wouldn't have dreamed of . . .'

There's a breeze as the door opens and two women walk in, both wearing black skirts and white blouses, likely waitresses from one of the more upmarket establishments in town. She wonders whether they are from the Metropole. Davidson stops to watch them as they cross to the bar, turning his back on Margaret for longer than she thinks it would be considered polite. The landlord is trying to light a pipe, cursing the tobacco which is refusing to kindle: 'Bloody matches are no good!'

'Allow me,' says Davidson, leaping up from his seat and producing a lighter from his trouser pocket.

'Thank you.' The landlord flicks the arm to produce a flame, and draws on his pipe until the bowl is glowing red, to match his nose. 'Nice one that,' he says, handing it back. 'Must've cost a bit.'

'It was a gift,' Davidson says, 'from a dear friend in the theatre.' He sits back down opposite Margaret, placing the lighter on the table between them. It is made of hammered metal and is in need of a good polish. 'This has seen some sights, I can tell you. From my travels during the war.'

'Oh yes?' Margaret hopes he will elaborate but he is looking around again, tapping his fingernails (which are in dire need of a trim) on the table top.

'Another drink?' he says.

'Not just yet, thank you. Perhaps in a little while.'

Silence settles between them. Across the room, the two girls she assumes to be waitresses start to sing: a dirty song, using words seldom heard, even in Blackpool. It is a parody of 'Old King Cole'. On it goes, becoming bawdier with every verse. Displaying no signs of disapproval, or concern about a woman like Margaret being exposed to such language, Davidson begins to clap along, joining in the chorus when it comes back around. Singing much as he might lead a hymn in church, at a volume noticeably louder than anybody else's.

The attention of the pub has turned to him now, which he acknowledges with a small bow when the song comes to an end. 'Shall we have another?' he shouts.

'How about "Antonio"?' says the postman, lifting his empty pint glass.

'I was thinking of something a little more . . . *Godly*,' Davidson says, bringing his hands together, as if in prayer.

There's heckling from the table in the corner of the room. 'Godly?' a man in a cap pipes up. 'You're in the wrong place, pal.'

('Hang on though. Isn't that . . . ? Can't be.')

('That vicar chappie? Nah.')

('The one from the barrel?')

('That's it!')

Davidson bows again. 'I'm afraid you've found me out!'

'Well bugger me!' says the postman. 'Is it really you?'

Davidson shrugs then smiles at Margaret and mouths 'I'm sorry'. But he doesn't look sorry at all. Just the opposite. The man in the cap rushes to their table to shake Davidson enthusiastically by the hand. The other drinkers crowd around too. Even the landlord is raising a hinged section of the bar to make his way closer.

('I paid a shilling to see you on't seafront. I wouldn't have wasted my money if I'd known you'd turn up in the pub.')

('Diabolical how you've been treated. Diabolical. I said as much to the wife the other day. Wait 'til I tell her . . .')

('Can I buy thee a drink, lad? And your lady friend.')

It takes Margaret a moment to realise that she is the lady friend he is referring to. 'A whisky and ginger please,' she says, with forced enthusiasm. She is going to need another if she is going to survive this.

'Right then. Jack – get theself back behind that bar and get serving.'

The drink arrives not a minute later, passed along the line which has formed in front of Davidson. He produces a pen from one pocket of his folded jacket and a stack of his postcards from another. Margaret watches him sign the first few cards with a flourish, and waits for him to pick up their conversation again. She looks for something to busy herself with, settling on an inspection of the lighter that is still sitting on the table. Why did he ask the girls on the street for a light when he had one in his pocket all along? He certainly strikes her as the forgetful type. The very fact that he brought her here tonight, that she is waiting patiently beside him, seems to have slipped his mind completely. But there is plenty to keep her occupied. She is close enough to study him; can see that he is generous with his time and his attention, paying considered compliments to every single one of his admirers.

'He's quite a character!' they say, as if that's a good thing. And perhaps it is. He is drawing all eyes to him; no one is looking in her direction at all. With him she doesn't fear she will be discovered. She could stare at any one of them as much as she wanted, could probably take out her notepad, and no one would notice: too dazzled by Davidson to see her hiding in the shadow he is casting. She should take the opportunity, take an inventory: how many people are here, what they are drinking, what they are wearing.

The singing has started up again. The postman's got his way with 'Oh! Oh! Antonio', and someone lifts the lid of a piano and starts to play an accompaniment. Aware that she should appear to fit in, she moves her lips in time, surprised to discover that she knows the words.

Davidson steps onto his chair and conducts the crowd with two forefingers, and Margaret is struck by a memory: her grandfather picking up knitting needles from her grandmother's sewing basket, tapping them on the sideboard to bring an invisible orchestra to attention, then beating out time in the air, both hands dancing away from each other before meeting again in the middle. One, two, three, four. Down, out, in, up. Sometimes she would sit at the kitchen table and watch her grandmother singing. *Oh, oh Antonio, he's gone away.* A quivering voice, arms outstretched in dismay. *Left me alonio, all on my ownio.* And then her grandfather would appear in the doorway, would step in and hold out his hand to her. The kitchen had barely space to walk, never mind dance, but she would stand on the tops of his feet and he would waltz her round in tight circles. Her grandparents didn't care how much of a show they made of themselves. Didn't care how they might look. As long as they made her laugh.

Every time Margaret finishes a drink, another appears. She has lost count and feels lighter somehow. Her limbs less stiff, her movements less practised. The piano starts up again: a Gracie Fields song, something about looking on the bright side. And though she doesn't know any of the words to this one, and the piano sounds like it needs to be tuned, and several of the singers are off-key, it doesn't seem to matter.

She stands and tries to find a way to the ladies', eventually discovering a doorway next to the bar: cracked green tiles arranged like brickwork on the walls and a stained sink that may have been white when it was first installed. Pushing against the cubicle door, she finds it gives too readily and she falls forward, her elbow knocking into the wall. She tries to focus on the writing on the cistern, but can't.

Attempting to pull her underwear down, she feels a warmth spreading down her leg. It is too late. Somewhere, at the very back of her mind, she's aware that her normal self will be disappointed in her. As if there is a version waiting at home, sitting in judgement. The thought amuses her. *That* Margaret would not like her gripping the sides of the toilet seat with both hands. Goodness knows when it was last cleaned. But she fears she will fall off if she doesn't.

If only she could make the cubicle stop spinning. She tries to move her head in the opposite direction to still it. But her neck is too tired. She lets it rest, leaning her cheek against the wall.

With her eyes closed she can still feel the twists and turns but at least she doesn't have to watch them.

'You going to be in there much longer?'

Margaret's eyes fly open and it takes her a moment to realise where she is. She manages to get to her feet but trips on the wet knickers around her ankles. She tries to pull them up again but they stick to her legs. She can't wear them now; the dampness might soak through to her dress, and people would see what she has done.

'Open up, will you?'

She takes them off, balls them up in her fist, looks for a place to hide them, but there's nowhere in this cubicle. If she tries to flush them the toilet might block, might overflow. So she stuffs them into her handbag instead.

'I'm coming!'

On the other side of the door, she finds the two waitresses. One of them is raven-haired and much more attractive, the other trying to compensate with make-up.

'It's her!' says the one with all the lipstick. 'The vicar's woman. Come on, love . . . you can tell us . . .'

Margaret can't catch her shifting thoughts, can't work out what it is she is supposed to be telling them. Has she got some information to impart? A report to file? 'I'm not sure what . . .'

'*Friend* of yours, is he?' One of the women drops her voice. Margaret is having trouble telling which is which. 'Is he . . . you know . . . ?'

Raven-haired says something, lips forming words with exaggerated movement as if she is shouting them but Margaret can't hear any sound coming out. The workers call it hee-hawing, or see-sawing, or something like that. They do it in the mills, mouthing messages to each other across the clatter of the looms. Mee-mawing – that's it.

'. . . a dirty old man?' Lipstick Woman says in a loud whisper, exercising her jaw as if chewing on a particularly tough piece of meat. 'No smoke without fire. We won't tell, will we, Nelly?'

The other woman shakes her head and leans closer.

'I'm . . . not in a position to say with any certainty either way,' Margaret says.

'No need to be like that, we were only asking!'

Raven-haired and Lipstick share words Margaret can't decipher, then disappear into the cubicle together, leaving her wondering how she failed to respond in an appropriate manner, what it was exactly that they expected her to say.

Fighting her way back through the pub she tries to remember which direction to go. It seems twice as busy as it was a few minutes ago. She can't see a doorway, can't see above all these heads. The atmosphere is thick with smoke and the heat of so many bodies. But with each step she feels the brush of something between her legs. The air against her bare skin, so cold that it makes her shiver.

'Are you alreet?' says an old woman who looks like she is wearing a hair net.

'Definitely,' Margaret nods, lifting a forefinger as though she is testing the direction of the wind. 'I just need to . . .' The woman *is* wearing a hair net. Margaret can't help staring at it. Does she realise she has left the house with it on her head? 'I just need to . . .' Extraordinary. She is wearing slippers too.

Suddenly Davidson is beside her, taking her arm. It is a relief to let him take her weight. 'Are you quite well?' he says.

'She's canned,' says the old woman with a chuckle. 'Look at her. She can hardly stand up straight!'

'I'll walk you home,' Davidson says.

'No—'

'I insist. Where do you live?'

She tells him. She is so tired, she tells him. But even as she hears the words, she is unsure whether she is actually speaking them. There is a lag somewhere. A disconnect. And talking over her own thoughts is the voice of Other Margaret, the real one, warning her that it wouldn't be proper. That she shouldn't let him know her address. Because the newspapers say he is not a man to be trusted.

'Stay here.' He leaves her leaning against the bar and returns to the table for their coats. 'Ladies and gentlemen, it is time for me to bid you goodnight!'

There's a cheer and he lifts his arms, as if to embrace the sound. There's a shout from one of the back tables: 'Going to see the lady back safe are you?'

'I'm merely doing my Christian duty!'

She could swear that she sees him wink to the room before he takes her arm and leads her out into the night. It is still warm. Not much cooler out here than it is inside. But it feels good to breathe the fresher air, every step waking her a little, bringing her closer to the usual self who is waiting for her at home.

'I think you may have drunk rather too much,' he says. And she thinks she hears a note of accusation in his voice. She is not going to be preached to, even by a man of the cloth. Especially not by a former man of the cloth. She would say so if she could, but as soon as she thinks them the words have fled. She frees herself from his arm and tries to quicken her pace.

'What's the matter? Have I offended you in some way?'

'No.'

'Then please, just let me see you home.'

She knows what she saw. He winked. And she knows enough about what winks mean to fear that he might have expectations of her. She is not laughing at the thought of Other Margaret now.

'I'll be fine.'

'I know but . . . Please. I feel responsible . . . All those people buying drinks. I've never been to that one before. I thought I might get away with it . . . I'm not supposed to fraternise with the customers, you see. They won't want to pay if they can see me in the pub. But what can I do? I'll go mad, in that blasted barrel all day.'

They take the backstreets. She tenses at every alleyway and doorway that they pass. Is he going to try to kiss her, touch her? It would be too easy for him. If he reached under her dress, he would find her exposed. He would think she wanted him to. That she had wanted it all along. Shame takes shape in her stomach and she grips on to the pain of its sharp edges.

But they are nearly at her lodgings. If he was going to try to overpower her, surely he would have done it by now. She is getting stronger with every step, strong enough perhaps to fight him off. They pass an elderly man sitting beneath a street lamp, his cap set out on the pavement in front of him, a handwritten sign: 'Unemployed. Hungry.' Davidson squats down and presses coins into his hand. 'Be sure to get yourself some good meals with that. Don't waste it. You know what I'm saying, don't you?' Margaret wonders whether he has made the gesture for her benefit, to impress her with his charity. But he says nothing of it once they walk on. And by the time they turn into her road she feels guilty for having doubted his intentions.

'Can I ask you something?'

'Of course,' he says.

'Why did you wink when we were leaving the pub?'

'Wink?'

'Yes. I saw you. You wanted them to think that we were . . .' She is already regretting starting this conversation. She should have prepared a suitable euphemism. She doesn't want to have to spell it out. 'You've come all the way to Blackpool and then you—'

'Give the people what they want.'

'Prove them right.'

'I keep them guessing. It's not enough to stand in a pulpit and preach; you've got to give them a reason to listen in the first place. And I need the money if I am ever going to appeal and clear my name.'

She is not convinced but is relieved that they have reached her boarding house. She is nearly safe. Though she realises, with some dismay, that Maude will have locked the door by now. She'll have to wake her: a transgression that will add another charge to this week's bill. 'Here we are,' she says, deciding it is safer to look at him so she can be prepared if he tries to lunge and force a kiss on her.

'Since we are asking questions,' he says, 'I have one for you. Which newspaper is it?' She sees a wide smile spread across his face, exposing his teeth. She mustn't stare at those teeth.

'Newspaper?'

'Come on, you haven't told me which one you write for.'

She laughs. No, it's a giggle. It sounds like it has come from

114

someone else. She is alarmed to note it sounds coquettish. 'A reporter? Is *that* what all this has been about?' It makes sense to her now. 'I wondered why you were so forthcoming . . .' She wants to stop this giggling but the relief is sudden and overwhelming. Her fears that he may have guessed she is part of Mass Observation seem suddenly ridiculous.

'So, who then?' Davidson is not laughing. No longer smiling. 'Who?'

'Who is paying you?'

'No one. Not really.' She must concentrate on what to say, without giving herself away. But her mind is blank. All her thoughts have darted. 'I just . . . I'm a researcher.'

'Researcher – is that what they are calling you now? Why can't they leave me alone? They got what they wanted—'

'I'm not sure what you—'

'Don't insult my intelligence further. It's immoral – the Bishop spending Church money on investigators. Money that should be spent on the needy.'

Margaret laughs again. This man is a fantasist. Must be. A moment ago he thought her a reporter and now he has cast her as what? Some sort of detective for hire? This is ludicrous. 'Surely you don't believe the Church would—'

'I must say, it was terribly deceitful of you to pretend you were on my side, make out that you were writing an article about my innocence.'

'I didn't say—'

'You sat there while I told you about myself and all along you—'

'Now hold on, I—'

'The other two, in London, at least had the good manners

to keep their distance while they followed me. Far more interested in paying off the woman who accused me. Plying her with drinks, buying her clothes. Paying for her lodgings so they could keep an eye on her until the trial.'

'I have no idea who you're—'

'I should have guessed.' His voice is suddenly calm.

'But that's not why I . . .' She leans against the front door, suddenly fearing that her legs will hold her up no longer. She tries to formulate the right words to explain but he has already turned and walked away. 'It's a misunderstanding.' She doesn't hear the footsteps behind the door or the key being turned in the lock and she falls back as it opens. She feels strong arms around her and doesn't have the strength to flinch or pull away. Instead she surrenders, and allows herself to be helped upstairs to bed, relieved to hear Maude's consternation about the late hour and the inconvenience of being woken.

She wakes late. After nine. Should have been up and out hours
ago. Will have missed breakfast. The thought of food turns her
stomach. She is still dressed in the clothes of the Margaret of
the night before. The Margaret who was unprofessional. What
a wasted opportunity. She'd had every advantage to make observations of the drinkers in the pub, but this morning she can
remember very few of the details. Some dirty songs. Green
tiles. A beggar in the street. She feels the familiar creep, certain
that she has embarrassed herself, exposed herself in some way.
That she cannot remember the specifics only intensifies the sensation, makes her mind turn over with possibilities. She didn't
close her curtains last night. Didn't even take off her shoes.
And she is naked beneath her dress, she does not need to reach
down to confirm it. Never reaches down there unless she has
to. Chooses not to think about the frill of flesh between her
legs. Has never seen what she looks like. Never wants to. Shame
prickles along the length of her body. She remembers that her
knickers are balled up in her handbag, and curses her traitorous
body.

Davidson walked her home. She can smell his cigar smoke
on her clothes. The memory comes back to her so suddenly
that she is disorientated. He knew she had been following him.
How had she become the one under suspicion? The accused?
She must stay away from him from now on. Best that she lets
him continue in this fantasy of private investigators and Church

conspiracies. At least she can rest assured that he has no idea about Mass Observation. Yes, she can get back to her reports without distraction. But she feels no sense of relief, only unease, a nagging sense of loss that she will never see him again. She should not care for his good opinion of her, but she cannot bear the thought that he thinks her the sort of person who would creep around and spy on him. She was interested, that was all. He was the one who first approached her, who invited her to tea. She wasn't to know that he had thought she was a reporter.

He is a strange man, of that she is sure, but he has a quality which she cannot put her finger on, something that reaches out and gathers everybody in the room, draws them close, whispers in their ears. In spite of herself, she is full of admiration for his skill at putting others at ease. Even her.

Thoughts of the night before are rocks in her stomach, churning, rolling over one another, knocking her from the inside out. Her muscles cramp. She has to get to the toilet but her body is not doing as it is told. It's as if it is playing dead, lying there on purpose, in protest. She hauls it off the bed, legs shaking, and the pain hits her. She must get to the loo. But she is not sure she will make it. She reaches under the bed for the chamber pot that she has been unable to bring herself to use since the day she moved in. Groping around for it with one hand, she is already lifting her skirt with the other, her fingers finding the cracked edge of the porcelain just in time to drag it out and squat before her body begins to purge itself of the night before. The burn, the smell, the humiliation. Whisky and ginger. Oh God, how many did she have? The weight in her stomach is rising now; the burn reaches her throat. Her brain is pulsing against the inside of her skull so violently that she fears it might swell and crack her thoughts open. She reaches up, parting her hair to check for injury. And even the touch of a fingertip is painful, every strand of hair as raw as an exposed nerve.

Finally, she stands, looking for water to wash her hands, but she did not fill the jug last night. She has to clean herself of the germs that caused this sickness. She must have caught a stomach bug, something nasty from the loo in the pub last night. It wasn't exactly clean, from what she can remember. She knows what Mother would say: she is lucky she has not caught something before now, living like this. It was inevitable she would be contaminated.

Though the prospect of walking seems impossible, she mustn't sit down on her bed, knows full well that she would not be able to muster the strength to stand up again. And she needs to get to work. She bends down to retrieve her balled-up knickers from last night, keeping one hand on her head as if it might fall off her shoulders. They are still damp from last night, stained, with a smell of stale ammonia. Tucking them between the layers of piled clothes that are waiting to be washed, she puts on a clean outfit and pulls a brush through her hair; every tentative movement feels like great clumps are being jerked out by the roots. Then she carries the chamber pot to the loo further down the landing, the smell prompting her to empty the remaining contents of her stomach, as well as the pot, into the toilet pan. She washes her hands and splashes cold water on her face.

Downstairs, the breakfast things have disappeared and, to Margaret's great relief, Maude with them. She had expected to see her landlady standing in the parlour, pretending to flick a duster over the bottles on top of the piano. Maude and her eyebrows. They appear to act quite independently of the rest of her face and are surprisingly nimble considering their proportions. But this morning Margaret has been spared *the look* Maude reserves for only the highest moral judgements; the look that would have communicated disappointment and dismay about the state she arrived home in. No doubt the lecture will come later, but for now Margaret is grateful that she can leave the house without interrogation.

Slipping out quietly, in case Maude is lurking behind the kitchen door after all, she turns out of the passageway and steps into the sunshine. Screwing up her eyes against the glare, she feels the pull of tender scalp against skull, and walks on, head bowed, towards the nearest parade of shops. A bell announces her arrival as she steps inside the chemist's, so loud that it greets her more as a warning than a welcome. But she is grateful to retreat into the shop's low light. Panels of dark wood line the walls; shelves are stacked with boxes of various sizes, rolls of bandage, and safety pins in coiled chains. A woman, who looks to be in her forties, is inspecting a display of perfumed soap and beautifying creams. She lifts a pot to look at the price hidden beneath, glances around, then pretends to read the ingredients. Margaret notes the reverence with which she sets it back down and predicts that she will continue to browse for at least a minute more. To turn and walk out now would make it obvious that she can't afford the prices here. Though the young man in a white coat behind the counter is paying no attention to her anyway. He is engrossed in a leather-bound book, tapping a pencil against its pages. Margaret can feel every beat as though he is hammering it directly onto her head. Behind him, mirrored glass makes the shelves look twice as deep, and twice as full. She assumes this must be a family business, estimates the décor has not been updated in at least fifty years. This man is perhaps the grandson of the original proprietor. Craning forward across the counter, she tries to read the labels on glass bottles filled with medicines of varying shades of brown. Her sickness has settled into a feeling of unease, deep in her stomach. She imagines the germs inside her multiplying, spreading like weeds, slowly choking her.

Walking the length of the mahogany counter, she stands in front of the young man, expecting that he will stop reading and offer her assistance. But he does not move, does not look up, does not stop the infernal tapping of his pencil. 'Excuse me,' she says softly, reluctant to create any sound that will cause her head to throb any more than it already does. But he continues to ignore her. She waits, then prompts him again. 'Excuse me.'

With a sigh, he lays the pencil carefully in the gutter of his book, then folds it shut. He will damage the pages like that. He will loosen the binding, make the spine misshapen. Does he not know? Or is he just careless?

'Can I help you with something?' He is in no rush to hear her answer; seems deliberately slow in raising his eyes to find her. She notes his accent is northern but self-consciously well-spoken.

'I need something for . . .' how should she put this? '. . . digestion.'

'A furred colon,' he clarifies. 'You're the fifth person I've had in today. Does no one realise the importance of keeping their system toned? I don't suppose you've ever considered a regular dose of syrup of figs?'

She looks down and shakes her head. 'No, I—'

'Milk of magnesium?'

'No, you misunderstand . . .'

'Ah,' he says, reaching for a round tin on the counter and rattling its contents as if to tempt her. 'I see what you are after – Bile Beans. Many young ladies swear by their side effects. Makes the weight drop right off.'

Margaret is tired. Tired of arguing with men who don't listen. 'I do not need a laxative,' she says wearily, but her words are lost as the bell on the shop door rings out behind her, and three teenaged boys enter.

'I'm sorry. You'll have to speak up, miss.' The man in the white coat leans forward and cups his ear with his hand. Does he expect her to announce her health complaint to the entire shop? He is still smiling, but not warmly, not encouragingly.

'I have an *upset* stomach,' she says.

The corners of his mouth turn downwards and he is quick to move away. 'I see. A stomach bottle,' he lifts something off the shelves behind him. 'Should ease diarrhoeal symptoms.' He says 'symptoms' as if the word itself is unpleasant, as if she might be experiencing them then and there. Margaret hears a giggle from the teenaged boys. He had to say it, didn't he? Had to say it loud enough for everyone to hear. 'Two teaspoonfuls in water, up to three times a day.'

The medicine is chalky in colour, and moves sluggishly as he tilts the bottle to read the instructions. She is about to complain that it is half empty, but spots another layer of clear liquid above the white and concludes that the ingredients have separated. Ringing it through the till, he wraps it in a brown paper bag and places it on the counter so that she can pick it up without any need for their hands to touch. She wants to assure him she has washed them, that there is more danger of her catching something from him than the other way around. But she takes the bottle and leaves the shop, avoiding the eyes of the teenagers who snigger as she passes.

Sickness swells inside her again. Bile rises to her throat and tears to her eyes. Clutching the brown paper bag, she navigates through the crowd and crosses the road. This is where she saw Davidson last night. This is where he asked those girls for a light, even though he had a lighter in his pocket. And now he knows she has been watching him. Oh God! The cramps that were in her stomach have moved up to her chest. So strong they knock the breath out of her; so strong that she stops and brings her hands to her neck. She takes the steps down to the lower walkway. People jostle and chide her, and she cannot fight the momentum of so many bodies carrying her forward.

The ground yields and she looks down to see sand beneath her feet, the space around her growing as people fan out in different directions to stake their claim to any plot of empty beach. She reaches out and grabs the tip of a vacant deckchair, anchoring herself as more people rush past. Managing to pull herself around to the front of the chair, she moves to sit, and for a split second feels as though she is falling – before she is caught by the fabric of the seat. She feels vulnerable in such a reclined position, unsure that she would be able to get up again in a hurry, not confident that she'd have the strength.

Unwrapping the paper around the neck of the medicine bottle, she unscrews the metal cap. The man in the chemist's said to take it in water but she doesn't have any and she can't afford to wait, can't risk having another bout of symptoms. She needs to take the cure, get better and get on with her day, so she takes a swig straight from the bottle instead, the contents bitter as they reach the back of her tongue. Her mouth feels dry, as though her gums are shrinking back from the taste, but she tips the bottle back a second time. Then another. Three doses a day. She may as well have them all now so she can get to work. But it is making no difference, bringing no relief. She unwraps the bottle further, tears the brown paper to check the directions for herself. The clear liquid is all but gone now, the bottom half of the bottle opaque with the heavier layer, a grubby white like the net curtains in Maude's parlour. She should have mixed the contents before she took the doses. That's what the label says: *Kaolin and morphine: shake well before use.* She does it now, watching what's left of the transparent liquid turning cloudy then disappearing as if it were never there.

Another sip. It tastes chalky this time. And she's retching. Fighting to swallow, her body rebelling against her once more. She needs to wash it down. Hiding the bottle in her handbag, she finds the hip flask she bought on James's instructions. A shake of it tells her what she already knows: that it is still full; she has not taken it out since she bought it. She can hear the liquid lapping against the metal inside. The fumes hit her as soon as she takes off the cap but brandy is known to settle the stomach, to calm the nerves. Brandy will take the taste away. And it does, filling her mouth and throat with a heat that burns through the bitterness on her tongue, almost sweet in comparison to the residue of medicine. She drinks, then drinks again. After every sip a sense of relief, a quietening of the thoughts scrambling to get to the front of her mind; a feeling that there is more space inside her chest.

She draws air into her lungs, tasting the alcohol on every breath; sinks back against the fabric of the deckchair, confident now that it will hold her, keep her safe; allows the hand holding the hip flask to hang loosely by her side; closes her eyes against the sun which is high in the sky above her. She can feel the weight of its warmth, her eyelids burnished pink by its insistent touch. The jumble of sounds seem to quieten gradually. If she stays very still, she can hear the sunlight itself, a gentle pulse that hums across her skin. The sea too. A chanting beat, drawing out the pain that was in her head and racing it away on the backs of galloping waves. Kicking off her shoes, she moves her toes in time to music she can feel inside her body. And when she opens her eyes, she can see its rhythm too: a little girl tapping the bottom of an upturned bucket to reveal a sandcastle, a boy lolling side to side as he takes his turn on a donkey ride. She has a vague sense that she should be making notes about all of this, making lists, but she cannot work out where she would begin, how she would untangle one thing from another. Closing her eyes again, she angles her face towards the sky, and feels even the corners of her mouth being drawn towards the heat of the sun.

The crowd's chatter is like birdsong, but there's another sound now too. A hum that's building into a roar, the very air vibrating with it. She can hear the light, hear it agitating atoms into music. And all at once the families further down the beach are dancing, leaping, twirling. Margaret sees a flock of birds swooping slowly down above them, floating on the breeze, turning this way and that; white feathers falling gracefully to earth, turned suddenly to black in silhouette against the sun. They are raining down upon the people now. Children jump to snatch them from the air, adults colliding as they look skywards and hold out their arms, none of them seeming to notice what Margaret can see: a winged shadow, racing across the beach towards them, cutting across the heads of fathers buried in the sand and grandmothers snoozing behind windbreaks. Margaret hears the roar again, looks up and sees what the shadow is chasing: an aeroplane low in the sky above it. So low that she can see the pilot, waving to the crowd below. He is shooing them out of the way. He is going to crash. She tries to stand up, to get out of its path, but she is stuck in her seat, her head swimming with the effort of trying to get a signal to her feet. Beneath the sound of the engine, she hears something else: a melody, the soaring of strings and the marching beat of brass. She hears it as clearly as if someone had turned on a gramophone.

She ducks as the plane passes over her head, squeezes her eyes shut tight. It is so close that she can hear the air buckle above her, can feel the stroke of its wing on her hair. She brings her hands up to her head and feels something resting there. A piece of paper. A single piece of paper. There are others on the ground around her, others still falling gently from the sky. Her eyes can't focus on what they say, a chaos of lines and symbols that make no sense. A young man runs and picks up a sheet that lands a few yards away. Two little boys, knees crusted with sand, fight over another until it tears between their hands.

'No good to you anyway!' says the first, as he stomps away in tears. 'You can't even play.'

'No, but I'm goin' f'ort learn!' The second boy bends down to retrieve the two halves then stops, shields his eyes and looks into the sky behind Margaret. 'Well . . . bugger me!'

Margaret tries to turn her head but she is too low in the deckchair; she tries to stand but the best she can manage is pushing herself sideways onto her knees on the sand. And there she stays, gazing up at it.

Blackpool Tower rises out of the promenade, circled by the buzz of a giant insect. Behind it the air is thick with a trail of black specks, pulsing like a cloud of gnats. Margaret watches as it turns, wings beating as they dip left and right into the deep blue of the sky.

'It's coming back!' one of the boys shouts. 'It's heading up the beach again.' They run off towards it. Margaret, still sitting on the sand, studies the paper crumpled in her hand. Her eyes are struggling to focus but she sees it now. It is sheet music. She can make out the staves, like ladders, and the clusters of crotchets and quavers that cling to them; lyrics skipping below, words elongated, waiting with outstretched arms to catch a falling note. She can make no sense of it, feels disconnected as though she is far away, watching herself through smeared glass. The pads of her fingers feel swollen, the tip of her tongue numb. No, not numb: alive with a sensation that she cannot place. Something like pins and needles or the tingling burn of cold.

She looks down at the sheet again. At the top, she makes out a title: 'Me and Jane in a Plane'. She can't remember ever hearing it, though Mother's insistence that she take piano lessons as a child should mean she can work out the melody. She tries to hum it to herself but the notes refuse to sit still on the lines, or stay in the gaps between. All around her, sunbathers are standing and dancing to a tune she cannot decipher, jumping to catch sheets of music that are falling from the sky again. The two boys run by with the prize of a copy each. Families are gathering up their picnic blankets and making their way towards the stairs up to the promenade; shells, cherished as treasures not two minutes before, lie discarded with the crusts of half-eaten sandwiches.

They are flocking to something. And she has a compulsion to follow them. There's an energy in the air, and she feels it like a force acting upon her, the pull of gravity towards something bigger than herself.

## 16

James opens the front door and finds her gasping on the step, sheet music clutched to her chest. 'Margaret. Are you . . . ? You look . . .'

'I brought you something for your collection,' she says, stepping past him into the hallway.

'You have?'

She thrusts several pages, now rather crumpled and damp, into his hands and watches his face as he flattens them out. He opens his mouth to speak but seems to change his mind and Margaret, impatient to tell him everything she has seen, continues into his office, taking a seat in the armchair in the corner before being invited. If he minds, he doesn't say so: too busy leafing through the pages of music.

'It fell out of the sky.'

'The sky?'

'Yes, look at the title.'

He studies the pages again and reads aloud. 'Me and Jane in a—'

'Plane, it's the new one by Lawrence Wright. He played it for me himself just now.'

'Lawrence Wright played it for—?'

'Did you see the aeroplane go over?' She is grinning now. Sitting forward in her chair.

'Aeroplane?'

'With Jack Hylton's band.'

'I'm sorry, you've lost me. Margaret, are you quite well?'

'Yes, of course.'

'You don't seem quite yourself. You're so . . .'

'Now you mention it, I have been feeling peculiar. Very thirsty.'

'Stay there. Don't move,' he says, rushing out of the room. She likes this feeling of being looked after, and does as she is told, grateful to catch her breath. He returns with a cracked mug emblazoned with the Lyons Tea logo. 'There you go. No clean glasses I'm afraid.'

'Thank you.' She takes a sip. Never has she needed a drink of water more than this one. Never has it tasted so good.

'Now, Margaret,' he says. 'Start again from the beginning.'

'Lawrence Wright hired a plane to fly Jack Hylton's band over Blackpool.' Margaret can see the disbelief on his face. This is going to be one of those stories. One of those he will tell over and over again in future. That he'll forget he's told people a dozen times already. And he is going to hear it from her first. Right now, it is her story to tell, hers alone, but she will give it as a gift to him. He is staring at her, waiting to unwrap every detail. 'It was terrifying at first, racing across the beach towards us, but then I heard the music. The band was inside. All of them. Playing their instruments. And then sheets of music started falling. All the children were jumping. People singing. And then Lawrence Wright. Performing. I went to his song-plugging booth. On the prom.'

'The prom! Indeed.' He smiles, gratified that she has used the short form favoured by the locals.

'I followed the crowd. There was a sing-along. To get people familiar with the tune.' And she had joined in, her body jostled from side to side by the movement of so many people. She'd felt the touch of skin and realised that the young man beside her had taken her hand. A woman on the other side had put her arm through hers. And she had been taken by the vibration in the air, of so many people singing at the same pitch. She could feel the notes running through the length of her body, touching every nerve and making it ring out with the clarity of a tuning fork.

'And then everyone bought the sheet music. The full song.' She stops and corrects herself, looking down at the pattern on her dress. 'Well, I'd estimate eighty or ninety per cent of them did. Families that is. Obviously members of the same household will have only needed one between them. Or will have bought additional copies as presents, I suppose . . .' Now she has started talking she can't seem to stop; she looks up to find him studying her with a curious expression. '. . . and if it's a one-off . . . a limited print run . . . well, there won't be many copies and I thought it was worth . . .'

'Having in the collection,' he says. 'Thank you for thinking of me . . . of the project.' He studies the pages and falls silent for a moment. 'And how's your report coming along?'

'It's nearly there.'

He looks up. 'Marvellous! I knew I could rely on you!'

Shame grips her suddenly as she thinks of last night, of Davidson, of her behaviour: she could not even rely on herself. On her body. 'Well . . . I am a little behind.'

'Still working your way through all those sideshows?' he says. 'From what I hear there's a new one opening every day. Perhaps we should draw a line under it now. Be like painting the Forth Bridge otherwise.'

'I'm sorry?'

'As soon as you got to the end, you'd have to start again at the beginning.'

'Yes. Yes, I suppose I would.'

James stands and walks to the piano. 'And what about your rector?' he says.

'He's not *my* rector.'

'Any rumours? Any more scandal?'

'No. Nothing like that.' She concentrates on making her voice sound bright, uninterested; wants desperately to change the subject, to think of anything but last night. But she wants to make sense of it too.

'I did hear one thing you might find amusing . . .' she says, a little more loudly than she had intended.

'Oh?'

'Someone in the crowd. I heard them say the Church had paid private detectives to follow him. Seems a bit far-fetched.'

'No, it's true enough.' He seems perfectly serious. 'Two detectives were called to give evidence at his trial.'

So, Davidson was right. She thought it was paranoia but his assumption is validated now. That she was following him. Spying. Gathering evidence. And for a moment she has to remind herself that she wasn't. Because she feels guilty. Complicit. As bad as the rest of them.

'Are you all right?' James says. 'You look deep in thought.'

'Suddenly rather tired, that's all.'

He turns and lifts the lid of the piano. 'Perhaps you should keep this music for your own collection? Do you play?'

'Me? No. I tried when I was a child. But I didn't have a talent for it.'

'I don't believe that! I bet you were good at anything you put your mind to.' He is laughing softly. Is he mocking her?

As she watches him arrange the sheets on the piano's stand, her own fingers are stretching out. Mother used to make her do warm-up exercises before every lesson. At first Margaret had been keen to go. Learning to read the notes had come easily enough but her progress was slow when it came to the performance. Still, Mother persevered. The new piano she had bought for the front room was not going to play itself, and wouldn't it be nice if she played some suitable music to entertain her father's managers from the bank when they came for drinks at Christmas?

'Would you like to play for us now, darling?' Mother called across the room to her, while giving each of the adults a top-up from the decanter she had bought for the occasion. Margaret sat; centred herself on the piano stool; lifted the brackets on the stand to secure the music; wiped her hands on the front of her dress. She could do this. She had practised for an hour every night after school. 'Für Elise', chosen by her teacher because it was easy enough for her to master, the tune so familiar that she could play it without looking at the music. She brought her fingers to rest on the first keys of the piece. Right hand: E, D sharp, B. Left hand ready to leap across the F, C, F of the third bar. As soon as she started to play, the room fell silent. She could feel them watching her. Could feel Mother's gaze. Relying on her to impress the guests; every beat counting out the money spent on lessons; every note a test of Margaret's gratitude. Little finger on E, she stretched out her hand to hit the octave above. But she grazed the note beside it, pressing hard enough to strike the string. Clumsy, Margaret. There was a laugh behind her and she felt someone step forward. Someone by her side. Again she missed a note. The piece too well-known for anyone to doubt that she was failing. 'Perhaps you could try something else, darling,' Mother said, her voice loud enough for the rest of the room to hear. 'Play the other one.'

Margaret reached out and put the second piece of music on the stand. A minuet in G major. But when she tried to read them, the notes made no sense. She tried to arrange her fingers on the keys but didn't know where to start. 'For goodness' sake!' Mother was no longer speaking loudly enough for everyone to hear. And Margaret found her hands were moving without instruction. She was hammering the keys with her two index fingers. Hammering them as hard as she could. The first tune she had ever learnt. The one Grandad had taught her. The one her mother used to play.

A hand came down and shut the lid on the keys, almost trapping Margaret's fingers. 'That's enough,' Mother said. 'I think you'd better go up to your bedroom.'

Sitting on the landing, she could hear the guests leave one by one. Could hear the clink of empty glasses as they were carried on a tray into the kitchen.

'"Chopsticks"?' she heard Mother say. '"Chopsticks", William!'

'I'm sure she didn't mean to—'

'She wanted to embarrass me. She can't let me have anything nice for myself.'

'Just high spirits, my love . . .'

'High spirits? And whose fault is that? She needs discipline. I know grandparents dote on children. And what with . . . well . . . I'm sure it was hard. But they let her run wild. No manners. No idea of the right way of—'

'There was nowhere else for her to go.'

'Yes, but that was then. I'm here now. And I can't cope with her, William.'

'I'm sure a few more piano—'

'You're not listening! I don't know what to do with her. I've tried. But there is something not quite right . . .'

'She'll grow out of it.'

'But she's not growing out of it, is she? And I'm fed up of being undermined. *I'm* her mother now.'

Margaret never saw her grandparents after that day. She looks down at her hands now, and realises they are clenched into fists. 'It was my stepmother who wanted me to play.' She says it softly, to James's back, and he turns to look at her.

'I didn't realise . . . Your real mother . . . ?'

'She died when I was three.'

'I'm so sorry, Margaret.'

She usually says 'it's all right' to spare the other person's feelings or to avoid her own. Instead, she says 'me too'. There's a moment of silence, then she nods at the piano: 'Are you going to give it a whirl then?'

He bows, flicks imaginary coat tails and takes a seat. Exactly like Lawrence Wright did, when Margaret stood in the music booth, when she felt lighter somehow. Floating like paper as it fell from the sky. 'I wish you'd seen the plane,' she says. 'It was wonderful. Quite wonderful.'

'I wish I had too.' His voice is quiet. 'Another time perhaps.'

'Another time.'

Her mother would have liked this man. She wants to tell

him, but the words won't come: it's as if she has already used up all the ones she knows. Though the moment seems to linger, she cannot keep up, cannot articulate the way she feels, and then the moment has passed and the emotion with it. She feels so tired. So drained. As dog-eared as the pages of music.

James flexes his fingers and begins to play, and she sinks back into the chair, listening as he works out the melody with his right hand and chords with his left. Sometimes, when she stays late to type reports upstairs, she hears him playing, laughing to himself as he sings the latest hit. Very occasionally she has heard him singing more softly to a sentimental song by Al Bowlly. And it leaves her feeling she is doing something she shouldn't, listening to something private. Though she is paid to eavesdrop on other people's lives, there is an intimacy in this. So she always leaves quietly so he will not realise she was ever there to bear witness.

But now here she is, sitting just behind him. Every part of his body animated as he plays, tentatively at first then growing in speed and confidence. The back of his head bobbing as his hands leap across the keys from little finger to thumb; his knees bouncing as his feet beat out the rhythm beneath. She knew he would appreciate the music. Watching him enjoy it stirs something akin to pleasure in herself. Pleasure that his enthusiasm is prompted by something *she* has done. It is warm in his office and the tempo of the song is soothing; her eyes struggle to stay open. James begins to sing along to his own accompaniment and she wonders if he has forgotten he is not alone. That she is in the room. That she is watching. Whether he has forgotten her altogether, like Davidson did in the pub last night. Or whether he just doesn't mind her being there.

He makes it to the end of the song and calls to her over his shoulder: 'Aren't you going to join in, Margaret?'

But she has fallen asleep in his chair.

# 17

Margaret wakes slowly, hiding behind closed eyes, pulling the covers around her chin. The blanket feels strange, as though it is holding her down. It is silky where it brushes her bare neck, but when she frees her arms to rearrange it from the outside, she finds the texture rough beneath her fingertips. Trying to make sense of such extremes of sensation, she strokes her thumb and forefinger along the edge, and discovers a line of buttons. There's a smell of pipe tobacco and menthol that's comforting. Her father used to smoke a pipe. He used to let her tap out the spent tobacco and refill it. And she would always take her time, knowing that she had his full attention, careful not to spill a single strand.

It takes some coaxing to persuade her eyes to open, still heavy with sleep. There's a feeble light, dusk falling outside. It is dark enough to need a lamp to see the corners of the room, but she can make it all out in an instant. Glass cases filled with novelties; shelves stacked with different brands of chopped meat; a desk strewn with toys and copies of the *Radio Times*. But she doesn't have the energy to disapprove of the disorder. Her mind has only one thought: what have I done? The lid of the piano is still open, the sheets of paper still creased upon the stand. She brought the music, he started playing the piano and then . . . then she must have fallen asleep right in front of him. In front of her manager. And before that – she flinches to remember – she was talking about her family. She was talking about her mother.

She sits up suddenly in the chair and the blanket starts to slip down. It is an overcoat. Not her own. It must be James's but how did she end up with it wrapped around her? Did he cover her with it as she slept? Thank goodness he was not here to see her wake. She should go before he comes back but she lingers, still not quite able to shake off the fug of sleep or the weight of the coat She has the feeling she would be cold without it, so she allows herself a moment longer in its company, bending her knees to bring her entire body beneath it, shivering as the lining caresses her skin. Pipe smoke and menthol. That must be what he smells of, up close. Now she thinks of it, it is not surprising. He bought a tin of Uncle Joe's Mint Balls because he liked the advertisement (red and blue with a picture of a smiling man who she assumes to be Uncle Joe himself) and quickly developed a taste for them. He once offered her one. 'The tin says they "keep you all aglow"!' he said. She wanted to point out that they weren't balls at all, but oblate spheroids, slightly squashed, like the Earth. She wanted to say that if the name itself was misleading, she doubted very much whether the slogan would live up to its promise. But she just shook her head instead and watched as he popped another into his mouth: 'You don't know what you're missing, Margaret!'

Right now, she does not want to go anywhere, do anything. She would like to stay here curled up under this coat in the dark. But the thought that he might come back and find her compels her to move. She stands, folds the overcoat in half and places it carefully on the back of the chair. Just like Davidson did in the pub last night. The thought brings a fresh wave of shame. His talk of private investigators was not paranoid delusion, his suspicions perfectly reasonable. Though his accusations were ill-founded, she feels as guilty as if they were true.

Turning to leave, her foot knocks against something on the floor by the chair. It's a plate. On it is a bag of crisps, and tucked beneath it is a note.

> *SUMMAT FOR YOUR TEA.*
> *DIDN'T LIKE FOR'T WAKE YOU.*
> *James*

She chokes on a surfeit of emotion, a rising sound, both sob and laugh: the realisation that James took the time to provide sustenance for her; the thought that he is a man for whom a bag of crisps constitutes a meal. He chose to call it tea rather than supper and, though it is impossible to tell from a written message, she imagines he was smiling as he committed it to paper (in what she can't help noticing is a shockingly untidy hand). The brand of crisps, Smith's, was one of his obsessions a few weeks ago. Goodness knows how much salt he ingested, taking out the little blue twist inside, tipping it into the bag and shaking it up. It was inevitably damp and clogged together, but James delighted in the ritual. He even wore a blue enamel badge with the logo on it for a week or so. She supposes he had found a bag here in his office and left it out for her as an after-thought. But it was still a thought – after or otherwise.

She could write 'thank you' on the back of his note for him to find when he returns, but she picks it up and puts it in her pocket, finding a scrap of paper amongst the chaos of his desk to use instead. 'Thank you' seems insufficient in the circumstances but she cannot think what else to say. It is only a bag of crisps af-ter all. She mustn't get carried away. Make herself look foolish.

Shutting the front door behind her, she takes the back roads to Maude's. At home in Northampton, she would never dream of eating on the street. Mother would be horrified at the thought of her doing anything so common, but there are very few people around to witness it. Besides, food will do her good after the unpleasantness with her stomach earlier. She hasn't had a thing to eat since last night and she feels hollowed out, desperate to fill the empty space inside her. As predicted, the salt inside the blue twist of paper has coagulated into one large lump and she is forced to stop and rub it between thumb and forefinger to crush it into smaller flakes. The crisps themselves are not crisp at all, but every mouthful is greeted by a grateful growl from her stomach (something else that would make Mother tut in disgust). She feels a small thrill of transgression. Rebellion. When a couple emerge from a side road and walk towards her, she doesn't hide the pack away. And once they've passed, she licks her fingers to taste the grains of salt clinging there. With such behaviour, she might pass as a local. Mother would be disgusted. But James would be proud.

It is the time of the evening that is neither one thing nor the other: too light for the lamps to be lit, too dark to see much more than contrast and shadow. She always thinks of Blackpool in the feminine, as one might a ship. A fallen woman whose face is painted with clashing colours. Sometimes, at the blush of sunset, her streets bathed in a tender glow like candlelight, she looks almost beautiful. But when the sun disappears into the sea, she seems to pine and pale and, stripped of her war-paint, the cracks start to show and she is quick to hide her true face behind night's curtain.

Hands still greasy, Margaret manages with some difficulty to knock on the front door. Maude appears almost instantly.

'Miss Finch.'

'Mrs Crankshaw.'

'Lucky I caught you.' Luck had nothing to do with it; she has probably been haunting the front window, waiting to pounce. 'Are you all right? You look jiggered!'

'I'm fine. Thank you.'

'Only you looked the worse for wear last night. Good thing I waited up.'

'It was.'

'And you didn't make it down for breakfast this morning.' She says all this as if it is news to Margaret.

'I'm fine.'

'I said as much to your gentleman friend . . .' She pauses and her head twitches from side to side, like a bird sizing up a worm. 'Came calling about an hour ago.'

Margaret concentrates on staying very still, so as not to betray any reaction. She can't understand it. Why would James come looking for her here when he must have just left her in his office? How long was she asleep for?

'I said I couldn't help. I told him: "Truth is I haven't seen her. She left without making her bed." "Very unlike her" – I told him that an' all.'

What else did she tell him? Margaret can feel salt and grease lying heavy in her stomach. She has to get upstairs in case she is taken ill again.

'He were here quite a while. Very polite he was. Very impressed with my lodgings. He asked to borrow a pen and paper to write you a note.' Another one? 'Quite a charmer. Asked me all about myself. And whether there was a Mr Crankshaw . . .'

She brings her hand up to fix the back of her hair. 'Like I said — a proper gentleman. But I were surprised when I took a good look at him in daylight. He's a little old for you.'

'He's not. We're not . . .' Wait, old? He can't be more than thirty-five.

'I'd have thought he'd be better suited to a woman more my age. And I shouldn't say it — but those *teeth*!' Davidson. Not James. Maude is talking about Davidson.

Margaret really is going to be ill again. There's a sharp pain in her stomach as though the crisps she has just eaten are scratching her from the inside. But her landlady does not appear to have noticed. 'Gat-toothed, my mother would have called him. You know what that's a sign of.' Margaret doesn't. 'It means his appetites are . . .' She drops her voice to a whisper. 'You know . . .' She still doesn't. 'Means he's a randy old bugger!' She shakes her head but is grinning at the same time and Margaret can't work out whether Maude considers these 'appetites' to be a blessing or a curse. She doesn't want to think about it.

'Now you mention it, I am still feeling under the weather. I'm going to go and have a lie-down.' She has to pass Maude to make it up the stairs.

'All right, Miss Finch. Don't forget your note.'

*Miss Finch,*

*I politely request that you desist in following me. If you see me again, please do not attempt to make conversation. I may be a forgiving man, but I am not a fool.*

*Mr Harold Davidson, Rector (former)*

The irony is not lost on her. Directly above a billboard which advertises 'The Starving Rector of Stiffkey: imprisoned day and night' is a smaller sign in the window of a boarding house, offering bed, breakfast and dinner. It was reading about his new protest in this morning's newspaper that has made her decide to come and see him. Since she read his note, she has struggled with the overwhelming urge to set him straight. To her it is a question of order. She cannot accept that this sordid version of herself exists, even in someone else's imagination. More than that, his accusations have tainted her own thoughts. Her observations are for science, for understanding, for the betterment of the less fortunate in society, but now, when she takes out her pencil and notepad to record a conversation, she feels like a voyeur. And by the end of the day her head is full of other people's words, with other people's lives. She wishes they would fly from her in sleep, that when her head hits the pillow they would empty from her thoughts, compelled by gravity to pour from her ear. But she is increasingly finding that every overheard secret leaves a trace, every discovered betrayal a bruise.

For days, she has tried to convince herself that she would be justified in contacting him, but his note was very clear and she didn't feel, in all conscience, that she could disobey his wishes. That changed the instant she saw news of his latest act. Surely the fact that he is risking his life by starving himself makes it her moral duty to do so now? She has seen similar performances before, variations on the same theme: a young woman self-imprisoned to raise money for her invalid sister, newly-weds who spend their honeymoon separated in neighbouring boxes 'without the sustenance of either food or love'. There are always volunteers desperate enough to sign up for the stunt: prize money of £150 offered to those who can survive twenty days with only a quart of water and 150 cigarettes. But she is shocked that Davidson has become one of them, that he has sunk to new depths. And she cannot bear the thought that he considers her to be one of the conspirators who has driven him to such an act.

According to the article, he is replacing a young woman who fainted in front of the crowds and has been taken away for medical treatment. The bulletin boards chalked up outside her side-show each day chronicled a staccato excitement on her physical state, expressing concern that visitors who did not pay to see her that day may be too late the day after. And they were right.

Perhaps if Margaret talks to Davidson, offers to help him with his appeal, he might reconsider; perhaps, if he knows he has a friend, another person of principle, he will stop putting himself in such humiliating situations. He doesn't need to risk his health, his life, or his dignity for her to believe him. The fact he is willing to do so is evidence enough. And if that means she has to clear up the misunderstanding between them, then she must.

Readying herself for their meeting, she has bought herself another bottle of kaolin and morphine and has taken several sips to calm her stomach and her nerves. She does not go to the front entrance where the public will soon begin to queue, but instead finds the side door via a gated alleyway beside it. She rings the bell, having to press it three additional times before she hears the bolts being pulled back on the other side.

'Sorry – I was feeding this lot,' says a middle-aged man with thinning hair greased back from his temples. She wonders which lot he is referring to; perhaps he is in charge of providing breakfast for the sideshow acts, though the striped cravat he wears seems a little exuberant for such a role.

'Good morning. I'm looking for Mr Davidson,' she says, but he is no longer looking at her. He is studying his own arm, his shirt sleeve rolled up to expose the thick hair growing on it.

'Harold. The rector . . .'

'I know who he is.' He gives a start and curses. 'Oh for goodness' sake!' She tries not to stare as he scratches at a patch of pale flesh halfway along his arm, dotted with red spots as if it has just been shaved. 'No table manners!'

She is beginning to doubt this man's sanity and, though curious to know what is causing his agitation, she deems it sensible to get past him as quickly as possible.

'So, can I see him?'

'Sorry?'

'The rector . . .'

'He's not receiving visitors at the moment,' he says, closing the door on her.

'Uncle Harold,' she calls before it slams shut, remembering the instructions Davidson had given her when they met for tea. 'I'm here to see Uncle Harold.'

'Oh, in that case.' He steps to one side, eyes still focused on his arm, and invites her to come in.

By now she has come to the conclusion that this man is quite mad, calculating that he may well lock the door behind her, leaving no route for escape. 'Are you all right?' she says, nodding at the patch on his arm, which is evidently still causing him irritation.

'Oh, don't mind them,' he says, stroking his arm more tenderly with a forefinger. 'They're playing up this morning. Worse than toddlers they are. And I've got hundreds to see to. They'll be easier to manage after breakfast. I'll introduce you?' He thrusts his arm towards her and, after the initial shock of such a sudden movement, her eyes adjust and, poking out from his rolled-up shirt sleeve, she can see four or five slivers of fine wire. 'Professor Fricke,' he says, tapping his chest with his other hand then sweeping it in the air above his exposed arm. 'And these are my stars!'

Margaret sees one of the wires twitch, and jumps back herself, repulsed. 'Fleas!'

'The very finest. Genuine European *human* fleas.'

'But they are . . .' He really is mad. He is standing there letting parasites suck the blood out of him as if it was the most natural thing in the world.

'As I always tell my audience – I live off them and they live off me! It's worked well for us for nigh on thirty years. Do you want a hold of one?' he points to two dark spots towards his elbow. 'That's Horatio and Samson. Both good boys but they do tend to get into scraps!'

'No thank you.'

'Probably right. Best not to disturb them while they are eating. Are you coming in or not? I've got to get on I'm afraid. Another ninety-five to feed before curtain up!' He steps further inside the door. 'It's all right. They won't hurt you. Can't go anywhere when they are tethered. Wire collars; I put them on myself. Anyway – they know what's good for them!' Margaret takes a deep breath and dashes past him as quickly as possible, not entirely convinced that Horatio or Samson may not be tempted to seek some variety in their diet. 'Through there,' he says. 'First room on the right at the top of the stairs – that's where he's setting up.'

'Thank you.'

'Say bye, gents!' He agitates the hairs on his arms to make the wires jump again. Margaret moves quickly into the darkness of the next room, resisting the overwhelming urge to scratch until she is out of sight of him, then telling herself she has no need to be worried about offending a man feeding fleas from his own flesh. What a story she could tell James about all this! But she has still not plucked up the courage to face him again.

There's very little light by which to follow the directions the man gave her. The windows have been covered, the room partitioned with temporary walls to create corridors and corners. In the first section, bulbs illuminate photographs hung on the wall: grotesque images from the Grand Guignol theatre in Paris. A man's eyes being gouged; a face being melted with acid; a tortured soul having its skin peeled off. She knows they are only actors with rubber masks and painted glass eyes, skin no more than sticking plaster painted red on its underside so it can be peeled off in strips. What disturbs her about the pictures is not the violence, but people's appetite to see it. She has learnt enough about history to know that people enjoy the spectacle of other people's pain: public hangings, stonings, the heads of traitors on spikes. The draw is the same in every case: that it is happening to someone else.

She has never been squeamish about the sight of blood herself. She remembers with fondness how, before she died, her mother would dress her grazed knees or clean the cuts on her arms. It wasn't that she'd hurt herself deliberately but there was a thrill in running too fast or jumping too far, just knowing that she might trip or fall and have to be patched up again. The memory causes her stomach to spasm; she takes the bottle of medicine from her bag, unscrews the lid and takes a large swig, then another, and turns the first bend into the exhibition.

Beneath a single bulb stands a creature on a plinth. Margaret steps back and almost knocks over the temporary wall behind her, reaching back with her hands to try to find the way she came. It is one of a line of figures standing perfectly still in their own pools of dim light.

Waxworks. Nothing more. She chides herself for being so gullible and pauses a moment to slow her pounding heart, taking another mouthful of medicine. She puts the cap back on the bottle then changes her mind, unscrewing it and drinking until she can feel it reach her veins; a sensation of calm laps the soles of her feet, rising to her chest and cresting into a wave when it reaches her head.

Everything has been staged to create a sense of drama and fear, arranged in curtained alcoves, each with its own plaque to name it: *Yanika, The Bird-Faced Man*; *Susi, The Girl With The Elephant Skin*; *Mermaidia,* who is half fish and half woman. She despises the freak shows above all the horrors Blackpool has to offer. She has long supported the campaigns to shut them down and free the specimens they exploit. But now she wonders where all the real people, displayed for so many years as curiosities, have gone. How do they make a living now that they have been replaced by models in a gallery? It's a question she has never thought to ask before.

Alone with the waxworks, she takes the opportunity to study them as though in a laboratory. She brings her face a mere inch from The Dog-boy and stares into his glass eyes, stops to appreciate the craftsmanship that has gone into threading the thousands of hairs into the wax flesh. She strokes his fur. 'Good boy,' she whispers. She is giddy. She knows it. Euphoric at the sensation of being separated from her thoughts, as if her feelings are floating at a distance, balloons tethered by a fine thread, the disapproving voice of Other Margaret carried to her only faintly as though through water. She walks on.

## 19

She pauses on a narrow staircase whose walls are encrusted with geodes, glass gems and fool's gold. The effect is garish but, through swimming eyes, rather beautiful: the glow from the bulbs strung overhead makes the light dance. She sits on a step halfway up, running her fingers along the surfaces, finding the coil of an ammonite hiding between two flowering clusters of crystal. She takes out the small compact mirror she bought after her outing with James, intending to take no more than a cursory glance, but she lingers on her reflection, tilting the glass to make the colours from the walls touch her face. And something like wonder lands briefly in her chest.

Peeping around the door, she finds Davidson standing with his back to her, in a room much smaller than the exhibition space below. It is empty apart from a large glass case and two wooden chairs, cordoned off with a rope, much like you'd see in an art gallery or museum. She watches him take a puff of his cigar, the other hand on his hip as he studies the tank, which contains around a dozen bottles of what she assumes to be water, and several cartons of cigars. 'Excuse me for interrupting you.'

He turns and it takes him a moment to recognise her. 'I should have thought my note made my feelings very clear.'

'It did. But I came to explain.'

'Please don't waste my time or—'

'In the pub, that first night, you saw me making notes but they were not about you.'

'As I said, I am not a fool.'

'It's a misunderstanding.'

He shakes his head. 'Have you or have you not been following me?'

'No. Not exactly. A few times I . . . I was just . . . I was curious.'

'You and every person in Blackpool! You can join the queue. Pay your fee, like everybody else. Instead of all this pretending—'

'I wasn't.'

'You had neither the intention nor the opportunity to publish an article about me.'

'I did not say I was a reporter.'

'But you let me believe it all the same. I thought you could help me.'

'Perhaps I can . . .'

He turns back to the tank.

'As I told you before, I'm a researcher,' she says. 'I'm writing a report about the sideshows and I was interested to find out what the crowds made of you. You are all anyone is talking about.'

'That much is true.' She hears the hint of a smile in his words. '*And* . . . ?'

'That's it. That's why I was—'

'What *do* they make of me?'

'You're an angel or a devil as far as they are concerned.'

'But the vast majority think I'm the former – you saw them in the pub.'

'People do not always say what they really think, Mr Davidson. Frequently they say just the opposite.'

'Also true. And call me Harold.' He sits down on one of the wooden chairs and invites her to do the same. Finishing his cigar, he immediately begins to light another. 'So, you say you're writing about the sideshows? Miss— may I call you by your—'

'Margaret. Yes, it will be a significant piece of work when it's all put together.'

'And you're going to write one of your reports about me?'

She should tell him that she won't be, that James has said he is outside her remit, but Harold is grinning at her now, swinging his legs back and forth under his chair. 'Makes sense,' he says. 'There can be few persons in this country today who have so captured the attention of the Great British Public. Many thousands of strangers have objected to my mistreatment. Whether they think me guilty or not, they feel I have not had a square deal.'

'Perhaps that's it.'

'And that is why you hope to record their interest in my case? I am determined to be of assistance if I may. What sort of information do you gather?'

'The numbers of visitors who come, what their reactions are.'

'To what end? To whom do you report?'

'To a number of politically minded individuals . . . men with influence.' She is unsure how much she should say but has come this far. 'It's a scientific endeavour. The study of people.'

'And I'd be one of them? I'd be studied? My case looked into.'

'In a way, yes.'

'Then you shall have a front row seat!'

'There's no need, I—'

'Right here, beside the case. That way you will see the faces of everyone as they file past.'

'But—'

He raises his hands to stop her. 'You don't have to thank me. Anything that helps a noble cause, I never could say no. Should have learnt my lesson by now, but I can't change my character! I'll make sure you get what you need, I promise you that. This new act will bring the crowds back.'

'But starving yourself. It's so . . . I don't understand why you'd—'

'I can't let people forget me. I need to keep my story in the papers. Keep the pressure on the Bishop. And I've got my rations,' he says, pointing at the water and boxes of cigars. 'Should be everything I need. Though I'm not sure how I'm supposed to get inside.' He is already standing and climbing onto his chair. 'No door, you see,' he says, tapping the glass then lifting a corner of the top of the case, which is made of wood and appears to have air holes cut into it. 'Only a lid. I suppose I'm going to have to climb into the top.'

'But is there no one to help? To instruct you? Mr Gannon runs all the sideshows, doesn't he?'

'Mr Gannon?' The laugh escapes through closed lips, and a small puff of cigar smoke flares out of his nostrils. 'Do you know, the first day I came to Blackpool, I came to meet him. He stepped out of his big car and a tramp staggered towards him – a sorry sight; the sole was hanging off his shoe and he tripped and fell at Gannon's feet.' Margaret has to concentrate on not letting her face betray her feelings at the thought of a man like that approaching her. 'When he got up again, he looked Gannon straight in the eye and said he'd known him as a boy and understood him to be a very generous man. Would he consider giving him a little money to buy himself a new pair of shoes, for old times' sake? Gannon took a huge roll of banknotes from his pocket and said he could do better than that. And do you know what he gave him? The elastic band that was wrapped around his money. Nothing more. To hold the sole on his shoe.'

'But surely in your case . . . You're the star.'

'I have barely seen the man since I signed a contract with him. I receive messages when he needs to communicate. The last simply said my act was moving here and that I would be fasting.'

'And you get no say in the matter?'

'What can I do? I need to raise two thousand pounds for my appeal. Besides, I've signed my body over to him now – not my soul, thank goodness; that still belongs to God!'

He climbs back down and sits on the chair, consulting his watch before producing a bar of chocolate from his jacket pocket. 'Would you care for some?'

'No, thank you.'

He breaks off a piece and puts it into his mouth. 'Now, don't look at me like that. I don't start for another half an hour. Think of this as the Last Supper. Well, breakfast!' When she doesn't laugh as he expects her to, he goes on. 'I'll be all right. Gannon is working on some new ideas. Bigger ideas. Well,' he lowers his voice, 'if you can keep a secret, Margaret – *enormous*. He is planning to cast me as Jonah next.'

'Jonah?'

'Yes. He's got grand plans of getting hold of a whale. Stuffed of course. Goodness knows how one goes about a task that size, but God helps us find a way. And he mentioned something about roasting me on a spit. Devils poking me with forks. That will get them queuing up.'

'But I've seen the crowds. Surely with so many tickets sold you could afford to stop all this—' Nonsense. She wants to say nonsense.

He laughs again. 'Oh, Margaret! I only see a fraction. And the little I do earn is spent before I've even earned it.' His expression is suddenly serious. 'If I see someone in need I can't turn away.' He breaks off another piece of chocolate. 'As you know yourself.'

'Is that what happened with that girl . . . with Barbara?' She notices him wince at mention of the woman who accused him. 'She was very young when you . . .'

'Sixteen. Though she was already, one might say, a woman of the world.' He inspects the glass case again. 'Are you quite comfortable on that chair? You must tell me if not.'

'She was a . . .' she imagines Barbara with the body of the Headless Girl, '. . . prostitute.'

'She had no parents. No job. No prospects. I came across her one day.' His eyes shine. 'Near Marble Arch. She looked like a film star. I told her as much – so young and full of hope. Despite what she must have been suffering in her life, she saw me and she started smiling! So much life and vitality. But I could see she needed help.'

Margaret dares not speak in case she interrupts the memory.

'I've learnt to spot it over the years. Her shoes were scuffed, her hem was hanging down. The signs were there for anyone who chose to take the time to look. Not just to look but to see, really see, and decide to do something about it. I invited her out for tea that day,' he says, rather bashfully. 'We had a wonderful time. I enjoyed her company. A young woman of many remarkable qualities and we shared a love of acting. She wanted to be on the stage herself, and I really thought she had what it took to make it. She needed to be set free. And if not me then who?' In his memory it is a romance, in which he has cast himself as the leading man. 'You should have seen her in court,' he says, shaking his head and closing his eyes for a moment. 'She looked wonderful – posing for the cameras outside. So poised and confident. She changed her outfit halfway through the first day of evidence, so the papers would use her photograph twice. During the trial she became everything I'd always known she could be. She was a star. And part of me couldn't help feeling proud – because I'd been very fond of her you know.'

'You must regret that now.'

'Perhaps I should, but I know I tried my best. I gave her money, yes, but I gave her my friendship too. Good counsel. References for jobs. I was like a guardian to her. I became the one she turned to when she was in trouble.'

'Trouble?'

'Unsuitable men,' he says wearily, as if that's the only kind of trouble there is. 'She took up with a street performer. A strongman. Dixie Din he called himself. He threatened to smash her face in so I went and asked him, perfectly politely, to stay away.'

She suppresses the urge to laugh; can't quite picture Davidson's diminutive frame squaring up to a strongman, then remembers his bravery in stepping in to save her on the night they first met. 'What happened?'

'He was very understanding. Went back to his wife and left Barbara alone after that. Just as well or I would have had to fight him.' He is perfectly earnest. There is no hint of humour. 'The truth was that I did everything in my power but she didn't want to be helped. Kept taking up with the wrong sort. I got her various jobs but she wasn't prepared to get up in the morning. She wanted easy money. And yes, for a time I was giving it to her. Paying for her lodgings, taking her to the theatre to break the habits she was in. My only regret is that I failed to do so.'

Margaret believes him, at least about his feeling of failure. But his story doesn't explain the court's verdict. 'If that's all, then why did the Church . . . ?'

He stands again, picks up a carpet bag from the corner of the room, and sits back down with it on his lap. 'She stayed over-night in my room,' he says. 'A fact I have never sought to hide or deny. When she had nowhere else to go, I let her stay with me. I was naïve. But I am not a complete fool. I would never have . . . I was paying for her . . . treatment . . .'

'Treatment?'

He looks away and rummages in the bag. 'For a disease . . . an intimate matter. A woman of her profession is . . .'

'Oh.'

'What would compel me to attempt to sin with a woman whom I knew to be infected? It doesn't make any sense. It's all in here.' He hands her a large book, something like a photograph album. She opens it to find page after page of newspaper cuttings. Headlines, photographs; Harold posing outside court wearing a silk top hat, looking as carefree as though he had backed a winning horse; nothing like a man who stood to lose his position and his reputation.

'And the waitresses?' Margaret points to an article about him pestering staff in a Lyons Tearoom in Walbrook.

'Yes. Exactly!' She had meant it as a question but he seemed to infer some understanding on her part, suddenly standing and starting to pace around the room. 'Exactly that. Accused of making a nuisance of myself because I left them generous tips. Gave them theatre tickets. Because I was vocal in my calls for better working conditions and better pay. Those girls deserved more and I wasn't afraid to say so. And some had a real chance. Just like Barbara. They could have had a career on the stage. And I was in a position to help them. I know what directors are looking for. I have a good eye.' He stops in front of her chair and leans down towards her. 'Show me your teeth, Margaret,' he says, raising his finger as if he has just been struck by inspiration.

'My . . . ?' She can make no sense of what her teeth have to do with any of this. She must have misheard him.

'Smile!'

She does as she is instructed, too confused to muster the words to question him.

'Very good. Now open wide.' He reaches forward and takes her chin in his hand. She cannot make sense of it. She knows that she should be feeling something. Horror probably. The word is there in her mind but not the sensation. She is alone with him and he is going to try to kiss her. Her mouth is frozen in a grimace. She can feel him pressing on her jaw to encourage it open.

'What's the matter?' he says, looking genuinely bemused. 'I was looking for fillings. That's the kind of thing that can be picked up on certain camera angles, you see. Or on the front row of a show.'

'*That's* what you did to those waitresses?'

'Naturally,' he shows no signs of embarrassment. 'I was happy to give them my professional opinion. A good set of teeth is vital.'

He smiles broadly to reveal his own and taps them with a finger-nail. 'The Lord help any women who has a set like these! It would not have been right for me to offer encouragement without being confident they had the necessary qualities . . . I simply wanted to help.' He falls silent then sits beside her again. 'Margaret, do you ever feel that, despite your best intentions, people—'

'Yes. Yes, I do.' They are both misunderstood. Both failures when it comes to knowing what should be obvious. She can understand how his single-mindedness got him into trouble; his determination to continue on a righteous path no matter the cost. He is an infuriating man, that she cannot deny, but she admires his resolve. In certain ways she wishes she were more like him herself. He shares her clarity of judgement and purpose, but he does not seem to fear censure or disapproval. Instead of striving to understand the unwritten rules, Margaret observes, he simply makes up his own.

## 20

First, they solve the puzzle of how to get him inside. With Margaret's help, Harold climbs a stepladder, before lowering a chair, and then himself, into the glass case. Barely a few minutes later, the paying public begins to arrive. She can hear feet running up the stairs. The early arrivals bursting through the door, smug to be at the front of the queue. Anything can be turned into a competitive exercise, particularly by men, who will take any opportunity to be the first, the best (and even the worst if the top ranks are already taken).

During the course of the day, she records in her notebook the number of people who file past Harold in their tens, hundreds, then thousands. He busies himself combing through the transcripts from his trial. For a time, the glass of the tank becomes clouded, and he is barely visible behind swirls of smoke, which coil lazily from the air holes at the top. Margaret solves the problem by opening a window to the street outside to create some draw. Aside from these moments of activity, she remains largely unnoticed by the spectators, all eyes trained on Harold until they are moved along by the push of those piling in behind. They study him for an average of eight seconds, the majority apparently content just to say they have seen him.

However, on six occasions someone tries to cross the rope cordon. The first time, when a thick-set man starts to bang on the tank, Harold shrinks back in his seat and looks to Margaret for rescue. She stands to go for help and is surprised to find the action is sufficient to deter the spectator from hitting the glass again. It must have spooked him: a movement at the corner of his eye. He must have thought she was someone far bigger, someone with authority, someone who would have stood a chance of stopping him. He was mistaken on all counts, but she feels a sense of achievement nonetheless.

When it happens a second time, simply getting up from the chair is not enough. She doesn't know what to say; doesn't want to speak at all because she knows her voice will betray her fear. But she follows an instinct to protect Harold and stands silently in front of the tank to shield him from view until the spectator steps back. The room falls quiet. All eyes suddenly on her. And she stays perfectly still, holds her ground, considers the looks on the faces of the line of people, separated from her only by a line of rope. She is not sure what their expressions mean. But no one is laughing.

By the afternoon she is polite but firm in her regular requests for onlookers to 'keep moving please' or 'look but don't touch', and receives the occasional 'yes, miss' in reply. Perhaps it is the chair she is sitting in. Perhaps it endows her with an official role in their eyes. But no one seems to question that she has the authority to keep things running smoothly. And though the bare wood seat becomes very uncomfortable within only a few hours, there are short breaks when she is required to step outside and lock the door behind her so that Harold can make himself more comfortable (she does not ask for the details). She has five minutes to use the privy and eat one of the sandwiches she has brought in her bag. It wouldn't feel right to take refreshments in front of a fasting man, but perhaps he is sneaking food when she leaves the room. She wouldn't be surprised.

She used to be so sure of what was right and what was wrong but she can no longer say who is exploiting who. Is he persuading people to part with their money to see a sham spectacle, or is he being drawn into making a spectacle of himself to feed a need in them?

A total of 7,681 people come. She calculates that they have paid just over £384 in admission. Only five make unpleasant remarks (not all who try to cross the rope are unkind) and only 162 look at him with what she considers to be obvious disapproval.

It is 9 p.m. when the shift finally comes to an end. Harold invites her to stay on after the last spectator files past. He wants to hear about her findings, what she plans to write in her report, but she is desperate to be alone, and more interested in the transcripts he has been reading than in sharing her notes with him. He does not argue when she suggests that she take his newspaper cuttings with her: 'I'm good at spotting things that other people miss.'

With the album tucked under her arm, she follows the arrows to an exit onto the road outside. She should head straight to her lodgings to get some sleep but she feels so full of energy that she is agitated, her skin itching, legs desperate to take some exercise. Besides, she finally has something worth filing, data that her fellow researchers could only hope to record. Her absence can't have passed unnoticed by the team. Since she embarrassed herself by falling asleep in James's chair she has avoided going to HQ at all, certain that he would be relieved to be spared the awkwardness of seeing her. But at this time of night the offices should be empty – there's a higher probability anyway. She can't stay away for ever or she will lose her job.

The street is dark. She stands and counts the doorways until she can identify HQ, hidden in shadow. No chink of light seeping through any cracks between its curtains. Deciding she is safe to go on, she continues down the road and up the path, the glass above the front door as black as the painted step below it. She finds the key in its hiding place and lets herself in, standing still in the hallway and straining her ears for any sound of movement from the rooms upstairs. It's still possible that one of the researchers has brought a woman back, but the silence satisfies her that she really is alone.

Setting to work under a desk lamp in her usual spot upstairs, she chooses not to turn on the main light in case it should give her away. Being here after hours alone makes her heart beat faster. Though she has never been told specifically that she should stick to particular office hours, she is not sure that she should be in the building so late. There's a thrill to working in the darkness. She always adheres so strictly to the rules, takes refuge in boundaries and regulations, but it feels good to cross a line. Even a line so faintly sketched that she is not certain it exists at all.

With no distractions and no one to disturb her, the report should write itself, but she can't settle to it. Halfway down the first page, she makes a mistake. It's something she could cross out and correct but she rips it out of the typewriter, crushes it into a ball and begins again. She wants this to be perfect. But she finds herself unable to resist the urge to open the album of newspaper cuttings.

The reports grow in size, inch after inch stretching out along the length of the page then curling into the columns beside; paragraph after paragraph snaking around photographs of Harold, and Barbara, the young woman he was accused of associating with. And like serpents they twist and turn back upon themselves, swallowing their own tails. So that, just when Margaret thinks she knows what kind of story she is reading, she is sent back to the beginning of an altogether different one. One minute, a parable with Harold the hero: the Prostitutes' Padre who devoted his life to helping unfortunate women escape from vice. The next, a bestiary of a predator who preyed on young girls in God's name. '*The defendant has, during the last five years, been guilty of an immoral habit in that he habitually associated himself with women of a loose character for immoral purposes.*' Habitually. Deliberately. Systematically. Meeting these women in bed-sitting rooms at all hours of the day and night. A wolf disguised as the lamb of God. What a story these reporters have found; men unsure whether to condemn or congratulate the audacity of such behaviour; men unwilling to let the mystery be solved either way. In Harold they have two stories in one and, even as they report the moment that the judge found him guilty on all four counts, they keep both possibilities alive: the saint and the sinner. Both just as compelling. Just as plausible. And that's what makes Margaret so frustrated. Because he can't be both. He is either guilty of the things he was accused of, guilty of inappropriate relations with women he purported to save, or he is not. There is one true story and one that is false. And, having come to know him, she can't help but believe in his innocence.

She studies the speculation and finds very few facts. From what she can see, the trial was essentially Harold's word against Barbara's. He was charged under the Clergy Discipline Act of 1892 on four counts. It is only now that she realises he was tried not in a criminal court but at an ecclesiastical hearing: the prosecution and defence making cases directly to a judge, without a jury. There was testimony from some of the waitresses he allegedly pestered, but she has seen firsthand that, though inappropriate, his behaviour isn't lascivious. And there is one detail that she finds particularly compelling: '*Mr Davidson helped upwards of 500 girls but only one gave evidence against him.*' Just one. If he really was the sort of man that couldn't control his urges, surely more would have complained?

His own suspicion that he had been the subject of surveillance by the Church is borne out by the reports, as well as his assertion that Barbara was given alcohol and money by private investigators. In fact, another woman, Rose Ellis, said she'd been persuaded to make unjust claims about him by the temptation of 40 shillings from a detective. Davidson confided that he set out to do one thing, only to be accused of another. Margaret concludes, from what she has read, that the Church's misunderstanding was wilful, its manipulation deliberate. That its intention was to attribute a far more sinister motive to his actions.

It's 2 a.m. before she has written what she came to and, though there is certainly room for improvement, she accepts that she will achieve nothing more tonight. At this moment she feels she could rest her head on the desk and fall asleep right there, too weary to make it back to her lodgings. But experience tells her that as soon as she gets into bed, her thoughts will sabotage any chance of rest.

Packing away her notebook in her bag, she arranges her typed sheets in a file, places them in the drawer she has been assigned in a tallboy in the corner, and switches off the lamp.

There are no windows above the staircase to cast moonlight onto her path downstairs and she decides it would be reckless to attempt the descent in total darkness. Turning on the landing light, just long enough to make her way down, will do no harm. But the effect is glaring. It takes a moment for her eyes to adjust and she sees her name on the noticeboard on the wall. It is here that the latest missives from London are posted (new areas of research or successes in other arms of the project); it is here that the researchers pin messages which may prove useful to another's project.

> *Bill — met bare knuckle boxer who may be able to get you into a fight. Drinks in the Fisherman's most evenings. Goes by the name of Stan. I can introduce you if you prefer.*
>
> *— George*

> *Joseph — betting ring operating out of the back of the fruit stall in Talbot Square. Worth making a note of how many men ask the seller where he ships his bananas in from. Seems to be a code of some sort. — Bill*

Margaret doesn't leave messages for her colleagues on the principle that they do not do so for her. But she finds three pieces of folded paper with her name on.

> *Dear Margaret,*
> *I do hope you are feeling better. I would be grateful if you would pop in and see me.*
>
> *James*

*Dear Margaret,*
*Perhaps we keep missing each other. Do come in during office hours.*
*As you know, I am usually here. James*

*Margaret,*
*I have been reluctant to trouble you. However, it is important that*
*we discuss your absence of late. Please come to HQ at your earliest*
*opportunity or, if you are unable to do so, send word and I shall*
*visit you at your lodgings. James*

Margaret has no choice, not if she wants to have a hope of keeping her job. She has to go in and face James. It may be too late, of course. It would be just like him to explain, at great length, why he has to let her go. He would put himself through the ordeal, just to spare her the hurt of receiving the news by letter. What makes it worse is the knowledge that she wouldn't do the same for him, wouldn't be able to cope with the awkwardness.

She lay in bed last night and played the conversation in her head. It was only with the help of medicine that she was able to fall into a fitful sleep; feeling as though her head was slipping underwater, waking up gasping for breath as she was jolted back to the surface. She has started to visit other chemists' shops now, has a route she takes to buy a bottle from each. She is careful to keep a note of which she has visited and when, so that she does not draw attention to herself; transferring the top layer of morphine straight into her hip flask and throwing the bottle and the kaolin away in a rubbish bin on the street, so that no one will hear glass chinking in her bag. It is no worse than drinking alcohol. In fact, one could make the strong argument it is better. She is nothing like the drunks she sees on the seafront benches, the young lads who fight and swear in the streets, or the women who let themselves be taken advantage of. Margaret drinks a little but often, taking the occasional sip to quell the sickness that is constantly creeping into her throat, and to calm her pounding heart. To make her better. That's what medicine does. And goodness knows she needs a little help this morning. She takes a dose before she leaves her lodgings and another just before she turns into Shetland Road.

James comes to the door. He looks serious when he greets her, jaw set. Margaret risks a fleeting look at his eyes, but he has already turned from the door and is walking into his office. 'Are you better?' He sits at his desk and motions for her to take the armchair. Oh God, the armchair where she fell asleep. She had hoped to get through this without drawing attention to how much of a fool she made of herself. But now, here she is, recreating the circumstances of her indignity.

'Margaret?' He has the tone of a kindly parent talking to a child, as if she might be about to doze again.

'Yes. I'm quite well now. Thank you.'

'That's good to hear.'

She thinks he looks genuinely relieved but knows she cannot trust her own judgement.

'I was growing quite concerned. But I didn't . . . well I wasn't sure it was my place to—'

'Bad stomach,' she says. 'Not sure what caused it. But I'm over the worst.'

'That's good to hear.' He has already said that. He is repeating himself. Going through the motions. Working up to telling her that her employment has been terminated. They both look at the floor. Margaret concentrates on a dent in the parquet, and wonders if he is staring at the same spot.

'Thank you for the crisps,' she says, to fill the silence so there is no space for him to say what he is going to. She doesn't want to lose this job. She is getting somewhere, thanks to Harold.

She finally has the chance to prove the other researchers wrong, to prove Mother wrong.

'The crisps. Oh yes. When you dropped off.' He pushes back a strand of greased hair that has fallen forwards. 'You looked very peaceful.'

He is being polite again. She has thought about this, frantically, every night since and is perfectly convinced that she must have looked monstrous: slack-mouthed and snoring. There is no way he could ever find a woman attractive after seeing her like that. Not that he would have done anyway. Not that she would want him to. Though she can't imagine women are exactly queuing up to be courted by him, but that doesn't matter when you are a man does it? You still get to do the choosing.

The conversation has stalled again and she tries desperately to think of something to keep it moving. 'The twist of salt is always soggy, don't you find?' What a pointless thing to say. She should let him get it over with. It's the least she can do. It's not his fault she is late with her report. Surely he is going to get cross with her now, or, at the very least, frustrated. She knows, because that's how she feels about herself most of the time. But she pretends to glance around the room so that she can take in his face for a moment, and is surprised to find a smile there.

'Soggy, yes!' He sits forward in his chair, rubs his open palms back and forth on the tops of his legs. 'I'd estimate at least seven out of ten bags are disappointing in that regard. I've opened them sometimes to find a lump as dense as a sugar cube. I suppose it must depend on the conditions when they pack the bags.'

'Humidity and such.'

'Exactly!'

'So, what do you do?'

'With what?'

'The lumps?'

'Oh, I keep them in the paper and crush them between my fingers. Well forefinger and thumb to be precise . . .'

She wants to tell him how much she admires him. Most men she has met are obsessed with appearance; not in the way that women are, not in the way that would make them wear a girdle or dye their hair. Women are concerned with taming their own bodies but men are determined to control other people's perceptions of their minds; every man a walking self-portrait which emphasises their strength, their wisdom and their power. And it must be exhausting, that inability to be wrong. But James is different. He doesn't appear to care how odd he seems to other people. Either that or he doesn't realise. But whichever it is, she thinks his lack of self-awareness a blessing. How liberating it must be to be comfortable in one's own skin.

He is still explaining, at length, how he salvages the salt: '. . . but that is not particularly successful either. So, circumstances allowing, I hack at them with a teaspoon to make them into grains again. More time-consuming than you might imagine. But worth the investment. Crisps without salt are just—'

'Fried potatoes,' she says. They look up at the same moment, and this time she doesn't move her eyes away.

'Margaret, there is something I'd like to talk to you about.'

'I know,' she says, resigned to what is coming, and determined to make it easier for both of them. He will probably ask her to hand in her notice so she can leave with some semblance of dignity. 'I appreciate it.'

'I'm so glad. Like I said, I wasn't sure it was my place but I'm concerned about you. None of us has seen you in several days and you've not filed any reports.'

'My stomach bug was . . . I've fallen behind. It's been difficult to concentrate—'

'I know, Margaret. And I hope I'm not speaking out of turn here. But I think there may be more to it than that.'

Oh God. She cannot hold his gaze. Does he know about the morphine? She has been so careful. Her medicine. If it wasn't for that she wouldn't have been able to work at all. 'I've been putting together a larger report,' she says. 'Working very long hours, as it happens. I didn't mention it because it was a delicate situation. I didn't want it to fall through.'

'That's what I was getting at,' he says, gently. 'Working day and night? Your dedication is commendable, Margaret. But you're going to be exhausted. You *were* exhausted. And you've made yourself ill. You fell asleep right there in that chair.'

'I'm sorry. I'll try harder.'

She glances up and finds him staring at her. 'No, you misunderstand. I think you are working too hard. Putting too much pressure on yourself. I'm not supposed to say this, but you are the best researcher we have, by a long way. And I don't want to lose you.' He looks down again. 'What I mean to say is, the *project* doesn't.'

The relief she feels is instant; a surge of joy. She has the overwhelming urge to share it with him somehow. 'Thank you.'

'Margaret, I'm under pressure to send the latest chapter of your report to Harrisson and I'm concerned you are being too much of a perfectionist. From what you have said, you have gathered ample data. I need it to be finished by the end of this week.'

It is achievable if she spends the next three days doing nothing else, but she has promised to meet Harold. 'The other thing

I've been working on, I—'

'You can come to that later,' he says. 'I just need to get that report to Harrisson. Can you do it?'

'It's just . . . I really think I'm onto something.'

'Could someone else take that over for you? If I ask one of the others—'

'No.' She is not going to let them take the credit.

'Can *I* help then?'

How?

'Just a suggestion . . .' he says, 'but perhaps we could go on a few missions together. I need to take my camera out again anyway. And two heads are better than one. Meet me here first thing tomorrow and we can make a start.'

Her standards must be slipping. Margaret barely registers the fact James pours their daily serving of fizzy pop into mugs. On the first occasion, she resisted the urge to go straight to Woolworths to buy him a set of glasses, but the cups (hers decorated with Blackpool Tower, and his with an advertisement for Bovril) have become an integral part of the routine they have settled into. She has become quite partial to dandelion and burdock, and no longer baulks at the sweetness of cream soda.

She is sure to show her face at HQ every day now. With his encouragement, she is able to submit her report on the sale of souvenirs at last. The relief is palpable, for both of them; celebrated with a fish and chip supper in his office, Margaret careful to avoid the addition of pea-wet this time. James is so amused by her account of her previous encounter that he reaches out for her shoulder to steady himself.

The report is forwarded to Harrisson, the panic is over, and they no longer need to combine forces. But neither of them mentions this fact, and the next day she arrives as usual. Having thought she had come so close to losing this job, it is important to look industrious, and James always makes time to ask about her latest findings. Together they consider new areas of study, and sometimes he accompanies her with his camera. At first, she thinks him tense again, almost resentful.

'Are you sure you have time for this?' she asks.

'Yes, it will do me good.'

And it does. At his suggestion, they head for quieter spots, out-of-the-way places — stretches of beach further out of town or cafés away from the seafront — and for an hour or two Margaret feels that she can breathe again. They take long walks, circuitous routes which take them past wasteland where a team of workers are digging deep into the ground. Neither one of them comments on it, not even when the steel supports are lifted in, and the walls are built; not even when the whole thing is covered with earth once more and the newspapers confirm that Hitler has held another rally in Nuremberg. But they both know what it means: the government is building shelters to protect a lucky few if the bombs start to fall.

In James's company she can push these thoughts away, but alone in her lodgings, they steal back, not into her mind but into her stomach. The days are passing too quickly; only a few more weeks before the summer season comes to an end, and she has still not received any indication that her role will be extended. Mother writes with news that their family doctor in Northampton is looking for a new receptionist. She has put Margaret's name forward and is already drawing up the terms under which she will move back home: her room is still just as she left it, though she will have to pay the going rate for board and lodgings and invest in outfits befitting such an important role, because Dr Speller has standards to uphold, having a brother who practises on Harley Street.

The letters are conspicuous in their silence on any other matters. There is no mention of the news. Only a cryptic reference to her father having 'one of his spells', and the toll it is taking on Mother. Margaret imagines him sitting in his chair, refusing to listen to the wireless or read the newspaper. But for someone like her, the evidence is impossible to ignore: the volume cannot be lowered on the conversations she overhears on the streets outside. There is no way to avoid what's coming. The only thing she cannot say with any certainty is which might happen first: the country sent to war, or she sent back to her old life. In both cases she is at the mercy of decisions made by men, so many miles away in London. But there is only one of those decisions she can possibly hope to influence.

All she can do is work harder to impress her superiors at Mass Observation. She is grateful for James's help and his company. His idea to observe how many fathers build sandcastles with their children (compared to mothers) yields some interesting results, and a moderate case of sunburn for both of them. They sit and watch players on the one-armed bandit machines and calculate the rate of wins to losses. But gradually they are drawn back towards the crowds, back towards the Golden Mile, where Harold is still on display.

Margaret does not tell James that she spends her evenings at his sideshow after closing time, because she knows he would disapprove of her keeping such long hours. She doesn't tell him that poring over transcripts of Harold's trial is the only thing that feels meaningful; the only thing she may have a hope of changing. She makes pages of notes, underlining questions that he might take to his solicitor. She identifies several witnesses who gave character references in his defence. The testimony of his landlady, in particular, chimes with Margaret's now firm belief that he was naïve about how his kindness might be perceived. She suggests they might persuade some of the other young ladies who he helped to come forward. 'A good idea,' he says, 'but thanks to me, they live respectable lives now. Many of

them with husbands and children. I could not ask them to reveal the details of their past profession in such a public forum.'

'But they could tell people the truth.'

'I'm sorry, Margaret, but it is out of the question. I gave
them my word.'

To get any more than a few hours' sleep is a rarity. It is as if
she doesn't need it any more, already living two distinct lives:
daylight hours spent in one man's company, after dark in another's.

Harold continues to starve himself for several more days
but the stunt is relatively short-lived. Visitor numbers begin to
drop again and he is provided with a glass coffin instead, with a
placard that warns he will 'Fast unto Death' if his appeal is un-
heeded. Margaret is relieved when the police, acting on the instruction of Blackpool's mayor, remove him. James reads aloud
from the newspaper the next day, describing how Davidson was
escorted to the police station clutching a cigar and a Bible. 'He's
being charged with attempted suicide,' he says, putting the paper aside to serve the two chocolate bars he has bought for their
meeting. Margaret does not mention that she was there when
the constables arrived. She had stayed up until 4 a.m. talking
with him, beside the coffin, the night before.

On the day of the hearing, she is due to be taking a survey of
the percentage of holidaying women who wear stockings and
how many brave bare legs. She manages to gather the data while
waiting outside the court, arriving three hours early to be sure
she will get a seat in the public gallery. But the queue is not
nearly as long this time. In her notebook she records the full
charge read out by the prosecution: 'Davidson has been unlaw-
fully fasting with intent to feloniously, wilfully and of malice

aforethought kill and murder himself.' She considers the inclusion of both 'kill' and 'murder' unnecessary and feels sure that is just the sort of detail James would find amusing. But she can't tell him, not without giving herself away.

Despite her intentions to make observations on the court proceedings and, in particular, the reaction in the public gallery, she finds herself spending the majority of the hearing watching Harold himself. He is unrepentant, vocal in his hope that his fast will bring the Bishop to his senses, but he looks small as he stands in the dock. Making attempts to entertain the court, he appears defeated. It is the police officer called to the witness stand who inadvertently raises the biggest laugh when he comments on the healthy appetite Harold has shown while in custody. But Margaret does not find it amusing. She is just glad his fast is over before he does himself serious damage.

'Acquitted!' James says, popping his head around the doorway as she sits typing the next day. 'Says here that he has vowed to lie in a coffin made of ice next.' He draws his arms tightly around his chest as if protecting himself from the cold. And Margaret cannot help but wonder how it would feel if he wrapped them around her instead.

'You'll crumple your shirt,' she says.

'I'm sorry?'

'You'll crease your shirt.'

'Oh.' He drops his arms.

Mother's embraces were rare, brief, and immediately followed by her patting down her dress, then heading straight to the hallway mirror to smooth her hair and reapply her lipstick. *Unnecessary fuss*, made only if Margaret had slipped and injured her leg, or fallen off her bicycle. She always felt as though

Mother was trying to make her smaller somehow; to tuck in her arms and straighten the angles of her elbows. Gripping her firmly enough to stifle her breath and quieten her crying.

She has never understood why adults do it to each other. To her it looks restrictive, possessive. With a man, whom nature has blessed with more physical strength, she could be reduced to nothing. Crushed. It stands to reason that the more parts of your body that are intertwined, the more difficult it must be to extract yourself. That's why sexual intercourse is so attractive to males: it reduces the female's ability to flee. You've only got to think of the barbed phallus of the cat, she thinks, to see the lengths that nature will go to.

'They seem to enjoy the suffering,' James says.

'Sorry?'

'The public – they like to see Davidson suffer, don't they? Starving and freezing. He really will end up killing himself at this rate.'

'Killing and murdering.'

'I'm sorry – what?'

'Nothing.'

'I was thinking,' he says. 'Harrisson wants a report on rides and attractions. How do you fancy a mission to the Pleasure Beach tomorrow?'

## 23

Her hair won't behave itself. It used to be as dependable as the rest of her, needing nothing more than a quick comb for her to consider it sufficiently styled, but today it is kicking out on one side. She tries to curl it under with her fingers as she walks. She didn't have time to tame it: waking to find her head on the desk, opening her eyes to see the keys of her typewriter, and realising she was going to be late. She drank a glass of water without drawing breath, and took a mint ball from James's office as she dashed out of the front door.

By some miracle, she arrives at the Pleasure Beach on time. James is already waiting, looking at his watch. 'You're here,' she says, not intending the words to sound so much like an accusation.

'Thought I'd get up early. Before the crowds. Take a slow walk over . . .' Margaret has an urge to reassure him, to touch his arm, but she doesn't. 'And I had something to tell you. Well, show you really . . . Thought you'd find it interesting. But it's . . . I wasn't sure whether it was . . . How can I put it?'

She sees colour rise to his face, and any curiosity she feels is overpowered by her desire to rescue him from his discomfort. He looks around, as if planning a route of escape. 'Have you had breakfast?' she says, nodding towards the food stalls lined up either side of the entrance to the Pleasure Beach.

'No,' he says. 'Have you?'

'No.'

'Then why don't we . . . ?'

She can't explain the awkwardness between them this morning. He seems nervous, as if they are strangers meeting for the first time. They begin to walk, pausing in front of a pie stall. 'Ninety-eight,' he says, studying the display with an intensity that makes her wonder if he can see right through the pastry and identify the filling inside.

'Sorry?'

'A typical stall has ninety-eight pies arranged in fourteen rows. Wasn't that what you wrote in your report?'

'Yes,' she says. 'Yes, something like that.' But she knows full well that he has quoted her words exactly and she can't help smiling.

'Your notes make my mouth water,' he says. 'I sit in my office and I can almost imagine I am smelling these pies.' These outings are probably the closest he comes to anything resembling proper food, Margaret thinks, unless his landlady is accommodating enough to leave him a cold plate for when he gets in at night. He still seems to exist largely on boiled sweets. 'Some extraordinary details,' he says, 'people making sandwiches of them. What do they call the bread rolls they put them in?'

'Barm cakes.'

'That's it. A pie barm!'

'Are you going to try one?'

He pulls a face. 'Far too heavy for this time in the morning. Now, oysters on the other hand . . .'

She points. 'That's the place. Always busy. The end stall, over there.'

'There's a queue. Let's get started with the observations before it—'

'No, please, you'll be no good without breakfast.' She wants him to have oysters if he'd like them. She wants him to enjoy being here with her.

'Only if you'll join me,' he says.

The thought makes her stomach turn. She has never tried one herself, has always considered the act of eating them performative. The idea that you should tip your head back and let them slip down your throat is a challenge, a test she is not sure she can pass. 'I have an incredibly sensitive gag reflex.' She hopes this will be sufficient reason to excuse her. But he seems amused. He looks towards the oyster stall but does not move. 'Come on,' she says, leading him into the small clutch of people gathered in front. Most have come to look rather than buy, and Margaret has little problem getting to the front while James follows. He clears his throat, holds up three fingers to the stallholder to indicate his order, then digs around in his pocket for payment. Taking his first shell, he douses it in vinegar and, instead of bringing it to his lips, lifts the flesh of the oyster between forefinger and thumb. 'When in Rome,' he says, turning to her before biting off a corner and starting to chew. He is imitating the way the workers eat them: taking their time, making them last.

'I wonder if they actually enjoy them,' he says, 'or if they eat them just to say they've done it. Not that there is anything wrong with that. That's what life's supposed to be about, isn't it? The experience.'

Margaret considers his question. It has never been her approach. There are very many things she has no desire to do. She doesn't need to try them to know that they aren't for her. She has always thought that people put themselves under too much pressure to be exciting, to be brave, to be reckless. That they make themselves look foolish by bowing to it.

'Are you sure I can't tempt you?' he says.

As long as she can nibble it slowly, Margaret thinks she can manage one. Following his lead, she takes a small bite, braced for her body's reaction and determined to overcome it. She must concentrate on chewing and swallowing as though she feels perfectly relaxed about it. The meat yields between her teeth. It is lukewarm and fleshy but relatively tasteless beneath the tang of vinegar, and she finds, to her surprise, that it is not unpleasant. Juice is running down her chin and she wipes it away hurriedly. But James doesn't seem to notice anyway, too busy concentrating on keeping his own shirt free of stains.

'Another?' he offers.

'Go on then.'

She still can't understand what all the fuss is about, why they are considered such a luxury, but she is enjoying the act of sharing them. There is novelty in the flavour: subtle yet unique, briny yet earthy, leaving a residue of rust in her mouth when she swallows. When they have finished a half-dozen between them, he looks for something in his pockets, a handkerchief probably, and when he fails to find one, she produces her own, wipes her hands and gives it to him to do the same.

They walk on towards the Pleasure Beach and begin their mission proper. She's had no cause to come here for work before, and no desire to come for leisure. 'What do you think, Margaret?' he says. 'Best if we pick a family and follow them? That's how you usually do it, isn't it?'

'Yes.'

'You choose then. You've got a much better eye for these things.'

For the good of the study, she should pick a family that looks lively, and is relatively small (larger families being less likely to be able to afford the number of tickets required).

'Do you think they'll ride the Big Dipper?' James says, looking up at the string of cars that rattles above their heads. 'I've always fancied that.' He sounds excited but there is something in his expression that Margaret can't quite resolve. 'I bet you've already had a go.'

'You want us to go on *with* them?'

'We'll have to, won't we? To observe.'

Margaret had assumed they were going to go as far as the entrance to each ride, then wait for them at the exit. She has no wish to be strapped into a carriage, thrown around at speed, dropped down dips or flung around corners. Now she scans the crowd for possible targets with her own criteria in mind: younger children will be too small to ride on the more thrilling attractions. She needs to find a family with little ones.

'There,' she says, pointing at a young couple walking towards them. The man is carrying a boy, who looks to be around three years old; the woman smiling as she runs behind a slightly older child, a girl – five perhaps – who is making a beeline for a rock stall. Taking Margaret's lead, James hangs back, keeping distance. For just under two hours, they follow the family. Margaret suspects that they don't have sufficient funds to go on the rides themselves, but they show no resentment or envy, apparently satisfied to watch others have fun. They spend nine minutes watching people hurtle down the sheer drop slide. Margaret notes that courting couples use the moment of peril as an opportunity to clutch each other tightly: young men place their hands on a breast or thigh in those few seconds of falling; young women hastily rearrange a lifted skirt as soon as they land.

From there, the father stops to study 'The World's Most Tattooed Woman', who is on a walkabout among the crowds. He accepts her invitation to try and rub the drawings off her arm, but declines her suggestion to step into the tent a little way along the prom and have one of the pictures inked onto his own skin as a souvenir.

'That was a lucky escape,' she says to James as they walk away. 'Was it?'

'If we were doing everything they do, you would have had to join the queue and get a tattoo yourself.'

'Not necessarily. This is your observation. Surely you'd have been the one to do it.' He touches the bare skin of her forearm for a moment. 'Now let's see. A ship or an anchor – what would suit?'

Up ahead, the parents are lifting both children up to peer in at the clockwork clowns outside the Fun House. Margaret risks stepping closer to listen to their reaction, but becomes distracted by James. He is fascinated, staring at the tableau as it jerks into life: a large clown holding a smaller one on its knee, both with faces powdered, large mouths that open in bursts of mechanical hysteria. The girl starts to imitate them, the laughter seeming to pass between the members of the family, infecting each in turn. And James too succumbs. Margaret is embarrassed for him. He is making a show of himself. This is infantile, an entertainment made for children – he is a grown man. She nudges him, but he reads it as a gesture of encouragement and laughs all the more, clutching his belly and throwing back his head to entertain the little girl, who begins to copy him.

'Stop it,' Margaret whispers under her breath. 'We're supposed to be blending in.' But he does not take any notice. She is becoming angry now; people are staring at him. At her. 'Stop it!'

'It's a marvel, isn't it? Just a machine, just a series of cogs and gears, but the effect it's having!' He turns to look at Margaret and his expression is so earnest, so joyful, that her anger is pacified. The family have made space and James has stepped forward to get a closer look at the clowns. They are all laughing again. All but Margaret. She cannot perform to order, cannot provide the response they expect from her. She tries to muster a modest giggle but the sound is strange, strained.

James is too busy with the children to notice when she turns and walks away, finding a spot on the other side of the carousel. Their laughter felt like something that was being *done* to her; something she was required to surrender to. Frustration rises to panic, reminding her that she is barren, lacking the vital components that others seem to have been built with. The clowns were mocking her. They all were. She takes a sip from her hip flask, and a deep breath. But she can't hide for ever.

'There you are!' he says, when she gets back. 'I was worried.' He does seem to draw a little closer to her than before. 'We could easily lose each other with so many people. Here – would you like a go with the camera?' He takes the strap from around his neck and places it around hers, their heads almost touching for a brief moment before he steps back. She is grateful to be able to hide her face, and makes a show of studying the scene in the viewfinder. 'Can you spot our little family?' he says. 'Left a bit and you should—'

'Got them!' She can't help but admire his skill in creating such a clever contraption.

'What can you see?'

'The mother is holding both children by the hand. The father is standing behind her with his arms wrapped — no wait, he's bending down. Picking something up off the floor. What is it? Something small. I can't see what—' She clicks the shutter and takes a photograph.

'A coin,' James says.

'He must have dropped it.'

'No. Guess again.'

'Someone else's then.' She watches but the man shows no sign of looking around him, of trying to identify who the money might belong to. 'He's put it straight into his pocket. Typical.' She is excited now. 'He's stolen it. I think I got it on camera. Just the sort of thing Harrisson's looking for.'

'I don't think we can say he has *stolen* it.'

Margaret takes the camera from her face and turns to him. 'Of course we can. He has taken money that doesn't belong to him. I'll bet he's going to spend it in the pub. Or on the gee-gees.' She looks through the viewfinder again. 'There look — he's off. Come on.'

# 24

They follow the family to an outcrop, as tall as a building, which has grown out of the pavement. It looks as though it has stood on that spot for millennia, carved by the waterfalls and streams that spring from coves on its surface. The bare rock is almost colourless, a mass of weathered grey, pitted like pumice. It's the lack of vibrancy that makes it stand out so conspicuously in the patchwork rainbow of the Pleasure Beach. Margaret reads the sign leading to a queue of people. 'The River Caves of the World.'

'That rings a bell,' James says. 'I think this was one of the first rides here. Little boats running on a track under the water . . .' The family join the queue, the two children jumping up and down with excitement. Margaret and James hang back to allow a young couple to go ahead of them. 'Must be a variation on the Tunnel of Love.'

Must it? She thought it was something like a fairy grotto, for children. But sitting on a ride that has a link (however tenuous) with love? The two of them. Together. Turning, she finds that several more couples have already joined the queue behind them, blocking any means of exit. James, meanwhile, seems transfixed by the mechanism which is transporting the boats so efficiently. 'I wonder how many people can ride at the same time,' he says. 'How many they could get round in the space of an hour. And how do they get everybody out if it breaks down?' They watch the mother and son climb into one boat, the father and daughter into a second. Up close, the rock looks artificial and the water unnervingly blue. Margaret can see palm trees stuck at intervals along the riverbank. 'Looks like it's our turn,' he says, rather too enthusiastically, as a bright pink vessel draws up level with them. 'Are you all right? I was only joking – I'm sure it won't break down.'

That's not what worries her. But she doesn't say so. He steps in first then offers his arm to help her down beside him. It rocks as they settle onto a bench with only just enough room for two; the sides of their bodies briefly touching as the boat jolts into motion.

'We're very low in the water, aren't we?' He reaches out and runs his fingers across the surface. Margaret tries not to think about how dirty it might be, of all the diseases it might be harbouring, not to mention the fact that his hand could get dragged into the moving parts beneath the boat. It feels as though they are being swept along by a current, until they reach a bend in the channel and there's the juddering shunt of metal against metal beneath them; vibrations pass through the thin gap of air between their bodies. Up ahead is the yawning mouth of a tunnel. She wants to step off but there is no walkway running beside them here, steep rockfaces looming either side to give the impression that they are heading underground.

'Here we go!' James says, craning back to see the arc of rock in relief against the sky as they enter. There's a wall of water falling from a crack in the roof. Margaret covers her head with her arms, but it stops automatically the very moment they pass under it.

'Are you sure you are all right?' James says. 'You're very quiet.'
'I'm fine. If those children can do it, I'm sure that I can.'

She welcomes the darkness that envelops them. There is music playing up ahead, and coloured lights. Now that the ride has begun, she will have something to concentrate on. Something to distract her. 'I really thought the father would keep that money for himself,' she says. 'Would have been a good example for Harrisson.'

'Perhaps. But I'm glad he didn't. That wouldn't have been the point at all.' She thinks she can hear a smile on his lips.

'The point?'

He says nothing.

'Wait . . .' There is something he is not telling her. 'How did you know he was picking up a coin?'

Still nothing.

'You left it there, didn't you? You dropped it deliberately.' Now she thinks of it, it was a rather clever idea: create a moral dilemma and observe how the subject reacts. But it is not in their remit to interfere. James told her so himself at her interview. They are there to observe. A zoologist wouldn't step in to save a gazelle from a lion. They only watch and learn.

'I wanted them to have the means to go on a ride,' he whispers. 'Just one. I could see how desperate they were to do it themselves, not just stand and watch everyone else.'

'But we're not supposed to get involved,' she says. 'When you were laughing at those clowns, they could see us; they were looking.' The embers of her anger catch again. There is something growing between them. A charge in the air.

'Come on, Margaret, we can't be invisible all the time.'

Why not? That's exactly what she works so hard to be. And she was succeeding, until he started to take notice. 'They are on holiday. We are here to work.'

'We are. But I've been thinking – shouldn't I try to *experience* the lives these people lead? To feel the things they feel?' How does he expect her to quantify that in her report? Emotions are subjective, highly distorted, unreliable. It is her job to stick to the facts. 'Working with you, Margaret. Reading your reports. You make me feel . . .' His words are swallowed by the tunnel. '. . .You moved to Blackpool. Alone. You're fearless.'

Fearless? She cannot respond without telling a lie. What could she say that wouldn't disappoint him, or betray herself? So she does not speak at all, allowing the word to reverberate. It's as if she can feel the corridor of air between her body and his start to quiver. She doesn't want to lose his admiration, even though it is undeserved.

But the moment is brief; interrupted by the increasing insistence of emerging light ahead. Margaret feels resentful of their little boat now, which carries them forward into the glare of a cave. Inside, a striped dinosaur is bending towards a hatchling in a large egg. An interval of darkness and there's another tableau.

'Triceratops,' says James, 'my favourite!'

'Completely inaccurate,' says Margaret, shaking her head at the caveman hunting with a spear. '*Homo sapiens* did not roam the Earth until 65 million years after dinosaurs disappeared.'

'Indeed. But I would have loved this as a child,' he says. 'All little boys love dinosaurs, don't they?'

'I could name them all by the age of seven. I borrowed a book from the library.'

'Do you know, Margaret,' he says, 'that doesn't surprise me. You are not like other girls at all.'

She is fairly certain he means to compliment her. But, though

192

she despises herself for thinking it, there is a small part of her that wishes she *was* like other girls. That, alone with her in the dark, it might cross James's mind to try to make love to her. If only so that she could rebuke him. It is not that she has ever wanted to be interfered with, but she resents never having had the choice.

'Tyrannosaurus rex!' he says, feigning fear, as they turn to watch the giant model attacking a mannequin of a primitive male in a loincloth. The boat turns again, taking them under the gracefully curved neck of a diplodocus, and into a much longer tunnel. For a few moments there is no light at all. James shifts on the seat. Now his leg is resting against hers. She fights the impulse to move away. She doesn't want him to think she is assuming any impropriety on his part, so she stays exactly where she is, steeling her muscles against the movement of the ride to prevent herself being knocked more closely into him. The roar of the dinosaurs is fading now, and she can hear the echo of whispered conversations from the boats in front, and the sound of falling water. There is light up ahead and they sit in silence, emerging into a large cavern. Brightly coloured creatures are suspended from the ceiling: starfish and seahorses, jellyfish and corals. The effect is other-worldly. Margaret knows the scene has been carefully choreographed to create a sense of magic, but she chooses not to look at the wires that hold each fish in place.

'I feel like we're underwater ourselves.' It is as if she has slipped beneath the surface. Sounds are muffled and distant, movements slowed. If she let herself, she would see the evidence: that all the noise and activity of the Pleasure Beach is just yards away, just the other side of a wall of artificial rock. But she chooses to ignore this too. She is not in Blackpool. Not on a ride designed to manipulate her senses. She is watching pearlescent fish flit by her in the darkness, fearing that a shark or electric eel might be lurking in the caves.

'Beautiful,' he says, a single word that echoes around the cavern, and she can hear something in his voice, something waiting there. 'What I said,' he whispers, so softly that she has to concentrate to make out his words. 'About you not being like other girls. I don't mean that as a bad thing . . . it's just that you know such a lot about all sorts of subjects. You're interested in learning about why things are the way they are. And you have such principles. Such a strong sense of . . . justice. More than any woman I've ever met. Or man, for that matter. That's all I meant . . .'

She knows what he meant. He is right. And it means that, even alone with her on a tunnel of love in the dark; even though their legs are touching, and the rough cotton of his trousers is catching on her stocking; even though the couple in front have been kissing since their boat entered the tunnel, it has not crossed his mind to embrace her, to take her hand. He admires her professionally. He just said so himself. She needs to hold onto that. It's all she could ever hope to expect.

Swept along, they enter a jungle: a gigantic boa constrictor coiled around a tree trunk; tribal masks strung up on lines between branches.

'Mayan or Aztec?' he wonders.

'I think we can assume they are supposed to be cannibals, wherever they are from.' She points to the display of skulls on spikes.

Travelling through another tunnel, they emerge into a dimly lit cavern that looks like the mouth of a giant creature: stalagmites and stalactites for teeth. A sign announcing 'The Valley of the Kings' takes them between hieroglyphs on pillars of artificial stone, past slaves fanning pharaohs, and on to Tibet, where elephants trumpet amongst crumbling temples. They can see daylight coming from around the next corner. 'Margaret. I . . .' His tone is suddenly abrupt, his words rushed. 'I wanted to ask you something.'

'Yes?'

'The Tower Ballroom. Have you been?'

'Was I supposed to? I can. Was there something in particular?'

'No. I'm sorry – you misunderstand . . . What I mean is . . . I've been in Blackpool for almost the whole season and I've never seen one of its most famous sights. I thought we should—'

'Yes. There would be some very interesting data about numbers of partners, average number of dances—'

'I mean go along, just to see it,' he says.

'Without making observations?'

'Yes. Just for fun. *After* work.'

He wants to go together. He wants to spend time with her. In this job, they work all hours of day and night, but the way he stressed the word 'after' seems significant: that he wishes to go as something other than colleagues. Does going to the ballroom, together, after work, mean his intentions are romantic? Perhaps he wants to embrace her after all. To draw her close to him. Because that's what people who are attracted to each other feel compelled to do. She fights an impulse to throw her arms around him then and there. Just to get it over with. Just to check that she will enjoy it. What if her body betrays her, what if her muscles tense up and reject him when the time comes?

'I've always fancied seeing the Wurlitzer and . . . in the past . . . before we started these missions together . . . I . . . well, I wasted too much time just reading about these things.'

She wants to say something but no words come. They have all fled. They do not trust her to use them.

'I was, I admit, rather envious of you,' he says.

'Of me?'

'Yes, going out every day and doing all this.'

'It's my job.'

'Yes, but it's the job you chose. I chose to work in an office all day, reading about the sights you were seeing and the people you were talking to.'

'I very rarely talk to anyone unless I have to.'

'But at least you are not on your own. Not lonely.' She realises that what he says isn't true. Being in a crowd of people has no effect on how alone she feels. None at all. She does not seek the company of others. Didn't, anyway. He clears his throat. 'So, the Tower Ballroom. If you fancy it . . . Understand if you don't but . . . well, I can't dance on my own!'

Dancing. Of course, it will mean dancing. It will never work. Even if she can persuade her body to let him put his arms around her, her feet won't comply. Not with so many people watching. She tried it once, alone in her bedroom, and she felt a fool. She looked a fool. She doesn't have it in her. There's a craving, rolling like a wave; gently at first but then it starts to gather pace, wild, white-crested. She should tell him that he is wrong. That he has misjudged her. Her skin is crawling with the feeling that she is deceiving him somehow.

'I can't dance,' she says.

'Oh, don't worry about that . . . Have a think about it.'

She doesn't need to think about it. She is not like other girls; he has said so himself. And this change in her, this need, will only bring pain. Another wave crashes over her, but this time it's anger. At herself. At her body, which will sabotage her. But she is not going to let it. Is not going to raise her hopes only to be humiliated in a crowded ballroom. She is not going to fail in his arms.

There's enough light to illuminate the walkway that was running alongside the river all along. Though she tries, she can no longer ignore the service doorways inside the rockface: the hinges, the handles and the bolts. The tunnel opens out into a brilliant blue sky and her brain is already noting the scaffold of the ride in silhouette against it. She cannot stop herself from identifying it as the Flying Machine, the oldest attraction on the Pleasure Beach; from estimating the ticket prices and duration of each ride; from calculating the cost per minute.

The smell of the food stalls reaches them even before the chatter of the crowds. Margaret is back in Blackpool.

# 25

'We've lost them,' she says, looking around as they step off the ride. 'I'll write up what we managed to observe this morning. I'd better be getting—'

'Hang on . . . Over there, look.' He is right. She can see the little girl above the crowd. The father must have lifted her up onto his shoulders. 'We can catch them.' He grabs her hand and pulls her through the crush of people. 'I can still see them.' He is excited by the chase, and she is now feeling something like exhilaration herself. The family have stopped to look at Noah's Ark, which looks as though it has been washed up in the middle of the attractions. It is rocking from side to side, life-sized models of various animals gathering as if preparing to board. She wonders what Harold would make of this cartoonish tableau – a Biblical lesson rendered in clockwork creatures. She rather suspects he would approve. The children seem to like it, the parents listing each animal they can see. They attempt a convincing vocal impression of each – polar bear, elephant, giraffe – but get stuck when it comes to the penguin.

James lets go of her hand. There is no need to hold it now that they have stopped to continue their observations. Margaret busies herself, taking out her pad and pencil to jot down some notes. Out here in the bright sunshine, she is unsure what just happened on the ride, unsure how they left things. She questions whether she was firm enough in her insistence that she can't dance. Did he think her reluctance a coquettish affectation? She wonders whether he will bring it up again. Whether *she* should. Whether it is too late to change her mind and go. Or suggest a different outing. One where she doesn't have to dance.

'It would be interesting to find out how many visitors consider its religious significance,' he says, while timing how long the family stand and look at the animals.

'Very few, I should think. It's a conventional ride inside. Jerking to and fro. Something like the Fun House, but with moving models of animals in cages. Not suitable for small children.' Now she thinks of it, it wouldn't be suitable for Harold either. The youngest child has begun to cry after a particularly convincing roar from her father, which Margaret suspects was an imitation of the bear which is standing near the prow of the ark. The parents look just as weary as the children, who have been out in the sun for several hours by now. They start to move towards the exit.

'That's that then,' James says, sounding genuinely disappointed.

'That's what?'

'No tattoo for you after all.' They are back on the spot where they saw the tattooed woman this morning. Now someone else is drawing a small crowd. James cranes over the heads to see, Margaret far too short to have any chance of doing so herself.

'It's a small man with a sign,' he says. 'Professor Flicke's . . . something.'

'Flea Circus,' Margaret says. 'Professor *Fricke's* Flea Circus.' She wonders whether Horatio and Samson will be performing.

'Shall we stay and watch?'

What's the harm in staying a little longer? She is in no rush to go back to her lodgings alone. The small gathering of onlookers is moving along quickly. People staying just a minute or two before stepping away and heading on to the next attraction. It is not long before Margaret and James are close enough to see a small trestle table, on which a series of miniature vehicles are involved in some sort of race. James is obviously fascinated. She predicts he is going to want some for his collection of Blackpool paraphernalia.

Professor Fricke lifts one, and brings it right up to the faces of the families further along the row. 'Here is an empty carriage, ladies and gentlemen, he says. My fleas travel in only the finest. A miniature version of the very coach which carried our king to Westminster Abbey for his coronation. I made it myself.'

James strains to look then turns to Margaret. 'But how does he get them to perform?'

'Tiny lassoes of wire,' she whispers, glad of the opportunity to demonstrate her knowledge. 'He keeps them on little tethers. Feeds them every day on his own blood.'

'He does *what*?'

'He lives off them and they live off him. A symbiotic relationship.'

He laughs and, though she hadn't intended it to be funny, she is gratified. 'You're not joking. He really lets them suck his own blood?' Perhaps he won't be wanting to keep his own as pets after all. 'How do you know all this?'

'I've been . . . That other report I mentioned to you . . .' Not choosing to tell him about Harold is one thing, but lying to him would be another. She hasn't been doing anything wrong. Perhaps the time has come to be completely honest. 'I managed to get access to the building where the Living Waxworks are on show. Do you know it?'

'Isn't that the one Davidson was at, inside his glass coffin?'

'Precisely.'

'And they let you in? Behind the scenes, so to speak?'

'Yes, a front row seat to observe the crowds. And I've got to know some of the acts. Some of them quite well, as it happens—'

'I bet you've seen all sorts!'

'You could say that!'

He stops suddenly and shakes his head. 'Margaret, you are a wonder! I was silly to think that . . . earlier . . . I shouldn't have . . .'

Shouldn't have what?

'Margaret . . . When I said—'

'It's all right. I understand.' He has changed his mind about the Tower Ballroom. She should be relieved but—

'Of course you do. Good old Margaret! This is exactly what I mean. I'm embarrassed I made a thing of it now.'

'Don't be.'

'Any other young lady, well – when it comes to matters that are . . . inappropriate. I mean obviously – I wouldn't—'

'Obviously.'

'But it's different with you, Margaret. *You're* not going to be offended. I should have shown it to you as soon as we met this morning.' He slips a hand into the top pocket of his jacket. 'Remember that school chum I mentioned – the newspaperman?'

'I . . .'

He pulls out a miscellany of papers. 'I asked him about the rector when he went on show in that barrel.' He grins. 'That was the day we first went out with my camera.'

'It was.'

'And I couldn't get over how many people turned out to see him. How many *believed* him!'

'There's a lot about his case that doesn't add up.'

She is not sure he has heard her, too busy sorting through the various notes and ticket stubs he has fished out of his pocket. 'I mean you just can't fathom some people, can you? It doesn't take someone with your skills of observation, Margaret, to see— Ah, there it is!' He waves a brown envelope. 'Obvious to you and I, but people fell for his story.' She wants to set him straight, to make him understand, but he is already handing it to her. 'If the newspapers had been allowed to print this, no one would have been left in any doubt. Though you can see why they . . . well . . . you understand . . . decency and all that.'

She lifts the flap, and slides out a thick sheet. Blank. Turning it over, she sees a face she recognises. He wears a solemn expression: lips parted, as if he intends to bestow some wisdom; his skin so pale where it meets the white crest of his hairline that you cannot see where it begins. Creases mark his suit, fabric pinched on the inside of his elbow, the flash catching the shine of his worn sleeve.

Behind him is a dark wall, papered with chains of vine; beside him, an aspidistra in a tall planter, its waxy leaves reflecting the momentary glare. But it is his collar that glows, like the moon, with borrowed light: a clerical collar which sits thick and starched around his throat.

He wears a solemn expression, and she wonders what thoughts are being shaped on his tongue. For he is looking not at the lens, but at a young woman, who sports the bobbed hairstyle of a starlet: jet black, cut into a blunt line to expose the curve of her neck. Strands fall across her cheek, curling forward into a sharp point just above her jawline. Are her lips parted in reply? Her eyes returning his gaze? It is impossible to see. She stands with her back to the camera, her head turned to his.

He wears a solemn expression. She is naked.

# 26

Margaret feels as though she is being turned inside out. As if her skin is no longer holding her together. She has to get away from all these people, from James. She wishes she could outrun herself: this stranger who she does not know at all. Everything they said about Harold was right. She has the proof in her hand. And she can no longer persuade herself that she knows better than other people. She is worse than the lot of them. Worse than the families who spend their money on pavement tricks and sideshow illusions. She has gambled her career on this man's lies, spent her time looking for evidence to support his deception, when she should have been concentrating on the job she was employed to do.

She should be angry with him, but instead she is consumed by sadness. Thinking not of Harold, but of James. She was a bigger fool to convince herself that he admired her. Any fondness he may have is for the person he thinks she is, the person she had thought herself to be. Not being like other girls was all right when she could believe she had the insight and intellect to analyse the world and see its truths. But now she has nothing. Is nothing. Any regard he has for her, misjudged. And now she understands this, she realises how desperately she craves his good opinion.

'Pretty conclusive, I'd say!' He is looking down at the photograph in her hand.

'Yes.' She tries to laugh along with him, but her breath catches in her throat, her eyes sting. 'I'd better go,' she says, turning and walking into the crowd, before the tears can start to spill. 'I'll see you later.'

He calls after her but she does not turn back.

She needs a drink. She needs a drink to calm her nerves and slow her thoughts. There is a pub on the corner and she goes in. Orders gin. A double. 'Another please.' Every thought is suspended for a few moments. It is as if each sip she takes allows the pressure in her skull to be released. She is not really here. Feels so far away from this bar and the people in it. Knows they are staring at her. Whispering. But doesn't care. They don't know her. Turns out she doesn't even know herself. The thought makes her laugh. The whole situation is farcical. She can see the corner of the photograph, peeking out beneath the envelope on the bar beside her drink. She uncovers it and looks again. A young girl trying to look older; an old man trying to look younger. Staring into her eyes as if he is leaning in to kiss her. As if she would want him to. The whole thing is ridiculous. Pathetic. She makes a sound. Perhaps a laugh. Perhaps a sob.

'Are you all right there, love?' The landlord pauses his conversation with three men at the other end of the bar. 'You look like you need another.'

'I do.'

He picks up her empty glass, fills it and places it back down on the bar beside her. 'What's that you're looking at then?' He turns his head to try to see, and Margaret spins the photograph to face him.

'The Rector of Stiffkey,' she says.

'My, it is! He's got his hands full too. Look at this, lads!' He calls to the men at the end of the bar, picking up the photo.

'Can I show them?'

Margaret nods and he takes it.

('I always said he were a pervert.')

('But to sit on the prom every day and tell everyone he's innocent!')

('Good luck to him, I say. He's making a living out of it.')

('And who could blame him when he were faced with that. Look at her!')

('What I wouldn't do for a view like that to go home to.')

('This picture's the nearest you'd ever get to a body like that.')

('Wouldn't mind a copy to put on my wall at home.')

('As if your Ida would let you get away with that!')

Opening her handbag, she thinks bitterly of Other Margaret who would have taken out a notebook and pencil and made a note of everything that's being said; who would tally up the comments supportive of Davidson versus those that were critical, as if she could find some definitive truth there. But these men don't care whether Davidson is guilty or not. They are too busy living their own lives. Just as she should have been.

She can't bear to hear any more about the Rector of Stiffkey or his sordid affairs. The first sip brought instant relief, but every mouthful that follows is merely chasing the same sensation. And it does not come. Shame is prowling inside her. She stands up, loses her balance and starts to fall forwards. She wills her body to right itself but it does not listen. Her forearm crashes into the edge of the bar and she manages to struggle upright. One of the men rushes to her aid.

'Get your hands off me!'

'All right, love. Just trying to help.'

Her limbs are still rebelling, still sabotaging her resolve to leave the pub with some respectability intact.

'Don't you want your picture?' One of the men holds it out towards her and she snatches it away. She needs to find another pub, another drink.

He'll finish just after 9 p.m. Leave by the side door and turn down here, the alleyway that runs beside the Living Waxworks building. That's when she will tell him what she thinks of him. The only way to get these clamouring thoughts out of her head is to say them out loud. He deceived her. He wasted her time. She needs to show him that she is not a woman to be under-estimated. That she knows the truth.

She waits in the shadows halfway along the passage, where it opens up into a slightly wider path. The bins beside her are overflowing with food; the lids must have been knocked off by a cat or the wind, and flies have moved in and made a home. She can hear the relentless hum of so much life, see the potato peelings churning with it, the top layer teeming with maggots. Other Margaret would have recoiled from this squalor, would have recorded it as an example of poor living conditions. But she is unmoved. It signifies nothing more than reality: it is the way things are. Flies lay their eggs where they can. And why shouldn't they?

It is already quarter past. He would usually be out by now. She is starting to lose her resolve. Perhaps, when the time comes, her words won't come out the way she has practised them. She is so very tired, and has to lean against the ginnel wall to keep herself standing. The stench of the rubbish bins pricks her eyes. It is the only thing that is keeping them from closing.

There's the sound of a door slamming and she looks up to see a figure stepping into the passage, a flame bouncing in the air, its movement stilled for a moment before it disappears. Davidson. Lighting a cigar. A smell more revolting to her now than the rotting food. She steps out into the centre of the path to prevent him passing.

'Dear God!' he says. 'Who's there?'

She doesn't answer. Her eyes have grown more accustomed to the darkness than his and she can see him straining to make her out.

'Margaret? Is that you?'

Still she chooses not to speak.

'It is you, isn't it? Thank goodness. I thought I was going to be robbed for a moment!' He pauses for her to say something, but she doesn't. 'What are you doing? Why didn't you come in instead of waiting out here?'

She promised herself she would stay calm, business-like; that she would not show emotion. But the arrogance of the man.

'Is there something I can do for you?' he says.

'You can stay away from me.'

'What's this, Margaret? What are you talking about?'

She forces herself back to the script she has rehearsed. 'It will not be necessary for me to carry out any more observations. I do not intend to write the report after all.'

'Don't intend to write it? Why ever not? Surely it is of great public interest.'

'It is a pointless exercise.'

'But all that time we spent . . . Margaret. I told you everything.'

'You told me lies.'

'I'm sorry, I don't understand . . .'

She takes the photograph out of the envelope and holds it up to him.

'What is that? I can't . . . Hold on.' Taking out his lighter, he makes a flame and can see enough to make out the photograph. 'That's not . . . It's not what it looks like.'

'Don't take me for a fool. How could it be anything else?'

'I'm the fool, Margaret. I let myself be tricked. I thought I was doing her a favour.'

'And what kind of favours was she doing in return?'

'Margaret, please! There is no need to be so crude.' Crude? A man like this, a man who had sexual relations with prostitutes finds her words distasteful?

'Do not lecture me about propriety.' She lurches forward and has to steady herself against the wall.

'She was the daughter of a friend of mine. An actress. She asked me to help her with some photographs that she could send to directors in the theatre. She knew that I was knowledgeable about such things. When I got to the house, she was wearing a bathing suit but she left the room and she must have taken it off. I had no idea until she dropped her shawl and the camera flashed. I was supposed to be cut out of the pictures. I was only there as an actor. Playing various roles, so she could demonstrate a range of expressions.'

At this Margaret starts to laugh. The very thought of it is ridiculous. 'And what role are you playing in that one? Leading man?'

'Villain, by the look of me. It's an abominable picture. I am ashamed of it. I look like the man everyone says I am. But consider, Margaret – why would I have agreed to pose for a photograph just before my trial if I had known that she would be . . .'

'Naked?' Margaret says, with some satisfaction at having shocked him again.

'You are not yourself this evening. Are you quite well? You've been drinking again. That's what all this is about, isn't it?' How dare he make this about her? 'Margaret, I've been wondering how to broach this subject with you. You think I haven't noticed that hip flask you carry but, I'm sorry to say, it is rather obvious that you are becoming reliant on it. And I've seen where it can lead. The girls I worked with in Soho—'

'You are comparing me to *them*? Women like that? Who let men put their hands all over them?'

'That's not what I'm saying. I have never thought of you as that sort of woman at all.'

She is not like other girls. Even to Davidson, a man who has degraded himself with the most desperate, the most debased. He has been alone with her on too many occasions to count. For weeks they have spent hours talking about his life and his hardships; she has walked with him in the dark, sat with him long after the sideshow has closed up for the night and he has never once tried to touch her. A man who could not control himself even among the most wretched of women. So, what hope would she ever have with a man like James? She starts to cry. Loud, gasping sobs that she is powerless to stop.

'Margaret,' he says, reaching out in the darkness to touch her arm. 'I'm sorry . . . I—'

She pushes him away, both hands on his chest, hitting him with all her strength. He stumbles backwards and in her rage she feels something else, as if a flame has been lit inside her. She steps forward and grabs him by the shoulders, her body knocking against him. He brings his arms around her to stop her from falling. She is shivering. She wants to be held. To feel the warmth spread through her. To be revived. It will never be James's touch she feels, but in the darkness she can pretend. Can ignore the smell of his cigar. In the darkness he is only arms and lips. She lurches forward and forces her mouth against his. If she can get this over with, perhaps she will be healed. Perhaps she will be normal. She just has to prove to herself that she can do it. Force her body to surrender.

'No, Margaret! What do you think you are doing?'

'I thought . . .'

'Is that what you think I am? After everything I've told you these past few weeks? I don't want to . . . You are drunk, Margaret. You don't know what you are doing. In the morning you'll realise how—'

She turns from him and starts to run away, her body slamming against the alley wall as she stumbles.

'Wait. I need to see you home safely. Margaret, please!'

But he doesn't follow her. She makes it round the corner before she is sick in the gutter.

# 27

Stale cigar smoke. She is aware of the smell of him even before she wakes; a memory pulling at her hair, tugging at her scalp. She is wearing no dress and no nightshirt. Only a slip. One torn stocking. Shame scratches at her bare skin, at the blush of bruises on her arm and the ragged flesh of grazed elbows and knuckles. She has no recollection of how she got home. Of undressing. Of getting into bed. But her muscles ache with the memory of humiliation, and she knows the truth is waiting to taunt her. She tries to turn from it and escape back into the oblivion of sleep. But it is too late. Maggots. Alleyway. Photograph. The rough skin of his lips. She threw herself at him, offered herself up like a sacrifice. But he was disgusted by her touch. Jumped away as though she was tainted, as though her flesh was on the turn. The thought takes her back to her observations at the lido. All that pimpled skin, the yellowed toenails. What would Davidson look like without his clothes on? He is an old man. A man who has proved he has no scruples, no morality. But she can't be certain that she wouldn't have let him go that far. That she would have stopped him dropping his trousers, lifting her skirt, doing the things she witnessed under the pier. She can't be sure at all. And though the thought of it is vile, it's the knowledge that he couldn't bring himself to do it that is worse. Men are supposed to want it all the time, their biology driving them to take an opportunity when it is offered (and in some cases when it is not). But he considers Margaret too freakish to respond to her advances, sensing perhaps the coldness, the void, the deficit. She is not like other women. And any hopes she had in that regard have been proved wrong. She cannot change who she is. It was ridiculous to try.

Laughter creeps in through the gap beneath her door. Chatter from the other young women who share her floor. They are laughing at her, at her humiliation. Too odd for even a man like that to take advantage. That's what they would say. And they would be right.

She may as well stay here and rot. Her breath is putrid; a bitter taste every time she swallows. There's a tightness to her face; she reaches up to her chin and picks at the flakes she finds there. Dried vomit. Another memory comes to mock her. Her stomach cramps and she feels the rise of nausea. She should get up and retrieve the bedpan in case she is sick. But she cannot muster the energy to move. If she lies still it might pass. There is no need to rise, to get herself cleaned up. She has nowhere to go, nothing to do.

She cannot face James again. Not now. Though she wishes she was brave enough to give him the apology he deserves. She rushed off and left him standing there. Dear James. If she ever sees him again, she should try to make him understand how much his little acts of kindness have meant to her. He thinks she is somebody that she is not. Somebody worthy of his admiration. All she can do is stay away. Stay in bed. If she is ill then they cannot compel her to go in. She will lose her job but that is no more than she deserves. It is over. She will leave Blackpool as soon as she is strong enough to face it. Return home to Mother and Father. Get a job as a doctor's receptionist.

The door handle shakes at intervals. Maude knocks, calls

through the keyhole, asks if Margaret is in there, tells her that she hasn't seen her at breakfast for two days, asks whether she would like her to bring some food up on a tray, points out that it goes against her usual policy, makes it clear that there will be an additional charge for the service. Margaret stays silent at first, hoping that Maude will think she left the house early to go to work. But when her landlady threatens to use her own key to unlock the door, she calls out some words to reassure her: just tired, under the weather, not hungry, needs to sleep it off. And none of that is incorrect. She has developed a fever, her body shaking so violently that the bedframe shudders against the floor. She has discovered that if she holds her jaw in a certain position, her teeth chatter and she tests herself on how long she can sustain the drumbeat: the only semblance of control over her obstinate body, which refuses all her attempts to console it. When it shivers, she tucks a blanket tightly around it, but it grows restless, and she wakes to find her legs have kicked themselves free. It forces her to rise just long enough to use the bedpan but refuses to grant her the energy to walk as far as the bathroom to empty it.

Her mind and body are at war now, one being suffocated by the demands of the other. But there is something gratifying about experiencing the pain so physically. Studying the tremor in her hands, she can watch herself suffer and know that she deserves it. That's the thought she holds onto; the rhythm that beats in her head; the bass note beneath the constant drum of craving. If she could just have a drink, if she could just get some gin or whisky, it would quieten, she would feel better. Her heart races at the memory of its taste. Without it, she wants to claw at her skin to let the pressure out. Knock at her head to interrupt the questions that circle in an endless loop.

Her body and mind are not at war with each other now; they are both at war with her. She is in control of neither, unwelcome in both. So, she will punish them in return. She will deny them any peace. At this moment she is grateful for the fact that there are no bottles of spirits in her bedroom. That she is not well enough to go out and buy more. Because this is the only fragment of self-respect she has to cling to.

'I'm not having it!' Maude calls from the other side of the door. 'You're under my roof and you are my responsibility. I'm coming in.'

Margaret hears the sound of a key in the door. 'No, no, please! I'm not decent.' The words come now she needs them to. She remembers how to pretend. 'I'm just getting up. Getting dressed.'

'I really think I should call a doctor.'

'There's no need. I'm feeling a lot better. Though I think some medicine might sort me out.'

'Medicine?'

'Yes. A stomach bottle. I don't want to impose but if you are going out today, could I trouble you to get me a bottle of kaolin and morphine please?'

'I have no plans to—'

'I'd pay you for the inconvenience, naturally.'

'Well, I do feel responsible for you. Think of myself more as a mother than a landlady.'

'Thank you. So that I don't have to trouble you again, I wonder if it might be wise to get two bottles. And I must insist that you bill me for double the service charge in that case.'

'If it will make you better, I'll go straight away.' Maude's footsteps are swift on the landing. 'But when I get back, I'm coming in to check on you!'

At first Margaret cannot muster the energy to move, but slowly the thought of medicine seems to appease her body, her limbs compliant enough for her to stand. But it is a hesitant truce, her movements clumsy and her muscles weak. She finds a film of dust on the surface of her washbowl but the splash of water on her skin is enough to rouse her to her senses. Suddenly aware of just how putrid the air in her room has become, she opens her curtains and window, pulls on her dressing gown and listens at the door to check the landing is empty. She makes sure to lock her bedroom door behind her to deter Maude from going in, and makes her way slowly to the loo, her hands shaking so violently that she almost spills the contents of her chamber pot onto the lino. Progress is slow but she uses the toilet, managing to produce a rusted stain of urine which clings to the side of the pan.

Undressing in the bathroom next door, she is surprised at how quickly her body has gone wild. The bruises on her arms have darkened. She is nothing but animal. Organs and cells. Component parts. A machine made of flesh. There's no more to her than the clockwork clowns. Human bodies are just another illusion. Clothes and make-up and even personality, just artifice to distract people from their grotesque physicality. And those are the tricks she lacks. Perhaps that's another reason why she is not like other girls. She has never learnt the strategies that others have, of hiding the ugly truth. But she must do her best now. Maude will be back soon and she has to make herself ready.

A knock on the door startles her. She pulls on her dressing gown and unlocks the door.

'Let's have a look at you,' Maude says, pushing the door open.

Margaret stands back for inspection, conscious of the fact that she was naked seconds before, gripping tightly to the two ends of the belt which is all that is keeping her covered. Something like shame runs the length of her, but it is thrilling. As though the robe might fall open and expose her, as though she might pull it open herself. She doesn't trust herself not to. Doesn't trust her hands not to move of their own volition. This body of hers feels unpredictable. Powerful.

'You're very flushed.'

'Yes, I'm really not well. Must have eaten something that disagreed with me.'

Maude tuts. 'I hope you're not suggesting my food—'

'No, of course not . . . I had oysters. At the Pleasure Beach.'

'Washed down with one too many in the pub!'

'I beg your pardon?'

'I'm not as green as I am cabbage-like.'

Margaret tries to make a mental note of the phrase to investigate later.

'When you run a place like this,' Maude says, 'you know what's what.' She taps her nose and smiles. 'But, I've got your medicine. I'll leave it in your bedroom for you.'

'No, no. I'll take it now.' Margaret tugs tightly on the belt then holds out her hands to receive the two bottles. 'Thank you.'

'And you'll be wanting something to eat. I'd already got the food in.'

'Yes. Of course. Perhaps some bread and butter?'

Margaret can hear Maude chuntering to herself about being taken advantage of as she heads back down the landing. She locks the bathroom door again, unscrews the first of the bottles and drinks from it. That familiar sensation of being held, of being touched in the very deepest part of herself. The liquid moving down her throat and into her chest, caressing her from the inside out, as though every hair that was standing on end is being smoothed, every tremor being stilled. She grips the edge of the sink. Unties the belt around her waist and lets her robe fall to the ground. Washes slowly, careful to coax her body into assent, touching it with the tenderness of a mother with a newborn, as if she is discovering its wonders for the first time. Wipes underneath her arms, gently at first, wondering at the sour tang that clings to the flannel. Then, swirling the rough fabric in the water and lathering up more soap, she takes a corner to the folds of skin between her legs. Uses the tips of her fingers to comb through the matted strands and part the hair to explore the dark creases of herself. And all the time she studies her reflection. She revels in her repulsion. Horror and excitement. A living waxwork.

# 28

Washing down the bread and butter with more morphine, she feels stronger. But it's an artificial sensation, something like false confidence, which she knows will not last. She has to get out of this bedroom while she is able. The medicine merely buys her time, gives her a headstart, but she can't outrun her own thoughts for long. She knows too well that they are still stalking her, will pounce, pin her down and begin the torture again.

A last swig and the first bottle is empty. She locks her door and heads downstairs, managing to make it outside without meeting Maude. The street is bright, the sun glaring. Her eyes have become accustomed to the dim light of her room. How many days and nights has she been up there? How much time has passed since she was in the alleyway with Davidson? She can't think about that now. Won't. She has to get to the chemist and stock up in case she is taken ill again. The route brings her past four pubs and she takes pleasure in resisting the draw to step inside; looks directly at their front doors as though staring them down; proves to an absent Davidson that she doesn't have a problem.

The man in the white coat behind the pharmacy counter recognises her instantly. 'I haven't seen you for a while, *miss*,' he says with a self-satisfied look that makes Margaret want to slap it from his face. 'The usual, is it?'

She nods and he reaches up to the shelf of kaolin-and-morphine bottles. 'Three please.'

'I wonder that you bother since it seems to be having no effect. Still no better?'

'Unfortunately not.'

Holding her eyes, he lifts each bottle and shakes it vigorously before placing it in a brown paper bag. She understands that he is making a point, that he is deriving some pleasure from making her wait for the two substances to separate. She supposes it gives him a sense of power, that he is trying to embarrass her. But it doesn't work. She doesn't care what he may think of her. Besides, she has already poured the morphine from Maude's second bottle into her hip flask, a secret that is resting at the bottom of her handbag. She feels like telling him so, but then it wouldn't be a secret any more.

'Thank you,' she says instead. 'How thorough you are. Very kind.' She doesn't need to ask how much she owes him; she places the exact change on the counter without a word. He raises a single eyebrow and begins to count the coins, as though she is a child who may have miscalculated. But before he has tallied up and placed the money into the till, she turns and leaves. And for once she does not jump at the sound of the bell over the door; she braces herself for its shrill jingle, and walks out without looking back.

Crossing to the beach, she pauses to remove her shoes. She didn't put stockings on today. She just had to get out of that bedroom, didn't have the patience to try to tame her body into further submission. And now she finds herself grateful to be without them. She can feel the hairs on her legs lifting at the touch of the breeze. It's the first time she has walked barefoot on the sand, which is already burning in the late-morning sun, and she is unsure whether the sensation is painful or invigoration: the prick of so many sharp grains, making something very deep inside her twitch.

Her steps are slow, each foot placed tentatively while she finds her balance, her toes disappearing beneath the surface. She has to keep her eyes down to weave her way between blankets, buckets and fishing nets. But the patches of beach begin to open up, the deckchairs less frequent, and she looks out towards the horizon. She can see the foam of the waves just a few yards away, so busy looking where she is going that she is not watching her feet. The cold comes as a shock, wet sand gripping her soles and holding her still. She has crossed a line, into darker ground saturated by the retreating waves; her footprints leave an impression as she walks on. And the sea is rushing to meet her now. Icy water that takes her breath from her, a pull that threatens to knock her off her feet. It creeps up her ankles and she lets her feet sink until they disappear completely into the sand. Two children, a little further along the shore, try to jump back before the waves reach their toes, shrieking with delight and shock every time they are splashed. The sand around them is splotched with the pockmarks of their dance. But the footprints will disappear as soon as the tide rises up to wash them away. Just as Margaret's will. There is something comforting in that. Perhaps the memory of her humiliation will fade. Perhaps Davidson will forget, in time. And James will no longer wonder why she rushed away.

'You're having me on!' She hears voices and turns to see two men walking the waterline towards her, their trousers rolled up to just below their knees.

'I'm not. Someone at our guest house said he weren't much to look at anyway. Just sat reading sommat. Not worth the ticket price, he said. Wouldn't have known it were him if it wasn't for the vicar's collar. Too late now.'

Davidson.

The men draw level and touch their caps, changing their path to pass behind her.

'Excuse me,' Margaret says. 'Are you talking about the Rector of Stiffkey?'

'We are. Did you see him before he went?'

'Went?'

'To his new act.'

'The whale?' she asks. Luke Gannon will have unveiled another stunt to keep the crowds coming.

'The what?' The first man raises an eyebrow at the other, then turns back. 'I don't know what you're on about, love. Only that he's gone. Set up somewhere else. Skegness, I think.'

'Skegness? But he—'

'Shame you didn't get to see him. Missed your chance now.'

Was he so mortified by her advances that he thought it best to leave the town altogether? She remembers – oh God – trying to kiss him. But her memory will give her no more than that. She ran away from him but did he follow her, or help to get her home? She has no recollection. And now, for him to leave Blackpool so suddenly. He had never mentioned that he had plans to go to Skegness. This man must be mistaken. 'Are you *sure?*'

'That's what the fellow at the waxworks told me. I was trying to buy a ticket to see the rector. But he's got a better offer. That's what the man said anyway.'

Margaret tries to move but her feet have sunk so deeply that she almost falls forward into the sea. 'Careful, miss.' One of the men reaches out and gives her his arm; she holds on and manages to free herself from the pull of the wet sand.

'Thank you.'

He touches his cap again and they walk on, Margaret turning and heading back towards the promenade. It is heavy going; her feet are thick with clumped sand, her handbag sagging with the bottles of medicine. She drops one of her shoes and can feel tears rising. She wants to be back on the pavement, wants to get home and wash the itch of dried salt from her skin. But first she needs to know. She needs to see for herself. Brushing the worst of the sand from her feet she puts on her shoes, and as soon as she starts to walk again can feel the blisters forming inside them; the burn of skin being rubbed raw. But on she goes, pushing her way through the crowds, past the music booth and the tea stand, past the cigar seller and rock stall, until she reaches the Living Waxworks. Davidson's sign is still hanging on the board above the entrance but a banner has been pasted across it: CANCELLED UNTIL FURTHER NOTICE.

He is gone. She has driven him away.

The breeze is no longer pleasurable. She can no longer bear the brush of her skirt against her legs, wants to scratch the sand off her skin with her fingernails. She turns down the ginnel where she last saw Davidson and stops to take a swig of morphine from her hip flask. Just enough to get her home, to bribe her body into moving forward and carrying her back to bed.

## 29

'Oh, you're here,' Maude's head appears around the doorway of the parlour as Margaret steps into the hallway. 'Just in time. He were just about to leave.' She jerks her head sideways towards the room, eyes wide with urgency. Margaret struggles to make sense of it, leaning back against the wall, careful not to knock down the framed list of rules which greets everyone who crosses the threshold of the house. Has Davidson come here to see her, to tell her he is leaving? He will want to talk about what happened. About what she did. Or tried to do.

'He's keen! Been waiting quite a while.' Maude's voice goes from whisper to overly cheery shout: 'I'll make another pot while you two have a chat.' Margaret watches her landlady gesture to the parlour then bustle off in the direction of the kitchen. She will have to go in and face him. She could turn and walk back through the front door instead, lose herself in the crowd again, but she hasn't got the energy. Her body won't allow her to run away. Not this time. It takes all her effort just to stand upright and let go of the wall. She should think of something to say but where to start? An apology, perhaps. But whatever she says will only add to her humiliation. She will just have to endure it. It is no more than she deserves.

'Are you all right?' As soon as she rounds the corner, he stands up to greet her.

James. The relief is so sudden that it makes her dizzy and she almost collapses into the nearest armchair. Her head is spinning, her thoughts being flung away, and what is left behind is a gathering darkness, growing bigger with every breath.

'You don't look well,' he says. 'Can I get you some water?'

'No, thank you. I'll be all right in a minute.'

'Mrs Crankshaw tells me you've been in bed since . . . After the Pleasure Beach the other day I was worried I'd . . .'

The conversation stalls and they both look around the room. Boarders are not usually permitted in Maude's parlour, which she guards jealously 'in case anything is broken'. She doesn't say 'stolen' but the implication is there, though Margaret can see now that there is very little to fall victim to either theft or vandalism. The room is rather bare: faded curtains and a glass display cabinet whose shelves are empty; starched antimacassars which cover the arms and backs of the chairs but fail to hide the wear on the seat cushions. There's a single photograph on the mantlepiece of a soldier in uniform. Perhaps there was a Mr Crankshaw after all.

'I'm sorry for my absence these past few days,' Margaret says finally. 'My landlady's right. I have been unwell.' He seems just as relieved with this explanation as she is. Silence settles between them like a truce. From out in the hallway, she can hear an intermittent jingle of china: Maude must be hovering just outside the door, listening. 'Do you need a hand with the tray, Mrs Crankshaw?'

There's a much louder rattle, then she appears. 'No, no. We're all set. It's just brewing.' She places the tray on a side table and sets about partnering cups with saucers and peering into the top of the pot to check its progress. 'Pay me no mind. I don't want to interrupt your little chat.'

With an onlooker in the room, the silence feels uncomfortable. They listen to the tea being poured into cups. 'It's very kind of you to come and check on me,' Margaret says to James.

'It is,' Maude pipes up, handing him his cup. 'Not many would do that for their workers. You must think a lot of our Margaret, Mr Timoney.'

'Yes,' he says. 'Yes, I do.'

Maude hands Margaret a cup and takes the opportunity to wink at her before leaving the room. 'I'll leave you to it.'

They wait until they hear her footsteps move away along the hallway before Margaret speaks again. 'I'd like to apologise. The photograph, it was . . .'

'I'm afraid I may have offended you after all—'

'No, it's not that. I . . .' She owes him an explanation. 'I haven't been honest with you about Davidson . . .' Her words stall again.

'I don't understand.'

'I'm afraid I got rather too involved.'

His eyes grow wide, his cup rattling as he replaces it on the saucer. 'Oh, I'm sorry I've spilt the—'

'Not involved *with* him.'

'Oh.'

'What I mean is, rather caught up in his case.' She needs to say this before she changes her mind. 'There were things that didn't seem fair. About his trial. And I got the idea I could help somehow. That I could see things other people might have missed.'

'Is that all?'

'Yes.'

'There's nothing else. He didn't . . .'

'No! Only that I thought I knew better.'

'Old girl!' He smiles now, and sets his cup down. 'And it

turned out you did. There's another reason I came to see you.' Reaching into his jacket pocket, he pulls out another brown envelope, and for a brief moment she imagines that he intends to give her another compromising photograph of Davidson. 'This arrived this morning,' he says, 'from Harrisson. He wants you to go down to London.'

'Me?'

'Yes.' He is sitting forward in his chair, his leg bouncing as if he is having trouble staying still. 'He has started reading your report about the sideshows and your notes on Davidson—'

'But I hadn't finished!'

'I looked in your file in HQ after you . . . well after you were taken ill the other day, and I decided to send it.'

Without her consent? The thought that James has sat and read it is bad enough, but Tom Harrisson too? She feels as though they have been picking over her private diary. The truth of how misguided she was, how badly she misjudged Davidson, laid out for all to see.

'It is an extraordinary piece of work, Margaret. So comprehensive. And you were right about the access you got. None of the other researchers have got anything close. I knew Tom would be impressed and I was right to think so.'

'But . . .'

'That's what he says in this letter.' He slips it out of the envelope and reads aloud. '"Please pass my compliments to Miss Finch for her excellent work in this matter and ask her to contact my secretary to arrange a mutually convenient time for us to meet to discuss her findings in person."' He folds it and looks up again. 'Margaret, your attention to detail—'

'But I hadn't finished. And it was . . .'

'It was enough to impress Harrisson. I've never seen him take an interest in an individual researcher like this before.' A few days ago, this would have been everything she wanted: to be able to stay with Mass Observation, to avoid returning to that house in Northampton. But the thought leaves her hollow now. She is a fraud.

'Who knows,' says James, 'perhaps you won't be coming back to Blackpool after this.' He is still smiling at her but she can see the corners of his lips are twitching, as if it is taking effort to keep them upturned. And she can understand exactly how that must feel because she is stretching her own mouth into the same unnatural shape. She knows his conflict must be disappointment or even jealousy that she has been singled out. But in her case, it is something else: the idea not just of leaving this place, but of leaving him. Because although she has spoilt any hope that their relationship could be anything other than professional, she finds she cannot bring herself to let go of the possibility.

'You don't look very happy about it,' he says. 'I thought this was what you wanted.'

'I did. I do. It's all a bit of a surprise.'

'But a good one!'

'Yes. Yes, of course. I'd better go and pack.'

There's a lively atmosphere on the platform: mothers swapping stories, children comparing sunburn, fathers sharing jokes. Friends call to each other over the tops of heads, singing songs they've heard at the pier show. Margaret boards the train, manages to get a seat beside the window, and is joined by a group of young women. They are a lively bunch, passing around a paper bag of sweets. The girl beside her takes her turn, then extends the offer to Margaret, who accepts a humbug with a smile.

'Are you all on your own, love?' The young woman holds the two top corners of the bag and swings it round to close the top.

'Mmmm.' Not anticipating conversation, Margaret has already put the sweet into her mouth.

'Never mind. You can buddy up with us. Can't she?' She turns to her companions, who nod their assent. Sitting so closely, it is difficult for Margaret to get a good view of the woman. She has fair hair, she can see that much, curled under just above the shoulder. And she is what Mother would disparagingly call 'shapely', encroaching a little on Margaret's seat. 'You haven't been on holiday on your own?'

'No, I work here,' Margaret says carefully, fearing the sweet may fall out of her mouth.

'I'd love to work in Blackpool, me. Be here all the time. There's so much going on, isn't there?'

'There certainly is.'

'Mind you. Then I'd have nothing to look forward to. It's

the coming for a week as makes it special. What do you do for a job?' She crunches the sweet loudly between her back teeth and Margaret wonders if she should do the same, just to get rid of it.

'I'm a researcher.'

'Researching what?'

Too late, she has missed the window of opportunity to chew and swallow, so tucks the sweet safely into her cheek. 'Holidays. How people spend their money, that sort of thing . . .' It's suitably vague. She is not giving anything away about the project, and she finds that she is interested in hearing this young woman's opinion. '. . . Whether they behave differently when they are away from home, take more risks.'

The woman thinks about this carefully and passes the bag of sweets back along the row. 'We might go a bit daft, but we don't change as people, do we? Anyway, the whole town's here together. We wouldn't get away with much. Even if we wanted to!'

'I'd never thought of that.' But it is obvious now she's said it; Wakes Weeks mean every community takes its turn, everyone holidaying with the neighbours they'll be going home with.

'We've had a grand time. I'm completely spent up. Not a penny left. My last shilling went this morning. The Headless Girl – have you seen that one?'

'I have. Horrible isn't it?'

'Yes!' She laughs. 'And clever. Amazing what they can do these days! I don't know how they think them up. Still can't quite work out how they did it. Magic!'

Margaret goes to explain the mirrored box but decides not to shatter the illusion. 'It was.'

230

The woman smiles and turns back to her friends, who are whispering about a young man sitting across the compartment. They are far from subtle in their attempts to sneak a look at him, but he shows little interest, engrossed as he is in a newspaper. The front page announces that Chamberlain has once again flown out to meet with Hitler in Germany, and Margaret wonders if the man has read the article in full. She pictures him in uniform, watches his reflection in her window; a muted image, projected against the blur of buildings and trees; a jaw and the bottom of a cheek, a hand scratching the dark curls on the top of his head. She can appreciate why these girls think him handsome.

He looks at the countryside outside and for a moment, the reflection of two dark eyes meets her own. Instinctively, she turns away. Her first instinct: panic. She pretends to study the magazine the woman beside her has opened. Then she feels foolish for thinking he would be looking. Just because she can see him so clearly, doesn't mean he can see her. He is probably watching Blackpool disappear into the distance, interested to know if he can still see the Tower from here, estimating how many miles they have travelled by the number of minutes since they boarded. She's surprised to realise she hasn't been doing that herself, and risks another look at him. Even if he has a view of her from where he is sitting, it isn't really her face he can see: just angles of light deflected off a sheet of glass. She thinks he catches her eye again but this time she does not turn away. She tells herself that they are just two strangers, watching the landscape fly past, spotting animals on hillsides, and church spires in the distance. But his eyes are not snagging on anything on the other side of the glass. They are completely still. Fixed on her.

They play an unspoken game: watching each other while pretending not to see. She lets him study her, busies herself by checking the contents of the carpet bag on her lap, and she can't be sure but she imagines she can feel his eyes on her cheeks, on her chin, on her lips. On her reflection. Only her reflection. But she wants them to stay there. Bolder now, she turns back to the window again, only vaguely aware of the changes outside – the greens of hills giving way to the dingy red of sooted bricks which steal the light and make her view of him sharper in relief. She barely notices that the carriage is falling quieter.

By the time the train pulls into Preston station, parents instruct their children to 'make sure you've got everything' in a whisper. There is a silent scramble to gather belongings. The girl sitting next to her drops her magazine on the floor. Margaret bends down to retrieve it. And by the time she looks back, the man's reflection is gone. In the moment before she steps down onto the platform, she scans the crowd for him, disappointed that she won't see his face in three dimensions. But at least he won't see hers. The reality would expose their imperfections: the blemishes and the scars. And what would she say to him if he tried to start a conversation? The window had not afforded her the opportunity to see who he had travelled with or how worn his clothes might have been. Perhaps he was a mill worker. Perhaps he believed she was the same: just another holidaymaker returning from Blackpool. Perhaps he looked at her and didn't find her lacking. She is grateful for that trick of the light.

Now she is boarding another train with the hope of new opportunities. But what does he have to look forward to? When she took the job with Mass Observation, James told her the worktowners lived by a routine of mere existence: long hours, dangerous conditions, poor pay, no prospects. For the first time, she feels guilty for play-acting a life that is not really her own; for dressing up, and pretending that she is one of them; for hiding her education and denying her advantages. If they knew, they'd think she was lucky that she could go back to her own life whenever she wanted. Though that would suggest that she belonged to a life somewhere else.

The exchange on the train has given her some confidence. Reminded her that Harrisson will not be scrutinising her, he'll be seeing her reflection in her work. She can use the data to show him what he wants to see. Davidson has taught her that. All she needs to do is make Harrisson believe she is professional, that she is worthy. All she needs to do is keep pretending. It's what she does best.

It's the white sheets on the hotel bed that disarm her. They smell so fresh, and have been pressed and smoothed so thoroughly that she is reluctant to turn them back and climb inside. This is the life that the worktowners would envy. A hotel in Knightsbridge with damask curtains thick enough to block out all the light, and a porter who carries her carpet bag up to her bedroom, unlocks the door and invites her to step inside. There is no chatter on the landing, no sounds of girls rushing between rooms. No Maude. She should be relishing every moment but she cannot sleep. There is not much medicine left and if she drinks it now, there won't be any to settle her nerves before tomorrow's meeting. Then again, unless she gets some sleep tonight, she'll be too exhausted to make a good impression anyway. She is no longer used to lying in the pitch dark;

best to open the curtains a little and let some moonlight in. That way, the rising sun will wake her in the morning and she'll have plenty of time to prepare, and find a chemist. All things considered, it's better that she has a sip now to help her on her way to sleep.

Even before she climbs out of bed she feels the rush of relief, her senses heightened as her bare feet feel their way across the floor. She drops to her knees and takes her time reaching for the bag, her hands lingering on the tapestry of the fabric. She is shaking now, delving to the very bottom where she swaddled the bottle in folded clothing. Lifting it carefully she unscrews the top: the scrape of metal against glass. She should save a little for tomorrow. Just in case. But she ignores the bargain she has made with herself and tips her head too far, holds it in her mouth as long as she can before swallowing, then reasons that there is barely a sip left in the bottle. She may as well finish it. She'll have time to buy more in the morning. She'll wake early. She always does. No need to open the curtains now. Sleep is coming to find her in the darkness.

Dreams dance just under the surface but dart away before she can reach out and touch them. She is somewhere far deeper. Unaware of the lack of broken bedsprings, unable to register the fact the frame does not creak every time she turns. But she hardly moves anyway. Her neck is stiff when she finally wakes, after being so many hours in the same position. It is still dark in the room, but the curtains are outlined with a margin of bright light. Margaret turns on the lamp beside her bed and looks at her watch. It is after eight o'clock. She is due at Harrisson's house in less than an hour.

She can feel the panic in her chest. Her heart beats with such violence that she fears it will split in two; it pulses in her throat, which tightens with every step. She can feel the sweat beneath her arms, can imagine how red her face must look, damp fingers burning with the effort of holding onto her carpet bag. Being late is what she dreams about at night, limbs mired in a pavement that turns viscous beneath her feet, body blown backwards by a relentless wind. It feels now as if those nightmares were prophetic: she'll never get to Harrisson's house on time. Ladbroke Road seems to stretch on forever. The houses are set back behind hedges and gates that make it difficult to read the numbers, each frontage so grand that it takes her between seventeen and twenty-two steps to cross them. The comfort of counting is the only thing that is moving her forward. If she doesn't keep her thoughts busy, they will spiral.

By the time she reaches number 82 she is six minutes late. She should rush straight up to the door, but she can't bring herself to do it. She stands instead on the pavement and contemplates turning back. Harrisson must be despairing of her. She imagines him sitting at his desk, looking at his watch. In fact, in all likelihood he will have put it back into his pocket by now. He will already have tutted and turned his attention to another task. Her lateness is unpardonable. There is no excuse for it, but if she goes inside he'll expect her to provide him with one, and that will be even more humiliating, will make her look even more inept. Any hope of impressing him is gone: not only is she late, but she is incomplete. Her body is standing on the pavement but her mind has raced away. It is untethered, wild, running in circles, untamed and unpredictable. She knows this feeling too well; there is no reasoning with it. She needs the hip flask but without morphine all she can do is wait for it to tire, to run out of energy; only then can she overpower it and put it back on the leash.

'Ah, Miss Finch!' She jumps at the voice and turns to see a tall, dark-haired man walking towards her. He is smoking a pipe, smiling widely between puffs, his gait unhurried and care-free, his arms swinging by his sides. 'Is it that time already? I always like to take a walk after breakfast. Sets me up for the day. And I very often lose all track. But, where are my manners?' He offers her his hand and she shakes it, conscious of the fact that her palm is slick with sweat. 'Tom Harrisson. Do come in.' He opens the gate and gestures for her to go through, then leads her up the stairs to the front door. Apart from a pair of white pillars, she thinks the building brutally angular. Within seconds of Harrisson ringing his own door bell, a maid appears, in a black dress and embroidered white apron, who welcomes them into a large hallway with a wide staircase that doglegs up to a landing above. Margaret hardly registers the fact that she has been relieved of her jacket before Harrisson strides through a doorway into a large room on their left. 'Do take a seat,' he says, gesturing to an armchair positioned in front of a desk. 'And, Hughes,' he says, sticking his head back out into the hall-way. 'Some tea please.'

'Yes, sir.'

Margaret goes to sit, but there is a typed document on the

armchair. There are piles of folders everywhere, held down with fossils as paperweights. Books and folded newspapers stacked at intervals on the floor. You couldn't call it chaotic – there appears to be order to the arrangement – but cluttered, certainly. The furniture is ornate and fussy, outdated and feminine. Every inch not covered in reports is home to a collection of china: Sèvres vases in dark green and gold, a pagoda that she assumes to be a serving dish. There's a sculpture of a moustachioed man in a bicorn hat who is fanning himself in the corner; the bronze of an elephant, barely visible amongst the correspondence on the desk. The effect is overwhelming.

'Ah, sorry. Let me . . .' he says, taking the paperwork from the seat and considering the piles on the floor for a moment before laying it on top of one of them. Margaret sits and silently tries to calm her thoughts, which are still zig-zagging.

'I hope the hotel was satisfactory, Miss Finch.'

'Very comfortable, thank you.'

'Quite a contrast to your usual accommodation, I should think!' He empties the contents of his pipe into an ashtray. 'I did my own spell of undercover work in Bolton you know. Quite an adventure. Fortunately, I had friends up there who would invite me to stay at weekends – so I could go back to civilisation. They let me keep some clothes there. One evening I wore clogs and a cap with my dinner suit. The other guests thought it was a riot!' Margaret is aware she is expected to laugh at this story, but she can't. She should, at least, take part in the conversation but she can't trust herself to say the right thing. Or rather, not to say the wrong thing. Her mind is trying to date the porcelain. French? Nineteenth century. It is all very ugly, whatever it is. She wants to ask him why he would collect such tasteless pieces. But she mustn't do that. 'So tell me, Margaret, what are your lodgings like? Are they filthy? Any problems with vermin? The sordid boarding house is, to the observer, what the entrails of the dogfish are to the zoologist,' he says, tapping his pipe excitedly, 'the material of science.'

'It's fine,' she says. 'Clean enough.'

'Oh,' he looks disappointed. 'But what about your landlady? I'll bet she's a character. These northern matriarchs are formidable women, aren't they?'

Margaret can feel herself becoming angry, and begins to fear that she will not be able to hide it. He wants to revel in the misery of her situation but she is not going to give him anecdotes to share with his friends at the next dinner party. 'She's been very kind,' she says, careful to keep her voice neutral.

'That's good.' He doesn't sound convinced and this irritates her more.

'In fact, I admire Mrs Crankshaw very much,' she says. 'It's a difficult life for her on her own.'

This detail seems to rally him a little. 'Is she a widow then or has her husband run off? That's very common amongst the working classes.' He reaches for a notepad under some newspapers on his desk and jots something on it. 'Worth gathering some data on that. I'll ask James.' At the mention of his name, Margaret feels suddenly vulnerable, as though Harrisson is testing her. But she tells herself he would know nothing of what has happened between them. Then reminds herself that nothing *has* happened.

Startled by a knock on the study door, she turns to see the maid carrying in a tray of tea. 'Thank you, Hughes,' Harrisson says. 'Just here is fine.' He clears some reports to one side. 'Miss

Finch has just arrived from Blackpool – say something to stop her feeling homesick!' Hughes pours the tea without a word. 'Don't be shy,' he pushes. 'Do that one you did for the chaps the other day. About the tea.'

Handing Margaret a cup, without making eye contact, Hughes speaks, in a monotonous tone: 'Ther's a brew for thee lass. I bet tha's spitting feathers. Go on. Tret tha'self to some sugar wi' it.'

Margaret takes the drink from her, aware that Harrisson is watching for a reaction. 'Thank you,' she says, simply. 'Which part of Lancashire are you from?'

'Burnley.' The colour coming to the woman's cheeks could be mistaken for embarrassment but Margaret senses the heat of defiance.

Harrisson chimes in: 'We like her to use her accent around the house. Cheers the place up! And I find I still have so much of it to study. You're a great one for dialect in your reports, Margaret. What was that one the other day – scrieking? Can you translate, Hughes?'

Margaret has a deep sense of shame that her work is being used against this woman, who is being exhibited like a sideshow act in Harrisson's home. These words, this accent, are no longer exotic to Margaret. Yes, she has collected their sayings as curiosities and she still enjoys guessing their derivations; working out how, over time, the speaking of a phrase in haste, or over the deafening noise of mill machines, may have led to a shortening, or distortion of the original. Words have lives of their own, journeys that they take. The relationship between what we say and what we mean is constantly shifting. But men like Harrisson view this richness of dialect and accent as if it is an

239

affectation, a deviance designed to entertain or antagonise him.

'It means cryin',' Hughes says, 'sir.'

'Cryiiin',' he mimics her vowel sounds. 'But of course you already knew that, Margaret. I suppose you've grown accustomed to the language while you've been living there.'

'It is what people are saying that is of interest, Mr Harrisson. Not the way they say it.'

For a brief moment Hughes looks up at her. Perhaps Margaret imagines it but she thinks there is the hint of a nod before she turns back to Harrisson, curtseys and leaves the room. 'Indeed! Do you take sugar?' he says, once the door is closed again.

'No, thank you.' She is really having to concentrate now, to remind herself that he is her superior.

He takes a report from a drawer in his desk and she sees it is her own. 'So, Margaret, I wanted to tell you how impressed I am with your work on Davidson. Quite a coup to get such access to the most infamous man in Britain. And though, ordinarily, I might say that it goes slightly off brief – that it is focused rather more on him than on the public's perception at times – I think it's an important piece.'

'Thank you.'

'James is a big fan of yours, as I'm sure you know. He told me I should take a look at this and as soon as I read it, I was desperate to ask you more.' He adds a little more milk to his tea. 'The thing is, it is not at all what I expected.'

'Oh?'

'The purpose of research is to look for patterns, to predict behaviour, to find certainty in apparent chaos. I'd assumed they'd all enjoy such a bawdy story. Moral standards are demonstrably low amongst the working classes. I thought they would be cheering him on – especially in Blackpool. But, according to your report there was some unpleasantness. Some criticism? And your findings were that people were split on the subject of his guilt.'

'Yes.'

'I find that curious. You've gone to pains to understand their thought processes. All these notes in the margins, you could almost make a compelling case for his innocence, but do you really think anyone buys it?' She wants to snatch the folder from his hands. 'Are they really that *gullible*?'

'Gullible is not the word I'd use.' Though it is. It's the word she hears inside her head, the word that has taunted her since she saw that photograph and realised how naïve she had been to trust him. 'Davidson is a very interesting man,' she says. 'I can understand how people got drawn into his story.' She understands that better than anyone. 'There is a lot of evidence in his favour. The public don't like to see injustice and no matter his guilt, the trial was not conducted fairly.'

'You could be onto something there,' Harrisson says, flicking through the pages of the report. 'He is a symbol of something more. They *choose* to believe him.'

'Perhaps. Though I get the impression it has less to do with their belief in him and more about their lack of belief in the system.'

'Ah yes,' he says. 'People in less fortunate situations like to blame those with privilege. It's always someone else's fault. On the face of it, Davidson is very different from them, but he is critical of the Church, of the elite, and so they take his side. A much deeper level of critical thought than I would expect from them. And, may I say, a very insightful observation on your part.

Was there anything that surprised *you* about your findings?'

This is a question she has not considered before. 'I don't know . . . I . . .'

'I find it odd that a man like that could have got away with it for so long. He's not exactly a Valentino is he?'

'It was never a question of attraction,' she says. 'Not on the part of the women anyway. He had the money and the position to make their lives easier.' The words are coming out now and she is too late to stop them. 'In all my weeks of observation, barely a single person showed any concern for the prostitutes. I doubt anyone can even remember their names. While the newspapers have been reporting Davidson's every move, not one of them has questioned what has become of the women he took advantage of.'

'Or perhaps we might say the women who took advantage of him!' he says, with a grin. 'So, what are you suggesting, Miss Finch?'

'That we should consider their view of things.'

'Hmmm. I suppose you're right.' He pauses. 'Society is like the sea, is it not? Most of it is uncharted by science. We should be diving down to explore the very depths to see what life-forms we find.' Is this what she has been working for all this time? Is this the man she admired? 'As you undoubtedly know,' he says, 'I am an anthropologist. I have studied the cannibals of Borneo, and now I am studying the cannibals of England.'

'*Cannibals?*'

'The working classes. Perhaps you could visit some of Davidson's old haunts tomorrow. Take some accounts on what the women there have to say about him.' He looks at his watch. 'You won't have time to fit it in before your train. But I'm sure you wouldn't object to another night in the hotel. Cast your net in Soho, Miss Finch,' he says. 'But be careful. God only knows what sort of deprivation these women are living in.' He shivers, but not with disgust, she thinks. With delight.

## 32

There is no rush. No panic to get there. No deadline to meet. She thinks she is safe to assume that prostitutes keep late hours; it is unlikely most of them will have woken yet, so she returns to the hotel to rid herself of the carpet bag and change her clothes. She did not have time to wash before leaving this morning. Her haste to make it to Harrisson's house made her sweat, and even after she had finished her tea and Hughes had shown her back out of the front door and into the fresh air outside, her skin continued to itch with anxiety, as if she could feel the salt crystallising onto its surface. Explaining to the receptionist that she intends to stay for another night, Margaret is insistent that she would rather return to her unmade room than wait for housekeeping to prepare another for her. All she wants to do is climb into the bath and make herself clean.

It is after midday by the time she makes her way across central London, having spent an uncharacteristically long time styling her hair and checking her reflection in the mirror. She knows she is stalling, unsure what she will say to these women even if she can find them. Prostitutes aren't going to want to waste their time speaking to a young woman, and miss out on the opportunity to engage in a contract with a man. The fact they are selling their bodies does not shock Margaret in the least. She wonders if perhaps it should. But it seems to her a much more honest way of approaching the transaction: the parameters clear, the rewards explicit before any bargain is made.

In romantic arrangements the contracts are based on hope, on trust, on expectation, and, from what she has overheard, are very often broken.

She takes a route along Brompton Road, past Harrods, and picks up the path that cuts across the south-eastern corner of Hyde Park. There is quite a crowd of bathers at the Serpentine. Some swimming, others drying off in the sunshine on its banks, and a few who, she assumes, have no intention of getting their costumes wet and have merely come to 'look the part'. She stops awhile, pleased to see women among them (just a few years ago they would have been fined for swimming there), and surprises herself with a brief desire to jump in herself. Already her dress is beginning to dampen and cling to her skin. With no sea breeze to cool her, the heat feels stifling.

Keen to stay under the shade of the trees, she takes a longer route through the park, emerging at Speakers' Corner where a middle-aged woman addresses the crowd about the Daughter of God. Her passion is clear but her words can hardly be heard above the heckling crowd. Margaret doesn't stop to listen. She is walking towards Marble Arch, the spot where Davidson first met Barbara. The details were given in court, they were reported in the newspapers, and he told her all about it himself, unembarrassed to relay the story of how he approached a young woman late at night. Proud of his charitable actions.

She heads east along Oxford Street, without slowing now. She does not pause to look in any windows, barely pays any attention when she turns off and passes the London Palladium. She could enjoy the riches that London has to offer, and delay her arrival in Soho a little longer. But she won't. She wants to get there now. She wants to hear what the women have to say about him. She wants to hear that she was not the only one to be taken in by Davidson's stories.

Fresh flowers are displayed outside the entrance to Liberty. The scent is familiar: the store Mother would bring her to twice a year as if it were a pilgrimage. They would make notes on the latest fashions; browse, but always buy second-hand elsewhere. She walks on and just a few streets behind it the world is transformed. The lanes become narrower, shop awnings on either side blocking out all but a thin strip of sky. They seem to trap the air below, heavy with the smell of exotic foods and the sounds of sellers who call to her to buy. Very suddenly she is navigating through market stalls, past piles of fruit she is unable to name and displays of spices the colours of clay and terracotta. She should stop and eat. A café on the corner advertises 'two eggs and a rasher for 1/9' but she can't stop or she might lose her nerve. It is necessary to harness the energy inside her, which she knows to be anger. She wants to know it all now; gather every detail about Davidson to fill the space that had been taken up by his lies.

Men in caps and trilbies stand in small groups, smoking and laughing. They do not pay her any attention as she passes, too busy putting the world to rights. There's a theatre on the next corner, advertising showgirls. Margaret sees a well-dressed couple studying the poster-sized photographs on display. The boy standing guard in front of the ticket office looks bored. He can't be much older than ten or twelve years old, his usher's hat slipping down over his eyes as he stoops to pick at his fingernails.

It is as if the street is divided. In the centre, it is daytime, the sun amplifying the pitch of every colour; but along the edges, underneath the awnings, it is twilight and it takes time for Margaret's eyes to adjust. She sees them in the shadows. She sees them in doorways and in the passages that run between the buildings. Painted red lips. A head of hair so blonde that it is almost white. She sees eyes rimmed with dark make-up and others barely visible behind the netted veil of a hat. She had expected to find pathetic cases, undernourished bodies, ragged clothing. She had expected to find desperation and despair. But they look like film stars, wearing their femininity as self-consciously as a man might flaunt his wealth. They are arranged in angles: an elbow leaning against a wall, a head held to one side on an elongated neck. Their bodies are posing questions: Do you want to buy? What are you prepared to pay? Some call out to men as they pass by but others feign disinterest.

'Excuse me.' Margaret approaches a tall woman. It is still only lunchtime but she is dressed for an evening at the theatre: a rich plum-coloured dress which is cut on the bias and clings to the curves of her body. Her sunglasses are an incongruous addition to the outfit and, Margaret concludes, totally unnecessary in the gloom. She is not fine-featured enough to be called pretty, but she is attractive, or gives the impression of it, having augmented what nature has bestowed upon her. Margaret can smell her perfume, which must have been applied liberally, competing as it does with the haze of smoke that surrounds her. The woman smokes a cigarette in a short gold holder and takes a draw on it before she turns to Margaret and raises a single pencilled eyebrow.

'I wondered if I might ask you some questions,' Margaret says, both envious and intimidated by her poise and indifference. She has a self-assurance that is captivating; a woman who understands the power her body possesses and is not afraid to harness it.

'Listen, darlin'. . .' As soon as she speaks the fantasy is shattered. It was illogical, but Margaret had imagined she would hear the accent of an American actress, a woman as well-spoken as she is well-dressed. But her accent is East London: dropped consonants and confused vowels. The disconnect between appearance and reality only makes Margaret admire the illusion more. 'You want my advice? Part-timers aren't exactly welcome. We've worked hard to establish ourselves . . .' Sunglasses Woman thinks she is asking for advice on how to work the streets? Margaret is shocked by the suggestion. But it is not moral indignation she feels, it is disbelief. She is not offended that she might be mistaken for the kind of woman who would use her body to extract money out of men, rather, she is amused by the thought that men would be prepared to pay. She can't even compromise herself for free. Not even with a man like Davidson. The memory of her humiliation pricks at her, but her current situation is so ridiculous that she cannot help it: she finds she is grinning. 'Forgive me,' she says, composing herself, in case her amusement is mistaken for condescension. 'I'm not . . . I wasn't clear. I wondered if I might ask you about a man who used to visit here.'

'Oh, I see,' the woman says, her demeanour softening. 'Look, I'm sorry if your fella has been going elsewhere.' She touches her arm so gently that Margaret can barely feel it. 'Take my advice. He's not worth it. Very few of them are.'

'No. He's not *mine*,' Margaret says. 'Harold Davidson. Do you know him?'

It is Sunglasses Woman's turn to smile. 'The randy rector?

We all do. Well, *did*. It's been a while.'

'Yes – he's living up north now,' Margaret says, encouraged that the conversation is on the right path. 'Did you read about his trial?'

'To start with, yes. A bit of it. But it was all nonsense after a while. The lengths men will go to, eh?'

'All those lies to persuade everyone that he was innocent.'

'To persuade them he was guilty!' She is laughing now.

'I'm afraid I don't understand.'

Sunglasses removes the stub of the cigarette from her holder and replaces it with a new one. She is taking her time. Enjoying holding Margaret's attention. 'Couldn't get it up, could he?' she says at last, lighting the cigarette. 'Ask any of the girls round here. It was common knowledge. Was always hanging around but when it came to it, he couldn't keep up his end of the bargain if you know what I mean. He just liked people to think he could.'

Margaret has overheard enough conversations to understand. 'You mean he didn't actually . . . ?'

'Don't get me wrong – he thought about it often enough,' she says, savouring her latest cigarette as if she hasn't had a smoke in days. 'He was a pest.' She calls to another woman who is standing a little further up the street. 'You seen Claudette lately?'

'Not for a while,' she replies. 'She's moved. Took up that empty room on Old Compton.'

'That's right,' Sunglasses says, turning back to Margaret. 'Come on, it's Claudette you want. Follow me.' Margaret does as she is instructed. Keeping up as she weaves a path through stalls and sellers, she is greeted by people as they pass, in recognition of some imagined friendship. 'It's one of these.' Sunglasses looks up at the window above a shop whose sign advertises 'Algerian Coffee'. 'Claud!' She shouts so loudly and so unexpectedly that Margaret jumps, but no one else pays her any attention. 'Claud. It's Norma. You up there?'

Norma. So that's her name. Margaret realises she hasn't asked her: so used to identifying surveillance subjects only by their appearance or their behaviour. She'd been preoccupied with which word she would use to denote Norma's occupation. She'd settled on 'prostitute', deciding that was the most official job title. But the word seems insufficient to describe her.

'Claudette! For God's sake! Someone here wants to speak to you. Could be worth your while.' There are no signs of life from the rooms above. Norma turns back to Margaret. 'She can't say I didn't try. Maybe you can come back later. I can't afford to stand here waiting—'

They hear the creak of a window being lifted, and look up. 'What is it?' An irritable shout from a woman leaning out on the first floor. Her hair is unbrushed and she is wearing a light blue nightgown in a sheer fabric doing little to hide the shape of her body beneath it. 'You woke me up,' she complains, picking at her eyelashes to dislodge the dried remnants of sleep.

'That's gratitude,' Norma calls back. 'I took the time to bring this reporter to see you. Wants to ask you some questions about—'

'Oh, I'm not a reporter,' Margaret says.

'Speak up! I can't hear you,' Claudette shouts. 'You want to ask me some questions?'

'Yes.'

'Better be worth my while. Meet you next door in quarter

250

of an hour.' She slams the window shut without waiting for an answer, and disappears. Margaret turns back to Norma, whose sunglasses have slid down her nose, revealing a swollen eye, the inside corner dashed with a purple bruise. It makes Margaret think of the pieces of over-ripened fruit on the market stalls, hidden at the bottom of the display, turned to hide the softened parts.

'That's what you came for,' Norma says, catching Margaret staring. 'Makes sense now. Have a good look then.'

'I . . . What do you mean?'

'The sob story.' She pushes her sunglasses back into place and walks away. 'We're either angels or demons. It's always one thing or the other with you lot.'

# 33

She has to keep her wits about her, stand her ground, hold her position. She lists these phrases in her head as she stands and waits. The pavement is narrow and people are rushing past, not looking where they are going, eyes hidden by the peaks of caps and the brims of hats. Margaret is waiting for a stranger called Claudette with no idea of who she is or what she might be able to tell her about Davidson. But perhaps this will be an end to it. Perhaps she will get the answer; the answer that she wants. Because Norma had said that Davidson didn't have sexual relations with the girls he was accused of taking advantage of. That he couldn't. And that would mean there is a lack in him, not in her. That would explain why he pulled away and rejected her – not disgust with her but disappointment with himself.

She could go inside and wait but it is safer out here. By the time she realised that the 'next door' Claudette was referring to was The Admiral Duncan, it was too late to argue. She has not been inside a pub since the night she confronted Davidson. Even out here on the street she can hear the sound of glasses being laid on the wood of the bar. Her mouth moistens at the thought of taking her time to choose, watching the landlord prepare her drink, feeling the weight of the liquid in her hand. It's the thrill of stepping close to the edge of a cliff; the possibility of losing her footing and falling.

But Davidson was wrong about her. She is in control. She could step inside right now and choose to have a ginger beer.

Prove him wrong. But her heart is racing again. She feels conspicuous, as if she has no business being here asking questions. She could find a chemist's shop but she does not remember passing any. Setting off in one direction or another, she might not find a place in time. She might miss her chance to meet Claudette.

She is right not to risk it. Here she is. Almost unrecognisable from the woman who leaned out of the window. Chin-length brown hair styled into two rolls sweeping back from her face, freckles visible through a thin dusting of powder, eyelashes darkened and curled. She is wearing a tailored dress and short jacket, as though on her way to the office rather than stepping into a pub. 'I thought you'd have started without me,' she says, walking straight past Margaret, through the door, and heading straight over to an empty table near the window. 'Pub'll be closing for the afternoon.' Margaret hesitates to join her; sitting down feels like a boundary she'll be crossing, as though the act of doing so will commit her to having a drink.

'Would it be better to speak in your rooms?' she says. 'More private.'

'It's a right mess up there,' she says. 'Haven't cleared up since last night. Anyway, we're here now, aren't we? Time for a quick one. Sit down and let's decide the fee.'

'Fee? You misunderstand. That's not how it works.'

'It might not be how it works for you.' Margaret is embarrassed by the directness of this statement, the unspoken suggestion that this woman is not just talking about the sale of information. The bell rings out for last orders. 'Least you can do is buy me a drink to compensate me for my time. Mine's a port and lemon.'

Margaret has to will herself to turn and walk to the bar. Every step heightening both desire and fear. 'Port and lemon please.' The barman does not bother to greet her. She hears the metal thread of a cap being worked loose, the gurgle of the alcohol displacing the air at the top of the bottle, the splash as it hits the bottom of the glass. A ceremony that quietens her thoughts momentarily. The ritual of anticipation. Just one wouldn't hurt.

'Anything else, love?'

The need within her makes her scalp burn. Her fingertips tingle. Perhaps an ale would be all right. A long drink. That hardly counts at all. And she wants to make this woman feel comfortable. 'Half a stout please.'

She wants him to hurry up and pour it. No, she wants him to slow down. To stop. To discover he needs to change the barrel. To close the pub before he can serve her. She watches him pull the pump down, flick it back halfway and pause; watches the dark cloud swirl inside the glass; doesn't want it to settle and bring the moment to an end. But he has already taken her money and Claudette is calling on her to hurry up. She lifts the two glasses and walks over to join her. 'There you go.'

'Thank you.' She takes a sip then leans back on her chair. 'But listen, if it's Harold you've come to ask me about, I've said all I want to. I've put that behind me now. Not interested.'

'I understand,' Margaret says, gripping her own glass tightly. 'I know him myself.'

'Harold?'

'Yes. I've been working in Blackpool. On a research project.' She traces a line in the condensation that has formed on the glass.

'About *him?*'

'No. About people. Holidaymakers. To try to understand them better.'

'So, what's he got to do with it?'

'He set himself up in a sideshow. Sitting in a barrel. Preaching about his innocence.'

Claudette rolls her eyes and lights a cigarette, and Margaret takes the opportunity to say more. 'I went along and started to make a note of what people in the crowd were saying about him. Whether they believed him. He found out what I was doing and offered to tell me his story.'

'I'm sure he did! Loves the sound of his own voice, that one. Bet he bored you to tears.' Claudette takes another large sip of her port and lemon but Margaret doesn't move. 'So, if you've heard it, chapter and verse, from the rector himself, why come asking after me?'

'Your . . . colleague . . .' As soon as she says it, she wonders whether her reference to their line of work, however oblique, may have caused offence, but can see no sign of discomfort on Claudette's face. '. . . Norma – she said you were the woman to speak to. How did you know him?'

'How did I know him? Are you kidding?'

'No, I—'

'Do you not read the papers? I was on the front page for days.'

Her hair is different but Margaret can see now. How could she have missed it? A little older and a little less attractive than she appeared in the photographs, but it's her. 'Barbara?' Barbara Harris. The one who gave evidence in court. 'But your name . . .'

'I changed it to Claudette after the trial. Don't get me wrong, those newspapers brought in a few more punters to start with but it put more off than it persuaded. Men don't want the services of a woman who's given evidence in court. Makes them wonder if they'll be next.'

'I see.' Margaret is still holding onto the glass. She is in control. She doesn't have to rush to take that first sip. 'He – Harold – told me for weeks all about the work he was doing to help girls who . . .'

'Girls like me, you mean? It's all right. You can say it.' Claudette smiles a little, but it is forced.

'He told me he was on a mission to help. But then I saw that photograph of him with . . .'

'That actress who was starkers?'

'Yes. I saw him for what he really is.'

'An old fool? Sad really. Didn't surprise me at all that those photographers tricked him like that. He's easily taken in. Needs to feel wanted. Desperate for attention.'

'You *believe* him? That he was tricked?'

'What does it matter?'

'Because all this time he's been raising money for an appeal to prove he's innocent. While you're still here. Doing what you do . . . You've had to change your name. Aren't you angry?'

'I hardly think of him these days. It was all right while it lasted. Trips to the theatre. He paid my lodgings for a time. Took me to fancy places. But he wouldn't play the game.'

'What do you mean?'

'Most men know what they come to me for. They pay for what they get. And with Harold – I just wanted to get it over with. Keep my side of things. That way we'd both know where we stood.'

'Norma said he wasn't able to . . .'

256

'That was the rumour among the girls. But I think he wanted to believe he was above all that. Better than other men. So, he sort of toyed with the idea. Always hanging around. Getting a right eyeful whenever he could. Coming to me in my room while I was getting changed. Getting into bed with me.'

'In court he said you were the one that tried to force yourself on him . . .'

'At least that would have got it over with and he might have buggered off. And yes, at first, I was taken in by him. He told me he could help me get work as an actress. Said he would introduce me to people from the theatre. But nothing came of it. And I soon realised what he was really after.'

'What do you mean?'

'He was always trying to change me. Wanting me to be respectable. Like I was some sort of pet that he could train. My saviour or something. Then those detectives came and found me and I finally thought I might have got my break – that was stupid an' all. I'm still here ain't I?'

For a moment, her composure slips. Margaret sees the slightest tremor in Claudette's bottom lip, and before she has time to stop herself, reaches out and touches this stranger's fingers with her own. 'I can see how you'd have believed him,' she says, gently. 'I made the same mistake myself.'

Claudette looks out of the window. She lets her hand linger underneath Margaret's briefly then removes it and busies herself with tidying her hair. 'That's what I can't understand,' she says, her voice suddenly brighter. 'Why would he go after you?' She studies Margaret, making no effort to hide the inspection. Margaret can hardly bear the intensity, the silence. She pretends not to notice. Reaches for the glass. Lifts it to her lips. Takes a sip of stout, another, then another.

'I can't imagine why he'd look twice at a woman like you.' Claudette's judgement hurts, but Margaret has spoken plainly to her without rebuke and it is only fair that she should do the same. 'You're too old for him for a start,' she says, head slightly on one side, still staring. 'He likes them young. So he can look after them. You've got everything going for you.'

Margaret takes another drink, barely giving herself time to swallow before the words rise inside her. 'You don't understand . . .' Soon she'll feel the swirl inside her head start to settle. She'll feel the liquid consume her; feel it carried, with every rush of blood, into the deepest parts of herself. But when it comes, it is not the familiar warmth of comfort that greets her. It burns. It rouses. It sharpens. Instead of surrender it brings fight. She puts the glass down. She wants to hear this. She wants to get what she came for. 'He wouldn't. Not with me . . . I'm not like other girls.'

'Lucky for you,' Claudette says, with an edge of resentment. 'You're clever – I can see that. And not bad looking either – if you made a bit more of an effort. Everything Harold's not when you think about it. He goes after girls who'll look up to him. And you don't need to be rescued, do you? You've got your own life to live.' She grabs her clutch bag and stands. 'But so have the rest of us.'

And Margaret is left sitting alone.

# 34

As soon as the train slows, Margaret gathers her belongings and makes her way to the door. The carriages are much quieter at this time of night, but her impatience has been building since she left London. She wants to be first onto the platform. There is no crowd to carry her through the exit onto the street outside, but she is compelled by her own desire to see it: Blackpool Tower standing proudly in the darkness, its prow cutting through a moon-drenched sky. She is home, greeted by the calls of the last of the street sellers, welcomed by the whisper of the sea which strains to find her on the breeze, the hairs on her arms reaching up to meet it. She feels as though she knows every inch of this town, every curve and every blemish. She knows its dazzling lights and its darkest corners. She has moved inside it. Crawled beneath its skin. Scrutinised it with the commitment of an obsessive lover. And it has laid itself open to her, let her undress it, probe, prise and examine; waiting patiently for her to realise that the secrets she was looking for were in plain view.

This town knows what it is, and so does everyone who comes to holiday here. It gives people what they want and they choose to play their part in the act. Blackpool's veneer may be thin, the mask it wears may be crude, but that's because it has no wish to hide its true nature. It is unapologetic in its reality, honest in its illusion. It knows that people do not look for the strings, the cogs, the powder. They look instead with wonder.

They choose to look with love. Because love, after all, is a pact. It is knowing that the paint behind the façade is peeling, that every light is pointed to exaggerate or flatter. It is not denial of reality, it is a question of where you rest your focus. You are not being manipulated if you are complicit. If you choose to step onto the ride.

It is illogical, ridiculous, but she feels as though she owes this town an apology. She has the urge to put her arms around it. Nostalgia perhaps, because she has already decided she must leave. Leave Mass Observation behind. Facts can never tell the full story; she realises now they are less reliable than opinions because they have a dangerous authority. In isolation they are immovable. As unyielding as rock, as symbolic as statues. Erected and revered as proof that something is wholly good, or wholly bad. But the same set of circumstances can be strung together to tell unlimited stories. How else could Barbara have thought her – Margaret – worthy of admiration? Clever, confident – at first Margaret snapped the lid shut on those words, which only seemed to taunt, and magnify the faults she knew were there – but she spent the journey back to Blackpool gradually unwrapping them, feeling their weight, turning them in her hands. She wondered how a stranger could look at her and see a woman Margaret has never recognised in herself. And once she sat with those words, once she could bear to think of them without flinching or turning away, they grew familiar as if they had always been there. Was Barbara's view of her mistaken because it did not match her own? Or could she come to know the woman she'd described? If only she chose to look for her. If she chose to look with love. To make a pact. With herself.

The prom is busy; there's a tension in the crowd, an atmosphere, the air unusually still, voices carrying through the heat of the evening. Walking into the entrance at the foot of the Tower, she checks her carpet bag into the cloakroom. She had intended to take the lift to the top, and take in the town in its entirety, but she changes her mind. Remembers what James said. She too has been in Blackpool all these weeks and has never seen the famous ballroom. She has spent her days – and nights – lurking in alleyways, looking beneath upturned stones for the things that crawl beneath. As if truth is always hard-won. As if it has to be scavenged, or mined.

She can barely make it to the door, couples spilling out of the entrance, young men and women cheering, embracing, lighting cigarettes and clinking bottles of beer.

('I'll drink to that!')

('It's put me in the mood to celebrate!')

('It's put me in the mood for sommat else!')

A man grabs her as she tries to push past, sweeps her up into the air and spins her round. 'How about it, love?' He puts her down again just as swiftly and pats her back good-naturedly. 'Sorry,' he says. 'I'm getting carried away. But why not eh? In the circumstances.'

'What circumstances?' She has to shout above the chatter, above the music.

He turns to a small crowd of people nearby. 'She hasn't heard!' Then, putting his arm around Margaret's shoulder: 'Chamberlain's only gone and done it. Arrived back with a piece of paper signed by Hitler. Peace for our time, he's calling it!' The group cheers and surrounds her. It's not going to happen. These young men are not going to be sent away. James is not going to be sent away. No war. No fighting.

Margaret is carried along and through the doors. She looks up. It's like stepping into a cathedral. She is mesmerised by the sheer scale of the ballroom, but does not pause to estimate its dimensions. Its exact size is of no consequence to her; of no consequence to the couples who are moving across the floor. They have no time to stand still and appreciate the architecture or decoration. It is as if the building itself is watching the spectacle of so much life below. Painted women gaze down from the arched canopy of the ceiling; classical statues above the stage, so engrossed that they seem oblivious to their own nakedness.

Two levels of balconies undulate around the walls on either side, each curve marked with lights that make the golden plasterwork shine. Every surface is patterned: the floor in herringboned wood, the walls with scrolled latticework and creeping vines. But none of it can compete with the mass of movement. It reminds Margaret of a hive of bees. It looks effortless, instinctive. Every couple charting their own path across the floor, without appearing to look where they are going. They swarm to the same beat, a rhythmic shuffle that moves every foot and bends every knee. When Margaret closes her eyes, she can feel it: the floor is pulsing beneath her feet, encouraging, prompting, insisting that she answer the call. It drives through her legs, up into her body; it shakes her from the inside: a rallying cry.

Opening her eyes again, she finds a point within the crowd; allows her focus to soften. Now she no longer sees the couples dancing, but a blur of colours. She doesn't have to try to make her body move, she only needs to stop fighting it. The music does the work, once she surrenders to it; it makes her sway from side to side, shows her feet how to take their turns to move, weight shifting from one to another. Her hips follow, her arms shaking gently by her sides. The rhythm makes its way into her neck, her head; it finds her tongue which rubs against the back of her front teeth as though they are the keys of a piano. No one is watching. Only the painted frescoes and the naked statues. And what do they care? What does she care?

'May I have this dance?'

Before she knows it she is holding the hand of a young man who is leading her onto the floor. 'I don't know the steps,' she tries to say, but he is not waiting for an answer. He'll never hear her above the music anyway. Finding a space amongst the couples, he slips his free hand around her waist and begins to guide her. Margaret has no choice; she is carried along by the movement of the couples around her. She looks down and tries to watch her partner's feet to see if she can discern a pattern.

'Are you going to let me lead or what?' he says, holding her hand more firmly as he manoeuvres her backwards.

'I'm sorry,' she says. 'I'm no good at this. You should find a partner who—'

'Come on. We're here now.'

A couple knocks into them and apologises, laughing as they change direction and dance away. Now she looks around there is a lot of that going on, small collisions and overcrowding, but it all seems good-natured. 'You need to relax a bit,' her partner says, raising his voice so that she can hear him, but forgetting his proximity to her ear. She closes her eyes again and tries to tune into the rhythm pulsing through the floor. 'That's it!' he says, keen to take the credit for any progress she might make. 'Hold tight.'

She lets herself be taken around the floor. She does not count the beats; she does not notice when the song ends and another begins; when the foxtrot becomes a waltz. When her partner talks to her, she does not listen. When he thanks her and leaves her, she continues to dance, swept up by another stranger. The steps are no longer a riddle to be solved, or a pattern to study. She goes wherever she is led, dizzy from all the turning. It's a feeling like the first sip of alcohol – a lungful of air when you are gasping for breath – but it is not wearing off. The sensation is so similar: the slowing of her thoughts, the dulling of pain. When she drinks the world becomes hazy and her own boundaries soften. She feels less conspicuous, less wrong, less lonely. That's how it feels now. As if she is moving so quickly that the edges of her are blurred. But the strange thing is that her senses feel sharper: the colours look brighter, the music so loud that she can feel it running through her. She can feel every muscle moving, the bounce of the ball of her foot. She can feel her hair lifting as she spins, exposing her neck, a strand catching on her lips. The mind has nothing to teach the body, she thinks. We do not learn how to breathe, how to digest, how to bleed, how to dance. We do it instinctively. Perhaps the mind should follow its lead.

She dances on until the very end of the night, declining several invitations from young men who offer to walk her home. Her feet hurt. She has blisters. Every step a stab of pain that has a sort of purity to it. Every step a process of forgiveness. A pact being made.

## 35

It's after midnight. Margaret doesn't have the energy to chase down sleep. It has fled too far for her to catch it and she doesn't have the patience to coax it back. Besides, she doesn't want to lie alone in her empty bed. Life feels precarious, as though it could end this very night. There's an impatience inside her to do the things she must, before she changes her mind.

From the end of the street, she can see there is a light on in James's office. She hasn't stopped and checked but she can feel the blisters on her feet are bleeding: warmth pooling in the bottom of her shoes, the feet of her stockings stiffening against her skin. Both arms are burning too, taking turns to carry the carpet bag she almost forgot to retrieve from the Tower cloakroom before she left. She stops at the front gate of HQ, and sits on the low wall to gather herself. Nearly there now. If she can just make it to the front door, she'll be able to take a proper seat and have a glass of water.

A knock on the door could wake the neighbours, so she taps gently on his window instead. No answer. She taps again, a little louder this time and, bringing her ear to the glass, hears movement from the other side, and steps back. The crack between the curtains is edged open and James's eye appears. She stands perfectly still, taking him in as he squints out into the darkness, unable to see her body, which is only inches from his. He opens the curtain wider still and she sees his face, his hair. Gently, she brings her hands to the glass, placing her fingers the other side of his. He detects the movement and smiles then. Relieved, no doubt, to find that it is not a stranger knocking on his window at this time of night. For a moment neither of them moves, then Margaret turns towards the door. She can't stay out here just looking in. There are things she wants to say.

'You frightened the life out of me!' he says, opening the door and stepping back to let her in.

'And not for the first time! I thought I'd come by in case you were still working.'

'And as you can see, I am. I should have finished up hours ago. Have you heard?'

'Yes, just now.'

'There's been talk of nothing else on the wireless. Peace for our time.'

'Apparently so . . .'

Neither of them will say it, just as neither mentioned the air raid shelter. Tonight is not the night to admit that they don't believe it; that they know, deep down, that war will come. For once, Margaret understands it instinctively. But the euphoria she felt in the ballroom is with her still, the air between the two of them just as heavy with joy, with possibility.

'Margaret – you're limping!'

'Just a few blisters. I'll be fine.'

'Come and sit down. I'll make you a cup of tea.'

It is such a relief to settle herself in his armchair. The memory of the time she fell asleep in this very spot brings not shame but fondness. She thinks of the bag of crisps he left out for her supper. His office is just as chaotic as ever. She can spot quite a few additions to his collection, including a pair of roller skates, each with its own paper tag, marked 'left foot' and 'right foot'.

She wonders if he has tried strapping them to his own shoes, and her amusement turns suddenly to sadness. She stayed away from HQ for too long.

On the wall next to his desk, he has created a display of the photographs they took that day on the pier. Standing, to get a closer look, she almost immediately regrets putting weight back on her feet, but she can see the mother eating the ice cream, and the group of boys fishing from the pier. There's a young woman with her back to the camera, looking out to sea, the sun shining on her hair. The camera has caught her unawares, but there's something about her. Something carefree. Margaret is certain that, though she cannot see her face, she is smiling.

'Do you like it?' James says, startling her. He is standing in the doorway holding two mugs of tea. 'I hope you don't mind that I put it up on . . .'

'It's me,' she says. It is not a question. Somehow it is not a surprise. She is the girl in the photograph. Putting down the cups, he stands behind her and all she can think about is her neck. The stretch of tanned skin that rises from her collar and meets the curl of her hair. She can see it in the photograph. A part of herself that she never usually sees. And right now his eyes are inches away from her bare flesh. His mouth too.

'It's a beautiful picture,' he says. 'You look so—'

'Happy.' She realises that it is true. 'It's been quite an experience working here.'

'Been?'

Neither one of them moves. She is still looking at the photograph; he is still looking at her.

'Yes.'

'I don't understand . . .'

'I'm sorry to do this at such a late hour but I wanted to tell you as soon as possible. I've decided to leave Mass Observation.'

'Leave?'

'Yes. I'll stay until the end of the season. But I can't see a future for me after that.'

She feels him step away, hears the creak as he sits on his desk chair. 'Is this? Margaret, I hope that what I said that day at the Pleasure Beach——'

'It's not that.' She turns around to face him now, leans back against the desk, gripping the edges with both hands.

'But you are so good at your job. Harrisson was delighted with your work.'

She can feel a blush of pleasure inside her, but she mustn't be diverted from what she has come to do. 'It just doesn't feel right, what we're doing. Treating people like . . . as though they are animals to be studied. And what good is all this research going to do?'

'I can't answer that,' he says. 'But surely doing something is better than doing nothing. At least we are trying to understand. Without understanding how will anything be done to improve them?'

'But what if they don't want to be improved?' There's an edge of anger in her voice. 'Don't want to be told how they should be living their lives?'

He shakes his head, confused. 'It's not about telling them how they *should* be living their lives.'

'Isn't it?'

There is silence and he looks around the room. He seems unsure what to say. Unsure why she is attacking him. She is questioning everything they have done here. Everything they have been working on. Together. 'Perhaps for some people,' he says, quietly. 'But I believe some good will come of it. How they *could* be living their lives, given the opportunity.' Then he looks directly at her. 'Margaret, has something happened?' he says.

'It's just a feeling. That I'm on the wrong side somehow.'

'Was it London? I thought you were coming back last night. I was concerned.' Had he been waiting to see her?

'I stayed on another night,' she says, attempting nonchalance, but her mouth is dry and she swallows hard.

'Harrisson then. Did he say something?' He looks away, as if turning from the answer.

'I went to Soho to speak to the girls there, find out what they thought about Davidson.'

'He sent you to Soho? On your own?' He stands from his chair and takes a step towards her, then stops himself. 'My God, Margaret, did something . . . ?'

'No. Nothing like that.'

'You'd tell me . . . if . . . I know it might be difficult . . . But I hope we are friends, Margaret.' He looks away again.

'Really, it was fine.'

'*Fine?*'

It does sound like a strange description now she thinks of it. An underwhelming word. A lazy one, her school teachers would have said. Inadequate in the circumstances, which surely qualify as extraordinary. She went to Soho and met with a prostitute. Found her and talked with her. Margaret Finch, from Northampton, who has spent her life doing what is expected. Watching quietly. Not speaking up. Margaret Finch, whose stepmother would fall into a faint at the thought of it. 'Yes, fine. Much less exciting than you'd think. I met one of them for a . . .'

She can't bring herself to say drink. '. . . a chat. Barbara, the one who gave evidence against him in court. I wanted to find out whether she was . . . what the papers said . . .'

She looks at him and sees his eyes are wide. 'But surely, Margaret, the fact you found her in Soho . . .'

'According to the articles she was a temptress. Or a victim. One thing or the other,' she says. 'But she was neither. She was . . . just a woman.' She shrugs. She actually shrugs. And this time the nonchalance is real. She feels light. Untroubled. As if she can see herself clearly. 'A woman trying to make her way in life. Like we all are.'

'I don't understand. Is this what has made you decide to leave?'

'No. Not exactly.' She does not know how to explain, can barely understand it herself.

'And you're sure it's nothing I said? That I haven't caused you to feel . . . uncomfortable. When I suggested we go to the ballroom – I give you my word that I won't repeat my invita—'

'I've been there tonight,' she says. 'Just now. When I got off the train. And it is quite marvellous. You must go and see it.'

He drops his head. 'I must.'

She feels suddenly tired. Needs to sit back down. She has said what she came to say, and more that she didn't intend to. She makes her way to the armchair and lowers herself into it.

'Margaret . . .' he says. 'Are you sure you won't change your mind? About leaving, I mean. I'll be . . . I'll miss you.' She knows it is true. She knows because she will miss him too. The way she feels is nothing like the romance novels Mother reads. There has been no chase. No capture. All this time she has been pretending to look the other way, but this fondness has gradually circled her, padding softly, stepping closer each time so as not to frighten her away.

'Me too.'

'I thought I was happy here, with all this,' he picks up the toy sailing boat from a shelf, turning it in his hands. 'On my own in my office. But these past few weeks. Our missions . . . I wouldn't have done it without you. Any of it. It's been . . .' He steps forward and kneels down on the floor in front of her chair and takes her hands.

'It has,' she says.

'I think you are extraordinary. Brave. This job, it's not easy. And all that work on Davidson. I was wrong to—'

'No. He wasted a lot of people's time and their sympathy. I was stupid to get so involved. When you said you thought I was struggling . . . it was true. If it wasn't for you helping me—'

'Perhaps we helped each other.'

'Perhaps we did.'

They find each other's eyes and neither turns away. They just look. Amazed but not surprised.

'And it worked out,' he says. 'Harrisson was impressed that you got so close to him. Even suggested . . . Ridiculous to even . . . That a woman like you would . . . with a man like him . . . Grotesque. As if you'd . . .'

As if she would. As if she would throw herself at a man like that. Try to kiss him. Be rejected. She pulls her hands away. Perhaps James thinks she feels repulsion at the very thought. But it's the memory that makes her recoil.

'Well, he's getting his punishment now,' he says. 'You wouldn't get me performing in that act for all the tea in China.'

'The stuffed whale?'

'I beg your pardon?'

'He was planning Jonah and the Whale.'

'Well, it's Daniel and the Lions now. Not stuffed. He's appearing with the real thing. In Skegness.'

'That's impossible.' Davidson, a man who ran at the sight of a church mouse? So spooked by a dog that he ducked into an alleyway. 'There's no way.'

'According to the papers—'

'He is the last man who would put himself in that position. It's a trick. It must be.'

'Well, if it is, it's certainly convincing everyone.'

She knows Davidson was desperate to keep them queuing up to see him, but not this. She thinks back to the last time she saw him and replays the moment. What has she driven him to? No, it can't be right. 'It will be another conjuring act. There will be some illusion or other. I'll work it out.'

She has always wondered why people do not say what they mean, or mean what they say; why they pretend, why they hide. It has taken her years, but she realises that she has learnt to do the same. Not only that, but it comes naturally to her now: to tame the impulse, to moderate the thought. But she is emboldened by how far she has come, can still feel the music pulsing inside her. She presses the ball of her foot against the floor, a stab of pain to spur her on. It's up to her now. She can spend her life watching, or choose to see; she can waste her time wondering, or she can find out if what she has feared about herself is true.

'Do you fancy a day trip?' she says, taking his hands again. 'We could go together. Just for fun. Get a bite to eat in Skegness, have a walk along the coast?'

# 36

They decided on the following Saturday as the most appropriate date, for despite the rather giddy mood of their planning,
there were James's commitments at HQ to consider. At least it
gave Margaret three days to recover from her trip to London.
She was glad of the time to gather herself, a little frightened
that something had awoken inside her: an impulsiveness that, if
unchecked, could sweep her too far away from the self she had
come to rely upon. But she was surprised the next morning
that she was not woken by the usual regret or shame. There
was something else instead, a similar sensation in many ways,
a churn in her stomach that she understood to be excitement.

Little thought was required to decide on an outfit for the
trip. She had only three dresses, and the yellow one she had
been wearing in the photograph seemed the obvious choice.
She took the opportunity to buy new shoes, however, and
made sure to break them in with short walks along the seafront to give her blisters chance to heal. At one time she would
have found the process of buying any clothing embarrassing.
She'd always felt a weight of expectation to have opinions on
the relative merits of bows versus buckles; to know whether
T-bars or ankle straps would be more flattering. It was one of
the many feminine instincts she did not have, and any time
spent considering how to elongate the leg or make the foot appear smaller had always only made her more painfully aware of
her shortcomings. On several occasions she had been so keen

to leave the shop that she had ended up with shoes that rubbed or pinched and had spent the next few years suffering the consequences. But this time she did not rush it; she allowed a shop assistant to measure her feet to be sure of the right size, and tried several pairs to find the most comfortable for the job. She didn't want anything to distract her from enjoying their day out.

Saturday morning comes, and she dresses in the clothes she'd laid out the night before.

'You're early for a weekend!' Maude lifts herself out of a chair at the dining-room table, her hair wrapped in a headscarf, a housecoat over her nightdress. 'I haven't got the breakfast on yet.'

'It's all right. I'm not hungry.' She couldn't eat anything if she tried. The sensation in her stomach is much more intense this morning, though she tries to persuade herself that she sees James all the time at work and should treat the day no differently.

'I can make you some toast.'

'No really, it's fine. You were having a quiet moment. I'm interrupting.'

'Don't be daft,' she says, reaching for another cup from the shelf and pouring her some tea without asking. 'Come and sit down!'

Margaret takes the chair opposite Maude's and helps herself to a spoonful of sugar. She's gradually got used to the strength of her landlady's tea, brewed for so long that it inevitably has speckles of brown floating on the top like soap scum. She is a woman who rinses every last drop of taste from every tea leaf. But who could blame her?

'Don't you look nice,' Maude says, refreshing the pot with more hot water. 'Off somewhere special?'

'Skegness.'

'That's the one they call the Blackpool of the East?'

'I think so, yes.'

'Bet it's not a patch on this place. There's nowhere like Blackpool is there?'

'No,' Margaret says. 'I can't imagine there is. And the weather's not as good over that side of the country. The prevailing wind, off the North Sea – much colder over there.'

'You're a smart one, aren't you?' Maude sits again. 'And good for you. In my day it were never good for a girl to show she were clever. Are you sure you won't have some bread before you go?'

'All right then.'

Margaret watches her cut a thin slice with enviable precision. 'You've never been to Skegness then?'

'Me?' says Maude. 'No, I've never been further than Fleetwood. Too busy with this place.'

'There's a lot to do. On your own . . . What happened to Mr Crankshaw?' It's the question she has long wanted to ask. But now she has said it, she fears she may have caused pain. Or embarrassment. And she wishes she could take the words back. 'I'm sorry . . . I—'

'Oh, it's all right, love. Simple answer is – he were no good,' she says, pinching her lips together so tightly that the colour drains from them. 'Walked out one day soon after we were married. Never seen him since. Another woman I shouldn't wonder.'

'I'm so sorry,' Margaret says. And she means it. She's grown fond of Maude in her own way.

'Better off without him. And I don't have it so bad do I?' She looks around the room. 'At least I don't have to look after a man on top of all this. No use moping on what I can't change.' She puts the slice of bread on a plate and places it in front of Margaret, wiping the crumbs from her fingers onto her house-coat. 'What about you, then? That young man who was here last week . . . He seemed like a good 'un. Quiet, but that's not a bad thing. Them as loves theirselves tend to love every woman an' all.'

'That's James. I work with him. He's the one I'm going to Skegness with today.'

'Is that right?' She grins. 'And do you like him? You know, *like that*?' She mouths the last words as though they are being overheard.

'Yes.' Margaret considers this admission, her cup halted half-way between table and mouth. 'Yes, I think I might.' There's something about forming the words that gives substance to her thoughts. As if the act of acknowledging has made them true for the first time. 'I do like him, yes!'

'Oh, I *am* glad,' Maude says.

And so is Margaret. In that moment, she is giddy with relief. With the thrill of having deciphered a riddle. And surely now she has drawn a line around this emotion, and labelled it, she can understand it. Can know she is capable of feeling it.

'I'll keep my fingers crossed that it happens for you,' says Maude. But, for Margaret, just sitting with the feeling is enough. Can't she just enjoy it without expectation? Without James asking anything of her, or her of him. Without complica-tion. She puts her cup down again without taking a sip.

'Never had children myself but I like to see you all settled,'

Maude says. 'Don't rush into it mind. That's what I did. Married the first one that came along.'

'No, no, I'm not . . . We're just friends. I—'

'Getting ahead of myself, aren't I? Think I'd have learnt my lesson by now. But I'm a proper romantic!'

James is waiting outside the entrance to the station, wearing clothes she has never seen him in before: a flannel shirt in light blue with an open collar. He spots her from a distance, watches her walk towards him, and the knowledge that his eyes are on her makes her mind stall momentarily. She fears she has forgotten how to move; the action of putting one foot in front of the other seems suddenly complicated, the voice inside her head telling her that she is doing it all wrong. But somehow her body carries on regardless and before she knows it, she is by his side.

'For you,' he says, thrusting a bag into her hand before she has had a chance to say hello. The paper is greasy and the contents warm. 'Scratchings from the butcher, fresh this morning.' Margaret is unsure how to respond. 'For the journey,' he says. 'I thought we could share them.'

'Thank you, that's very . . . thoughtful.' She smiles and he looks relieved.

'Shall I hold onto them for now?'

'Yes please. Shall we wait on the platform?'

'Let's.'

The conversation is easy and rarely falters. James reads from the timetable, lists the places the service will stop en route; they speculate about the weather that will greet them on arrival in Skegness. When their train steams into the station, he holds out his hand to help her step up into the carriage. The first compartment is empty and, though several people look through the glass and contemplate joining them, they do not come in and take a seat.

'I think we've got the place to ourselves,' says James, immediately blushing.

'Yes. People don't like to disturb a young couple. I mean . . . they'll assume that's what we are . . .' She is making it worse. She can feel the heat rising to her own face.

'Easy assumption to make,' James says. 'A man and a woman together. They don't know . . .'

'. . . that we work together,' she says.

'Exactly.'

She looks up at the tilted mirror beneath the luggage rack above him. From this angle she can see the hair on the top of his head. It is starting to thin very slightly on the crown. She wonders if he knows this.

'No talk of work today though,' he says, his voice unnaturally bright. 'We're here to have fun.' He gives her a smile and she returns it eagerly, as the train pulls away from the station.

They remain alone for the majority of the journey, joined only briefly between two stops by a mother with a small child asleep on her shoulder. James spends a great deal of time looking around: watching the changing countryside through the window, standing up to study the prints of the Pennines decorating the walls on either side of the compartment. She has never known him to be so quiet but she senses no discomfort on his part. He still pipes up with facts when they pop into his head, but he seems less frantic as the journey goes on. They begin to talk more about themselves, about apparently frivolous matters like foods they dislike. She tells him about steak and kidney pies resembling baby's heads. When he hands her the open bag of pork scratchings, she declines, and he does not appear offended, munching his way through them himself.

'I could do with a cup of tea,' he says, after finishing the bag. 'Shall we walk up to the dining car?'

'We are nearly there now, aren't we?' Her watch confirms it.

'Well, that's flown by!'

They find a tearoom close to the station instead and, on her way to the loo, Margaret takes the opportunity to enquire with a waitress exactly where and when they might see Davidson's show. But they do not dally over refreshments; both are keen to explore the town, the weather having exceeded expectations and greeted them with unbroken sunshine and a pleasant breeze.

Skegness has many of the same attractions as Blackpool: the beach of course, the stalls and rides. They walk along to the Fairy Dell, a landscaped garden of man-made streams that meander beneath bridges. While James wanders off to look more closely at a fountain, Margaret sits on a bench, and takes off her shoes and stockings. James turns back just in time to see her step barefoot into the shallow stream.

'Aren't you coming in?' she says, her voice cracking. The water is freezing and makes the new skin of her healed blisters sting. But it is something else that snatches her breath: she is proud of herself, amused at how horrified Other Margaret would be.

James scrambles to roll up his trousers and follows her, holding his shoes, the socks inside them stuffed in so hastily that one of them falls into the water. But he doesn't notice. She bends and retrieves it for him, wringing it out. Strange to think this fabric has been nestling against his skin. Most people's feet have very little to recommend them – bulbous toes, tufts of hair, rough soles – and she can't imagine his are any better. But she holds the sock in her hand a little longer before giving it back.

Small children rush past them, splashing their legs. 'We'll have to dry off before we go to the show,' she says, bending to shake the water from the hem of her dress. She looks up again to find him standing completely still.

'You still want to go then?' he says.

'Yes – that's why we're here, isn't it?' That came out wrong. They came to spend time together too. 'What I mean is – I want to see what the trick is. I still don't believe all this nonsense that he is performing with lions. They'll be puppets or something. Clockwork. He wouldn't do it.'

She cannot tell him that this is something she has to do. That she wants to move on with her own life now. That she must face up to what she has done.

## 37

The Pavilion-by-the-Sea looks like any of the amusements they might see in Blackpool. Margaret thinks its name is misleading. The building is unremarkable, flat-roofed and almost totally windowless, its only decoration the dozens of advertisement boards that shout about the wonders within. Davidson's next show is not due to start for another half an hour.

'My treat,' James says, thrusting sixpence for their admission through the ticket hatch.

'Well, you can ask for your money back when we see it is just a sham,' she says. 'Then you can give it to me, because I'll have won the bet.'

A red-headed woman behind the counter hands them two tickets: 'There's no refunds!'

'But your advert clearly says Mr Davidson is performing with real lions,' Margaret says, 'and you and I both know that is not the case.'

'I can assure you it is!' she says. 'What would you know of it?'

'My companion used to know him,' James cuts in. 'When he was in Blackpool.'

'Did she now?' the woman says. 'One of his "nieces" I expect. Suppose you'll want me to pass on the message that you are here. As if I'm his secretary.'

'If you would,' says Margaret, angry with her tone and her implication. 'I'm Miss Finch.' The words are out before she has had time to consider them.

James has been noticeably quieter since he put on his socks (one dry, one wet) and laced up his shoes at the paddling fountain. He said very little during their early supper at a fish and chip shop on the seafront, and now he is saying nothing. Margaret is glad of the silence. She wouldn't be able to concentrate on conversation anyway; she can feel the anticipation building inside her: the same hunger and repulsion that she felt when she'd stood at the bar in Soho. Even if Davidson gets the message she is here, he may not agree to see her. And then there will be no opportunity to make this time different.

The wooden benches are uncomfortable but at least, in coming this early, they've got the best seats. There are very few people here yet, but making a quick calculation, Margaret estimates there's room for 80 to 100. They are so close to the front that she can reach out and touch the dark green curtain that is covering the small stage. It's only around 15 feet across, raised a foot or so from the ground. Checking there are no sideshow staff to witness it, she lifts the bottom of the fabric and sees the thick bars of a cage. She can smell something animal, so strong it is almost sweet: the ammonia of stale urine and the musk of damp fur.

'Are you Miss Finch?'

She drops the curtain. A man in dirty overalls is walking down the aisle between the benches.

'Yes.'

'Rector says he'll see you. Follow me.'

James moves to come with her, but the man raises a hand: 'He didn't mention a fella.'

'You keep our seats, James,' she says, relieved that he will have to stay behind. She has long thought of him as James in her head, but it is the first time she has called him by his first name, and she sees him register the change. 'I won't be long.' She has to go. Has to do this. But she wants him to wait here for her. She wants to find him sitting in this same spot when she gets back.

Following the stranger through a side door, she is led through a corridor and outside again. She can hear the sea just the other side of a high fence that has been built to cordon off the back of the building. There's a large covered trailer and various wooden sheds. 'Over there,' the man in the overalls says, nodding to the far corner. Margaret sees a figure sitting on an upturned crate. If it wasn't for the fact he is smoking a cigar, she might mistake him for a child, his body hunched over, staring so intently at the ground that he doesn't notice as she walks up beside him.

'Margaret,' he says, looking up. 'How delightful to see you! What a lovely surprise.' His smile looks too heavy for his face. 'I suppose you've come to find out what Skegness makes of my new act?' He brings his cigar to his lips and she sees it shaking in his hands. Clamping his teeth around it only exaggerates the tremor.

'I came to find out if it was true.'

'What?'

'That you are risking your life in a cage of lions!' He forces a laugh but she doesn't join him, and he looks surprised. 'Or whether it's just another . . . performance.'

'Think of it,' he says, straightening his back and raising his voice, 'as another test from God. He has sent many obstacles, but still I cleave to Him.'

She hasn't come to hear another of his sermons. She wants to know why he left so suddenly. She wants to know if it was what she did. If she doesn't ask now, she fears she will change her mind. 'The last time I saw you . . . I was—'

'The Lord saved Daniel from the lions and he does the same for me. Three shows daily. It's the perfect analogy for my trial, don't you see?'

'That night. I was upset and, yes, I'd had too much to drink—'

He waves his hand, shooing her words away, and continues on his own subject. 'I had . . . objections . . . at first. Concerns about the lions, of course I did. But I decided to trust in God.' He is talking very quickly now, not pausing to exhale the smoke before he speaks again. He draws on the cigar in sharp bursts as though gasping for air. She can hear the click of his tongue sticking to the roof of his mouth. 'Besides, as you know, people are fickle. They constantly want something new. Otherwise, they'll stop coming. They'll forget.' His eyes are wide and he spreads the fingers of his hands then curls them into fists, laying the knuckles on the rough-hewn wood of the crate either side of him. She has come all this way to prove something to him. To herself. But he has not given her a second thought since they last met; her humiliation is so unimportant to him that either he does not remember or he does not care. He is not even prepared to listen.

'I could get you a good spot,' he says, snatching the cigar from his mouth again. 'If you want to listen in to what they are saying for your report. Perhaps you could stay on in Skegness for a while. Find out what they make of me. And my lions.'

He is still pretending they are real. 'Can I see them?' she says. 'The lions?'

'Yes.'

'If you must.' He nods to the covered trailer parked close to the fence. 'It's always the lions – I sometimes wonder if people come to see me at all.'

'Aren't you going to show me?'

'They don't like the smoke from the cigars. I'll stay and finish this one. You'll be all right. Just around the back there.'

Margaret approaches the trailer cautiously, braced for some trick or other. It is claret red, paint peeling on the edges, bubbles of rust on the overhang of the roof. As she reaches the back, she can see light shining through it: the bars of a cage.

She doesn't need to see them to know they are there. A smell so aggressively masculine that it makes her throat tighten. She can hear movement, a brief rattle of metal, and can feel a shift in the air around her, as the trailer shakes. There's the sound of breathing, which she realises is her own; short gasps which feel as if they make it no further than her back teeth. But beneath this is something deeper, louder. She can hear them sniffing the air, can feel them testing her scent in a quickening rhythm. There's a long, slow growl, so low that it is pure sensation: a rumble that passes through her body like the motion of a train. She takes another step and can see a mass of fur. The bars are spaced widely enough that she could reach through and run her fingers through it. The possibility makes her doubt herself. What if her arm moved unbidden; what if she couldn't stop it?

The lion knows she is there. It doesn't need to move, to stand, to turn. It doesn't need to see her. Another low growl. A warning. She should step back but she wants to go on. Moving sideways along the length of the trailer, past a tail that flicks from side to side, she can see the mane, the back of its head. And behind it, lighter fur spread out across the floor, a chin resting on a paw. A second lion. A pair of eyes that open and look straight at her. It springs to its feet so suddenly that Margaret staggers backwards. Then it turns from her and rubs its cheek against the planks of wood that line the solid back wall of the cage. This one's a lioness. No mane. A chiselled muzzle.

'What are you doing back here?' A girl emerges around the front corner of the trailer, struggling to carry two buckets. 'You can't just—'

'I'm here with Harold . . . Mr Davidson.'

'Of course you are.' The girl sighs, dropping the buckets heavily to the ground. 'Where is he?'

'Sitting over there.'

'Sounds about right. I've told him, this is not a zoo. I need to keep them calm before a show.'

Up close Margaret can see that the girl can't be much older than fifteen or sixteen. She has not yet lost the freckles of youth or gained the curves of adulthood, and is wearing what looks like a man's shirt, sand-coloured, the hem at the back hanging midway between her knees and bottom. Her brown hair is worn simply, just below her chin with a fringe that makes her look even more child-like.

'I didn't realise . . .'

'It's not your fault. He doesn't listen,' she says. 'Can't blame you for wanting to see them. They are magnificent aren't they?'

Margaret thinks the girl is pretty magnificent herself, as she watches her climb the small set of steps at the back of the trailer and retrieve a key that is hanging on a chain around her neck. 'I didn't believe it. I thought they'd be . . . But they are real.'

'Every inch of them — especially their teeth.'

'And you look after them?'

'I'm in training to be a tamer.' Unlocking a padlock which secures the cage door, she turns to the animals. 'Right, you two. Let's get you ready for the show.' She does not hesitate in pulling back the bolt, opening the door and stepping inside. 'Freddie, for goodness' sake, you've got half your dinner around your mouth!' The lion looks up and slowly gets to his feet, lumbering over and rubbing the length of his body along her legs. Margaret can only just see the very top of the girl's head. Even on all fours the lion is almost as tall as she is. She calls down: 'What's your name?'

'Margaret.'

'Well, you may as well make yourself useful now you are here. Pass me a cloth from that bucket.' Margaret hesitates and the girl steps up to the bars. 'You don't have to come in. Just pass it through here.' Her hand reaches out, palm open. Margaret sees that one of the buckets is full of water and, plunging her hand inside, finds it is lukewarm. She lifts out a small hand towel that is frayed and full of holes.

'That's it. Wring it out. I don't want to get my costume wet.'

Margaret does as she is asked and reaches up to pass the cloth.

'Freddie here is not known for his table manners, are you, boy?' The girl cups the lion's chin and wipes his beard. Margaret can see streaks of pink on the towel, dried blood mixing with the water. 'Can you pass the brush please? The other bucket, there.'

It's the sort of brush one might use to groom a horse. Again, Margaret does as she is asked, sliding it along the floor of the cage so she doesn't have to reach through the bars.

'That's better!' the girl says, pulling the tangles out of his mane tenderly. 'You're almost presentable. And what about you, Miss Toto?' At the sound of her name the lioness steps forward and stands still as the fur on her head and flanks is smoothed down; she starts to buckle at the knees and sway a little, evidently enjoying the sensation. 'I'm afraid you're going to have to go and take your seat now,' the girl says, laying down the brush and turning back towards the cage door. 'I'll be taking them in for the show. I hope Harold's ready.'

Margaret watches the girl ease back the lips of the lioness to reveal four yellowed teeth, each sharpened into a point longer than her own fingers. It reminds her of the moment, weeks ago, when Davidson tried to do the same: inspecting her as though she were an animal herself. 'Tell him we're on in ten minutes, would you?'

'I will.' Margaret stays long enough to watch the girl conclude that the lioness 'looks dazzling' and plant a kiss on its nose. Walking round to the other side of the trailer, she spots the crate but no Davidson, just the stub of a cigar on the ground beside it, the last embers still burning at its tip. She tries the door to get back into the building but it must be locked from the inside. James will think she has forgotten him; she has been gone much longer than she intended. She tries another door, also locked, and walks further, hoping that she will find a gate to get back to the main entrance at the front. In the narrow passageway that runs between the wall and the fence, she is relieved to see Davidson's back. He is talking to someone. Two people. So deep in conversation that he does not hear her coming. His arm is raised, bearing his weight against the brickwork. He looks relaxed, nothing like a man who is about to step into a cage of lions.

Even from this distance she can hear his voice. 'Those tickets got you in all right, ladies? No problems at the gate?' The two young women watch her approach but he remains oblivious. 'I'm afraid you've missed the chance to see Freddie and Toto,' he tells them, 'but if you'd like to come back here again after my little performance, I'd be happy to introduce you.'

Margaret taps him on the shoulder and tells him the show will start in ten minutes. 'I'll be there,' he says. But he does not turn to look at her. 'That's Miss Finch,' he tells the two women. 'She is writing a report on me. All top secret. But I wanted to help her get ahead, get noticed by her superiors, you know. And she has been very grateful for the opportunity.' He pauses and speaks over his shoulder. 'Followed me all the way to Skegness, haven't you, Margaret? To write about my new show.' He still hasn't turned to acknowledge her; hasn't introduced the two women.

'That report's all finished,' she says.

He turns to face her now. 'Surely not. There's still a lot of interest in my case.'

'I can't see that there is anything left to say,' she says. 'I think I got a pretty good idea of the sort of man you are.'

'So you haven't come to——?'

'No. But I'll stay and watch the show. I want to see how you do it. Knowing you, there will be some sort of artifice involved.'

She doesn't pause for him to answer; she is already walking away. 'I'm glad I got to see you again,' she says, to herself. And she is. She has got what she came for. She doesn't need to look back to know that Davidson will not lift a hand to wave goodbye. He will not notice she has gone. Too busy acting; too consumed with playing the lead role in his own life to take note when someone enters the stage or leaves it.

# 38

She finds James sitting just where she left him, staring at his hands, which are laid, palm down, on his knees. He does not notice her until she takes her seat beside him. 'Are you all right?' she says. He does not look up at her. 'I saw the lions. I was wrong, they are real.'

'Oh?' One of his legs is jiggling up and down.

'A lion and a lioness. Freddie and Toto. I'm on first-name terms.'

'Oh, right.' She watches him tap his fingers on the tops of his thighs. There's a good minute of silence and then he says, 'What were they like?'

'Absolutely terrifying!' He turns to her then, and she feels such relief. Perhaps there is still a chance she can make things right. She shifts very slightly along the bench – an inch, maybe less – but it's enough that she can feel the heat from his body. She tries not to react when they make contact. 'It's getting crowded in here now, isn't it?'

'It is.'

'I'm sorry I left you sitting here on your own.'

'I understand.'

'Do you?'

'I think so.'

'I had something I wanted to ask him.'

'Right.' He worries at a small spot on his trouser leg – a spill from the fish and chip supper, Margaret assumes.

'And did you?' he says.

'No.' He is only going to make the stain worse, rubbing it like that. He'll work the grease into the fabric. Best to leave it until he can wash it properly. 'In the end there was no need. To ask him, I mean.' In the end she knew the answer herself. Davidson hadn't left because of her. She hadn't upset him. Shocked or offended him. She was beneath his notice.

Margaret looks around at the rows behind them. Families pass bags of sweets along the line to each other, children complaining that a brother or sister is taking too much time or more than their share.

James speaks suddenly. 'I should have come with you. I didn't like you being alone with him. A man like that.'

'He's harmless!' She turns to look at him but his eyes are still fixed on his knees.

'But he might have . . .'

'There was never anything like that. Not with me.'

There is silence and then he speaks again. 'But those women. The trial. He was guilty of—'

'—of wanting to feel important.'

'Improper relationships, Margaret. That's what got him into trouble.'

'Yes, and I admit it – I believed him. There were many things about that trial that didn't seem right – didn't seem fair. And I thought I could save him, I suppose.' She looks around the auditorium. 'I thought I could save him from all *this*.'

'And now?'

'I don't know. I'll never know.' Because there isn't only one version of it. Of him: Davidson, Harold, the Prostitutes' Padre, the Rector of Stiffkey. 'And what does it matter, in the end? I believe he used those girls. There's more than one way of doing that.'

Davidson told her once that his story was a tragedy but she sees now that it is a farce. A man whose biggest fear is that he won't be talked about or remembered. 'There was never any danger he'd be inappropriate with me.'

'But come on, Margaret. He must have had thoughts . . . I wouldn't blame him . . .'

'You wouldn't?' She means the question as a joke. For so long, the idea that she could inflame anyone's desire has been ridiculous. She thought she'd proved as much that night she tried to kiss Davidson. But James is not laughing.

'Of course I wouldn't. You're . . .' He finds her hand, which is resting on her lap. 'Any man would . . . But I'm not . . . I have grown very fond of you these past few months. But I can't ask you to waste your time on someone like me.'

'Someone like you?'

'I've never had the . . . I hear the other researchers talking at HQ and it's . . . I'd come to terms with the fact that I'd probably spend my life alone. That I'd be happier to . . . But then, all this.' He squeezes her hand beneath his. 'It's rather confused things.'

'It has.' She is grinning so widely that she can hardly get the words out, her throat so tight that her voice sounds strange.

'You think I'm ridiculous.' He takes his hand away.

'No, I . . . It's me. I'm the one who's . . . I'm not like other women. You said it yourself.'

'But I didn't mean . . . I'm not making myself clear, I—'

'It's all right. I've always known I'm—'

'Exceptional,' he says, turning so suddenly towards her that she doesn't have time to look away.

'I was going to say different.'

293

'That too! Extraordinary, uncommon, marvellous!'

She reaches for his hand again and wraps her little finger around his, grasping it tightly. And she tells him everything: in that tiny gesture she pulls every part of him towards every part of her. His forefinger grazes her thigh and she does not draw away from the touch.

'What a coincidence,' she says. 'Those are exactly the words I would use to describe you!'

'So . . . ?'

She nods, and they sit side by side, both staring at their entwined hands, neither saying a word. They jump as music strikes up from the back of the auditorium, and turn to see the last few audience members settling in. Margaret watches as two girls walk down the steps of the central aisle and take the two last seats on the end of their row.

'I saw them backstage,' she whispers. 'Friends of his.'

'He is friends with a lot of young women.'

'He is indeed.'

'*LADIES AND GENTLEMEN, GIRLS AND BOYS . . .*' The announcement makes Margaret grip the front of her seat.

'This is it!' she whispers.

'I'll get to see the famous rector at last.'

'I hope you're not disappointed!'

She hears a metallic squeak and watches as the curtains judder into motion. At every sideshow she has ever been to, Margaret has noted how the crowd leans forward to get a better view. The curtains part, slowly at first, revealing the girl standing in a spotlight behind the bars. She is still wearing the sand-coloured shirt and on her head is a safari hat. She is perfectly still, her arms outstretched, and as the curtains widen the audience can see metal chains wrapped around her hands, attached to something hidden at the dark edges of the stage. The curtains stop suddenly, swinging back towards each other. She tugs on the chains and both lions growl, making the audience cower so violently that several people cry out. James reaches for Margaret's hand again and she hooks her thumb around his little finger to keep it there.

'. . . FREDDIE AND TOTO . . .'

The curtains are fully open now. Everyone is sitting completely still, not one of them taking their eyes off the lions.

'. . . AND MR HAROLD DAVIDSON, FORMER RECTOR OF STIFFKEY.'

There is a commotion at the back of the room and Margaret turns to see Davidson walking towards the stage, pausing to shake the hands of men sitting either side of the aisle. She can feel James's hand twitch on hers, as though he is about to move it, but she squeezes his fingers gently.

'Welcome!' Davidson says, lifting a cane in greeting. 'You will know, of course, that the Bible tells us the story of Daniel . . .' Another sermon. Margaret already knows it will be a variation on the theme she has heard innumerable times before, about his innocence and the hypocrisy of the Church, but in this incarnation he is not Diogenes in a barrel, or the starving rector; he is not being prodded by mechanical devils or encased in a coffin of ice. 'Daniel, who was thrown to the lions, punished for his faith in our Lord God . . .'

The lions sit obediently in the cage behind him, wearing the disdainful expression of two housecats woken from a nap in the sun. One licks its paw and begins to groom behind its ears, the other stands slack-jawed. Margaret can see it sniffing the air, its whole head twitching as it draws in breath through its mouth.

Davidson talks for several minutes more. She can see his eyes sweeping across the rows of people in the audience; there's a brief moment of recognition when he sees her, but he does not linger. It's only fair that every person who has paid should return home saying they have seen the real Rector of Stiffkey and that he singled them out. He stays with each one just long enough. But Margaret watches his eyes snag on something. She doesn't need to look to know that he has spotted the two young women he saw backstage. He seems distracted now. Has lost his train of thought.

The crowd is beginning to get restless: more interested in watching the tamer unwrap the chains from around the necks of the lions. They didn't come to hear from Davidson, they came to see him risk his life in that cage. He will struggle to hold their interest for much longer. He raises his cane at intervals, and uses it to strike the bars of the cage. There, that got their attention. Both lions climb their front paws up the bars. Standing on their hind legs they must be ten feet tall.

'And the Lord,' he shouts, 'sent an angel to prise open its jaws and save Daniel from the lion!' He drags the cane along the bars and two paws swipe to catch it. The audience is rapt now.

'Should he be doing that?' James whispers.

It will all be part of the act. The tamer knows exactly what she is doing. But Margaret doubts any of them have noticed the look on her face. Or the fact that she has begun to move slowly backwards. She doubts that they can see that, without turning her back on them, she is pulling back a bolt on a door at the side of the cage and stepping out.

Davidson steps forward and opens his arms to the crowd

– a posture reminiscent of the crucifixion. It's all deliberate, Margaret thinks. All designed to put on the best show. And it works. Margaret can see him growing; she can see the brightness in his eyes: his own light reflected back at him by the crowd. He opens a second cage door, just behind him.

'He's really going to do it. He must be mad!' James says. 'Margaret, are you sure you want to . . .'

But they both know it is too late to leave now. There's a cheer as Davidson steps into the cage, bolting the door behind him. Then absolute silence. The lions fall back onto all fours with such force that the stage shakes.

All part of the act. All rehearsed. All under control.

They are pacing now, back and forth along the length of the cage. Margaret hears the tamer's calls to 'calm down now, just calm down', and is unsure whether she is talking to the animals or to Davidson himself. He lifts his cane, and the lions lower themselves to the floor, both rolling onto their backs as playfully as kittens. The crowd calls out in delight and Davidson flashes a smile and begins to pace back and forth.

He taps the cane into the palm of his other hand, as though deciding how next to subdue them, and there is laughter from the audience and suggestions to 'put his head in its mouth' or 'take a ride on its back'.

His eyes keep returning to the girls in the crowd. He winks. A huge smile on his face. Margaret sees him stumble, step on a tail. And there is a flash of movement. So sudden that she can't make sense of it.

She hears screaming, even before she sees the blood. She doesn't know what has happened, but the lion is on its feet and Davidson is lying on the floor.

She knows that the person crying out a few rows back is a plant to cause hysteria. It is very well done. People are running out. James tries to pull her by the arm. But Margaret cannot move. She is fascinated by how Davidson is doing it. She knows, of course, that the blood that is seeping into the sawdust on the floor is carmine dye and glycerine. If these people wait long enough they will see it set too hard; they will see it is all a trick. Artificial claws paint lines of fake blood across Davidson's face. Artificial blood on sharp teeth. They look like wild animals but Margaret has seen them stand while a young girl grooms their fur. She knows that they have been trained to perform: to roar and swipe, to lift Davidson as Freddie does now and carry him just as tenderly as they might lift a cub by the scruff of its neck. And Davidson is playing the role of his life. Kicking his legs, shouting out for help. His arms flail as his head disappears into Freddie's jaws. She wonders if he keeps his eyes open. What it is he can see in there. And then he falls still.

She begins to clap. But nobody else is joining her. Surely James can appreciate the art of it. The tamer is unbolting the cage door. She is going inside. She is lashing out at Freddie with a rake. She is shouting get back. Get back. She is crouching down. Pulling Davidson by the foot. Dragging him towards the door.

The stage curtains are pulled across. They hide the blood that's pooling in the sawdust on the floor. They hide the safari hat that has fallen off the girl's head.

All part of the act. All rehearsed. All under control.

But still no one is clapping. No one but Margaret. She leans forward to lift the curtain but James pulls her back. They can hear shouting from the other side: Get him out. Call an am-

bulance. Lock the cage. For God's sake, lock the cage. She has
to get out. She has to get backstage. To see the trick. If she is
quick, she will catch them laughing. She will congratulate them
on their performance. She runs to the side door and down the
corridor to the compound outside.

He is lying on the ground. Not moving. His shoe has come
off. That must have happened when the girl was dragging him
along the ground. His trousers are torn and he is covered in
sawdust. And blood. He is covered in blood.

'Where's the ambulance? Is there a doctor? Anyone who can
help?' The girl is frantic. Shouting at a small group of men who
are standing a few feet away. But no one is moving.

Oh God. Margaret stumbles towards him, crumpling onto
the ground.

'He's still with us,' the girl says. 'Harold, your friend is here.
The young lady. Harold, wake up. The ambulance is on its way.'

Margaret leans over him. She can see puncture wounds either side of his face. 'I thought . . . I thought it was . . .'

She can see the blood draining out of him, the colour from
his face.

'The Lord sent an angel to prise them open.' His voice is
so soft she has to bring her ear to his mouth to hear him. But
the intonation is there: the fire from the pulpit, lines delivered
from a stage. 'And they all saw it, didn't they? They were all
watching. They'll tell the papers what happened.'

Oh God. They were all watching. Even the children. They
saw everything. And it wasn't a trick. It wasn't for show.

'I'll recover and then they'll come.' His eyes are flickering
open. 'They'll all want to see the man saved from the jaws of
death. It will be a sell-out!'

She takes his hand. It is cold and limp in her own. 'You must stay awake, Harold. Don't shut your eyes.'

Two men run in carrying a stretcher. 'We need to get him to hospital.'

She stands and steps back and feels a hand on her shoulder. 'James?' As soon as he catches her arm her knees give way. 'I thought it was . . . But his face, it's . . .'

'I know. Don't look.' He pulls her into his chest. 'Don't look.'

A small crowd of backstage staff has gathered. No one says a word as the two men position themselves – one at Davidson's feet, one at his head – and lift him carefully onto the stretcher. Margaret's legs buckle again. 'Can somebody pass that crate for her to sit on?' James calls out. 'And something to calm her. Margaret, no, please, don't look.'

The woman they'd seen at the ticket booth steps forward with a hip flask.

'No . . . I . . .' She mustn't. She has stopped that. She doesn't want to go back.

'Just a sip. It'll do you good,' the woman says, pushing the flask into her hand.

The metal is cold against her skin but the sensation warms her. She can feel the weight of the liquid inside, can hear its surface shifting: small waves inside the chamber.

'Go on,' says James. 'You're shaking.' This time is different. As she lifts the flask to her lips, the fumes reach her nose. She can already taste it, can already feel her body shiver, her skin prickle. As if every nerve is keening for the numbness that will be delivered. One sip. 'That's it,' he says gently.

It burns her tongue. She should swallow it down but she can't. It is as if her throat has closed up. Liquid and fumes trapped in her mouth. Eyes watering. A spasm in her stomach. She tries again to swallow but it only makes her cough, retch. The burn of acid rising in her neck. Liquid forced out between tight lips.

One, two, three, up. The men lift the stretcher and Davidson reaches out a hand to her.

'Margaret,' his eyes are wide. 'Get word to the papers. We might still make the morning edition.'

# Epilogue

The air is surprisingly still; the breeze has dropped. A single russet leaf floats soundlessly onto the carpet laid by last night's storm; trees shaken of their newly deepened colours before they'd had fair chance to wear them. The melted frost has turned the paper of the leaves to pulp and Margaret holds tight to James's arm. If one of them should slip, they'll be kept upright by the other. Either that, or they'll fall together. Both options bring her comfort.

It is four months since she has seen him – neither of them stayed in Blackpool once the season was over. Her work on Davidson really did get her noticed: Harrisson mentioned her research to an old school friend who works for the government, and Margaret was invited to Whitehall to discuss opportunities to help her country. They need researchers with an eye for detail and an instinct for recognising patterns. And though she is not allowed to discuss the specifics with James, when he told her he had been recruited as a meteorologist for the RAF, they already knew that war was coming.

He has been posted at a base in Norfolk, and she is working for a government department at a large house at Bletchley in Buckinghamshire, sharing digs with three other women in a nearby village. Within the company she keeps, she is not considered unusual, and does not feel herself to be different. She can sit alone and lose herself in a book in the canteen at lunchtime, without judgement or censure. She can spend a whole day barely saying a word to another worker, without disappointing any expectations. If she misunderstands a comment or misreads a situation, she feels perfectly at liberty to ask for clarification.

But she is very often in the mood to seek out her friends (and she has come to consider them as such). Sometimes in the evenings they sit by the wireless and play cards, and occasionally she accepts their invitation to join them at the local pub. For a long time, she avoided going for drinks altogether, fearful that proximity might open up the seam of an old weakness within her. But gradually she built up trust in herself and now, if a bottle of sherry is opened to mark a birthday or engagement, she will join them in a toast. A glass. Just one. To prove to herself that she can.

But the taste never lives up to the thrill of watching it being poured. That first sip chokes her with disappointment and beyond that, memories as sharp as fish bones in her throat. Memories of Other Margaret. Just the smell of it can take her back, can make her feel invisible again. Every swig from a hip flask or a bottle of morphine blurred her thoughts, smudged her edges. But she doesn't need medicine. Not any more.

She wants to believe this.

She wants to feel every moment. Here. Now. With James. Because just knowing they'll face the pain of parting again tomorrow makes every moment more precious. They've already walked the seafront at Sheringham with the low sun in their eyes. They've stopped at a café and warmed up with a cup of tea. And now here they are. This is what they came for.

'It must be here somewhere,' he says, stumbling on the uneven ground. They both agreed the church was smaller than they had expected, as they sat at a pew in the back. Margaret whispered Davidson's story of the day a church mouse had interrupted his sermon and there was something about the silence in the empty church, something about the feeling that they shouldn't make a sound, that made them both laugh. And tears rose to Margaret's eyes. Tears of relief.

James never tires of her stories. Especially her account of the day she met Professor Fricke and his fleas. Sometimes in his letters to her he asks her to tell it to him again, to write down memories of their time in Blackpool, just so that he has something to read. Something the censors won't remove.

'It's so peaceful,' she whispers.

It is. This is the coast. Nothing like Blackpool, which is the seaside. The only chatter here is from birds; the only other souls they've seen a group of cocklers walking back to the village with their harvests, skirts tucked into their waistbands.

'He must have conducted the funerals for a lot of these himself,' James says, pausing to look at another name on another headstone.

She supposes he must. 'What about that one?' Margaret points towards the back corner of the churchyard, where a grave stands apart from the rest.

'There he is.' They draw close enough to read the inscription. 'He's in a nice spot here,' James says.

'Yes.' Though she can't help thinking he'd rather be in the thick of it with the others. She lets go of James's arm and reaches down to scrape away the drift of leaves that is covering the bottom of the headstone.

*He was loved by the villagers who recognised his humanity and forgave him his transgressions. Rest in peace.*

It's a fitting epitaph, she thinks. Suitably ambiguous, like the man himself. A man of goodness. A man of weakness. Both things are true. But beyond that she does not know what he might have been. And is it wrong to choose to think of him with fondness, like his parish does? He is remembered in Stiffkey as a man who gave his money to the poor and turned a blind eye to those he knew were poaching. Reporters continued to come, weeks after his death, and the villagers had been keen to share their memories. But over time they refused to stop and talk to strangers; would change the subject if Davidson's name was mentioned in the pub. Perhaps, like Margaret, they came to realise that he was seduced by something much more dangerous than lust. That he lost his reason, sacrificed his dignity, with a craving far more insatiable.

Margaret too had a taste of it, briefly intoxicated by the same thrill, the same arrogance. She had wanted to rescue him from humiliation, never pausing to see the truth: it wasn't that he wanted to clear his name. He wanted to be known. Whatever the cost.

He didn't make it into the morning edition of the papers, and had slipped into a coma by the time his accident made it into the following evening's edition, the shock of his injuries causing his body to shut down. The coroner concluded that the circumstances constituted death by misadventure. There was scant mention of the girl who had dragged him out to safety, though Margaret read that the sad incident qualified her as a fully fledged tamer, rather than trainee. The irony, lost on all but Margaret it seemed, was that the man who had insisted he had devoted his life to saving young girls had been rescued by one himself.

But by the time she had got him out it was too late. When Margaret and James returned to Blackpool they passed a barrel on the seafront, covered by a blanket like a shroud. There was no need of a sign of explanation. Everyone knew to what it was referring; punters paused to pay their respects for a moment before being tempted into the latest exhibition of starving newlyweds. The show in Skegness closed for two hours on the afternoon of his funeral, just enough time to put up a new banner advertising 'The Lion who Killed the Rector' which, as far as she knows, hangs there still.

'Shall we get back then?' James offers her his arm and they start to walk. 'You're shivering. Here, take my coat.'

'Then you'll be cold.'

'In that case I'll have to warm you up myself.' He wraps both arms around her and pats her back vigorously. 'There you go, old girl.' He is still the only person to call her that.

She presses herself close to him, burying her face in his scarf. She still marvels at the change between them; the change within herself. Muscles softening, skin yielding. Something new and yet familiar. His hands fall still and they stand in silence, neither daring to move, his chin resting on the top of her head. And then, the gentlest touch of his lips on her hair. When this war is over, they will be able to be together every day. And not knowing when or where that will be doesn't frighten her as much as perhaps it should. Theirs is a contract made with hope, with trust. And with patience. It is as if they are unwrapping each other slowly, every letter sent another layer removed. She looks up to him and closes her eyes. An unspoken code they both understand. His lips on hers.

'Let's get back, shall we?' he whispers finally.

Reluctant to leave the warmth of his embrace, she looks up slowly. 'Let's.'

'I'll treat us to something for supper.'

'Supper?' She nudges him with a grin.

'All right, *tea*. Fish and chips?'

'Go on then.'

They drive back to Sheringham with the roof down, wrapped up against the cold, singing songs from Blackpool's seafront. Melodies lost to the wind as soon as they leave their lips; words snatched up and scattered into flight.

# Author's note

This novel is inspired by several real people and events in Blackpool during the late 1930s and imagines what might have happened had they collided. To set these meetings in motion I have brought them together, in the summer season of 1938, as the country braced itself for war.

The exception is the flight of Jack Hylton and his Orchestra, which took place over Blackpool's prom more than a decade earlier in 1927.

Mass Observation began in 1937. Though Margaret Finch is a fictional character, many of the details in this story are taken from notes made by its Blackpool researchers, which are held in the Mass Observation Archive at the University of Sussex.

The real Harold Davidson was defrocked by the Church of England in 1932 and his Blackpool sideshows entertained crowds, on and off, for four years. He was mauled by a lion in Skegness in 1937, and died of his injuries. His grave stands in the churchyard in Stiffkey, Norfolk.

# Acknowledgements

This book is dedicated to my grandparents who, every year without fail, made the thirty-five-mile journey from their home in Wigan to take a holiday in Blackpool.

I'd like to thank everyone who has supported me in writing and publishing this story. Most notably, two of the best in the business, whose wisdom, insight and patience have helped to shape it: Louisa Joyner, my editor at Faber, who has my trust and my admiration; and Laura Williams, my agent at Greene & Heaton, who always has my back.

Thanks to my publicist, Josh Smith, and Faber's sales and marketing team for spreading the word, Anna Morrison for designing the cover, Anne Owen for overseeing its transformation from manuscript to book, and Hayley Shepherd for seeing the things I failed to spot. The reps who get stories onto shelves; the booksellers who put them into hands; the book bloggers who plant them in people's minds; and the readers who take them into their hearts.

Natalie Gray, my colleague at ITV News Anglia, first told me about the Rector of Stiffkey and set this story into motion. Dialect consultancy was provided by John and Julie Darbyshire, Northern powerhouses Lisa Timoney and Susie Lynes, and my wonderful mum, Susan, who gave me a first-hand account of her outing to see Blackpool's Headless Woman as a child.

I am lucky to count many incredible writers as friends, and much of this novel was imagined and written in their company. The Historical Ladies: Jenny Ashcroft, Lucy Foley, Iona Grey, Cesca Major, Sarra Manning, Kate Reardon and Katherine Webb. The Cliterati, including Clarissa Angus, Callie Langridge, Emelie Olsson. Louisa's Angels: Claire Adam, Ingrid Persaud and (my book wife) Bev Thomas. Not forgetting Elodie Harper – colleague, fellow author and friend – and Lizzie Speller, who is both mentor and inspiration.

Special mention goes to two women who have saved me on more than one occasion. My unofficial Little Big Sis with whom I share every detail of my life. And my dearest S, with whom I share a brain and (often, I might swear) a soul.

Richard – former husband, forever friend.

And, last but not least, K and F – the biggest thanks goes to you, always.